RAVEN

AND THE

PANTHER

John Fennell II

TO

BARBIE
AKA
"THE RAVEN"

CHAPTER 1

"Would you like another drink?" Mike asked with a smile. It isn't often that he served such a beautiful customer.

"Yes, please, and this time, make it a double," Raven answered. She took the final swig from her first drink and placed the empty glass back on the counter with her gloved hand. Mike noticed that both of Raven's hands were gloved. He shot a nervous look at her.

He turned, grabbed a Crown Royal bottle from the mirrored shelf, and reached under the bar to retrieve a glass. After filling it with ice, the bartender poured the Crown into the glass and finished filling it with Coke. He removed her empty glass and placed a new small napkin on the mahogany bar then gave her the mixed drink. Raven accepted the drink with a smile and took half the drink in one swallow. She set the glass down on the bar then began to swirl her index finger around the top of the rim. Raven looked up into the mirror behind Mike and noticed that no other patrons were in the downtown Charlotte bar. She refocused her mind back to the drink and the forthcoming task.

"Raven, you've been coming to my bar off and on for the past four years. Now, don't you think I know when you're troubled?"

Raven slowly raised her head up and gave Mike a stern look. At this point, Mike knew something was seriously wrong. She refocused her mind to the drink.

"What? Go ahead, spill it, Raven. Is it something I've done or said? Is the drink too weak?"

Raven's brows dropped down creating a wrinkled forehead. Mike was almost annoying because what troubled her was much more serious. Raven took the second swig from her glass; her lips savored the last drop of Crown. She returned the empty glass to the napkin and said, "Mike, I know you're an operative for The Foundation because The Panther has dropped off my assignment packets here; this is old hat." Raven slowly looked up at Mike and placed her right hand under her jacket lapel. A look of fear poured over his face. He knew judgment day had arrived. Mike had a hunch the Foundation was on to him.

"Keep both hands on the bar, Mike. Don't give me any reason to collect the seventy-five thousand dollar contract that the Panther has on you." Raven slowly pulled out her 9mm Glock and placed it on the bar with the barrel pointed away from the duo. Mike slowly looked down at the Glock then back up at Raven. He nervously said, "Now, Raven, I don't want any part of this." Mike's hands began to sweat.

Unemotional, Raven explained, "Here's the rule. The first one who picks up the Glock and kills the other lives, got it?"

Mike began slowly shaking his head left to right, as he painfully analyzed the situation. Beads of sweat formed on his forehead. His parched throat became a nuisance as he tried to plead with Raven. His mouth was moving, but no words could be heard.

"Cat got your tongue, Mike?" Raven asked with a firm, serious tone.

Mike continued to stare at the loaded gun, he knew Raven's reputation but never saw her in action. His uncertainty carved at his confidence. Mike heard that she was fast and her temperament kept her in the right state-of-mind when she had a job to do.

"I'm going to ask you a series of questions, and if you answer correctly you will live, understand?"

Mike sucked saliva into his mouth then pleaded in a weak tone, "Now, Raven, let's talk this over; you know I'm no match for you."

Raven smiled almost in a trance-like demeanor and said, "Mike, I don't know if I am or not, I haven't seen you in action, now have I?"

Mike stared down at the Glock, taking deeper and deeper breaths. His arms began to tremor; she could hear water trickling onto the wooden floor behind the bar.

First question, Mike," Who is The Panther?" A silence fell over the bar. "Hey Mike, focus buddy; answer the question. Who is The Panther?"

Tears were now running down his cheeks. Raven knew he didn't know who The Panther was. She sat on the bar stool and wondered who in the Foundation trained this sorry ass and placed him in the field?

"Mike, Mike, get a grip," Raven demanded. Mike now was almost hyperventilating taking deeper and deeper breaths.

She stood up from the bar and slapped him in the face, which brought his attention back to the questions. Raven returned to her seat.

"Question two, who is The Preacher?" Mike was now more composed, and he gave Raven an answer, "He's Rothman's right-hand man, you know that Raven."

"Do you know his location?"

Mike shook his head indicating no while he stared at the loaded Glock on the bar. Raven took her left index finger placed it under his chin and forced him to look at her cold eyes. Half a minute passed before she spoke.

"Okay, final question, what were you doing down in Miami last week with The Preacher?"

Mike looked Raven straight in the eyes and said, "I wasn't near Miami, you've got to believe me, Raven."

Raven shook her head in disagreement then said, "Mike, Mike, Mike, you know you were there with him. The Panther has too many witnesses that have verified your appearance in the Bear Den nightclub with The Preacher. I saw the surveillance footage. It's a damn shame, Mike. I liked you."

Mike stood stone-faced trying to think of a way out of this; he knew he was guilty.

Raven stood at the bar in the ready position to start her game with the Glock. Mike began to sweat again. She looked up from the Glock into Mike's eyes and said, "Go for it, I'll give you the first move."

Mike looked at the Glock and made a play for it. Raven's right hand was on it before he moved his hand an inch. She smiled as she pointed the gun at Mike and said, "Why didn't you walk away? There is no video of you in the Bear Den? There are no witnesses, just an anonymous phone call to the Panther."

A fear poured over his face because he knew her reputation. She had the upper hand, and Mike knew it. Raven raised the Glock, gently squeezed the trigger and terminated another defector of The Foundation. She quickly turned and walked over to the door, flipped off the electric open sign, locked the door, and made her way to the rear of the bar, where she escaped to the rear alley.

A fury of gunfire met her in the ally. Raven, surprised, located the assassin and opened fire that gave her a split second to take cover behind the dumpster. Raven knew that this could be The Preacher. Perhaps, he found out she was slated to terminate Mike for his treason. This convinced her that there was a mole inside the Foundation, and she needed this person alive.

Raven inserted another 17-round clip into her Glock. She pulled out another handgun to aid in her defense. She then slowly glanced up to the second-floor level and quickly scanned the set of windows the firepower came from. Raven caught a slight movement in the second window she looked at. She noticed a dresser mirror reflecting a dark image of a person holding a handgun perched inside the window frame.

Suddenly, across the ally, a door just below the window swung open, and an Asian man carried out a bag of garbage to place in his dumpster. She instantly ran towards the open door with both guns aimed at the second story window. The assassin appeared in the open window, and Raven opened fire forcing him to retreat. With the speed of a cat, she found the stairwell and in four strides was at the top of the stairs. She found the door of the room and crashed through firing both handguns to give her the advantage that she needed. Caught by surprise, the gunman didn't have a prayer. His body fell lifelessly to the floor. Raven scanned the room then placed one Glock back into the side holster, and then she kicked his firearm away from his lifeless body. She checked for an ID and found none. In his shirt pocket, she found one Morgan silver dollar dated 1921. Odd as it seemed, she placed it in her jacket pocket, took out her iPhone, and snapped several pictures. Raven then turned and exited the building with no other encounters. During her escape, she wondered what the significance of the silver dollar was.

CHAPTER 2

TEN YEARS EARLIER

"Barbara Ann, come in here, and set the table," Stella shouted as she tended the cast iron skillet filled with fried chicken. Stella knew that she could count on Barbara to help around the house. She worked at the Summersville Grade School as a cook, and at her age, the years began to slow her down.

The seventeen-year-old Barbara cheerfully entered the room and hugged her mom. Stella stood guard in front of the stove as if the chicken might escape.

"Now, stop that, Barbara Ann," Stella said with a grin even though she loved having her granddaughter living with her.

"Oh, Mom, you know I can't help it. I love you so much," Barbara returned as she sneaked a soft kiss on Stella's left cheek.

Barbara grew up in Stella's care. She took a particular interest in children having raised ten of her own. Barbara always meant something special to Stella. Maybe it was Stella's age, knowing that her days were limited for raising more children. Barbara was very grateful for having such a fine home to be raised in. Even though she wasn't raised with traditional parents, Stella taught her Christian values. Her independence from a conventional upbringing helped develop her personality. She learned early on to work hard at home and with her studies at school. She wanted so much to make a difference in the world. She strongly believed in helping others, not by giving handouts, but by providing opportunities to them and removing obstacles in their way. Barbara believed in self-reliance through education and work values, and she believed that she was put on this earth to make a difference. She was a natural born leader, joining all the clubs at school to learn and help in her community. Barbara loved animals. She brought home every stray cat and dog in need. Stella used to get so mad at her but resigned to the fact that Barbara was not going to change no matter how much she complained.

She opened the cabinet door and placed six dinner plates on the table.

"Is Bill coming home tonight?"

"Now, Barbara, you know we never know when he comes in. Just set the table as usual, and we'll see."

"Okay."

"Tell Beth and the kids to wash up. Supper will be ready in five minutes," Stella commanded as she placed the chicken in a large serving bowl. She shook flour and milk in an aluminum shaker then poured it into the hot chicken grease to make gravy. Barbara walked into the front room to deliver the message then returned to the kitchen and began to mix the boiled potatoes with milk and butter. Stella placed the homegrown green beans mixed with bacon and onions on the table.

"Let's eat," Barbara announced. She opened the oven door; the fresh baked hot rolls made her smile as the aroma filled her nostrils.

Just as they began to eat, the kitchen door swung open, and Bill entered. He smiled as he placed his lunch pail on the counter and began to wash the dust off his hands and face. His two children smiled as he turned around. Bill walked over between them and patted their heads. His iron discipline dictated the children were seen not heard. They only spoke when spoken to. Bill kissed Beth and then followed up with Stella and Barbara.

"Did you work hard today?" Stella started the conversation just to feed Bill's ego.

"Hell yes, and don't you know by now? I work hard every day," Bill quirked with his distinctive laugh that could be heard clear up to Wilma McClung's house located several hundred feet up Irish Corner Road.

Bill worked operating a percussion air track drill at the new highway Route 19. Once a pattern was complete, explosives were loaded into the vertical holes drilled in the sand stone. The explosive expert detonated the powerful explosives with a simple press of a button. The once solid strata were reduced to small chunks of rock and dust for removal by large earth moving machines.

Once the modest meal was consumed and the children are excused, Bill slid the metal dining chair back just enough to cross his legs. He reached into his breast pocket to open a new pack of Camels. He pounded the top of the pack on the back of his left hand out of habit before he opened the pack. He picked the sliver off the clear plastic cord with his index finger and thumb, and in one swift motion, the top of the pack came off. Bill placed it on the table while he reached into his tan colored work pants and retrieved a silver lighter. The distinctive click of the hinged metal lid precluded the spin of the metal wheel that brought the blue flame to life. Bill raised the lighter up to his Camel and took a long draw, which produced instant pleasure to his deprived lungs. He removed the pleasure stick from his mouth and exhaled. Bill closed the lid with a distinctive click then returned the lighter to his pocket.

"Where's my beer, Barbara Ann?" Bill barked in a commanding voice.

"Just hold on a second," She returned knowing his bark was worse than his bite. "I've only got two hands, you know." She pulled out a cold Bud from the refrigerator, opened it, and set it down in front of him. Bill looked up at Barbra and smiled. "You do okay for a girl." She took the dishtowel resting on her shoulder, grabbed both ends, gave it a quick spin, and snapped it on Bill's left ear with a loud crack.

"Damn it, Barbara Ann, that hurt," Bill yelled out as he placed his left index finger on the sore ear revealing a touch of blood.

"Don't dish it out if you can't take it." Barbara snapped. "Isn't that what you always taught me?"

Barbara grew up with Bill living at home. From an early age, he taught her to be independent. He wanted her to grow up with the ability to take care of herself. With her extreme good looks and sexually developed body now that she is in her teens, his decision to teach her independence was a wise move. Bill's self-defense training, while he served in Viet Nam, proved to be valuable to her. Not only did Barbara like the physical challenge but also she adored the mental discipline it taught. Along with the self-defense, Bill's expert rifle background in the military proved valuable to Barbara. Bill also loved hunting, so he taught her gun safety. The two of them spent long hours in the woods hunting and at the gun range improving their skill set. Bill believed in the second amendment and thus transferred his beliefs to Barbara. He was like a father to her; their love for each other grew by the day.

Bill looked at Barbara and smiled. "You are a good student, Barbara Ann."

Stella sat down at the table next to Bill just in front of the flour bin. She reached into her apron pocket and pulled out a deck of cards, which indicated to everyone that she wanted to play Setback.

"Is Naci stopping by this evening?" Bill asked.

"Yes, he called and will be here at seven," Barbara answered with an excitement in her voice. Bill quickly shot a glance at Barbara.

"Who is this guy anyhow?" Bill said.

Both Barbara and Stella gave Bill a strange look. Barbara commented, "He's been coming out here for a year. You've certainly quizzed him enough times by now; you should know everything about him."

"He only says so much. I want to know more," Bill demanded.

"Aunt Margaret checked him out." Barbara defended. Then the room filled with a long silence.

"Well, what the hell did she say?" Bill asked.

"He comes from a good family. His dad is a coal broker for a large coal firm, Tasa Coal Company, located in Pittsburg Pennsylvania. Tasa buys locally mined coal for resale on the open market. They help the small coal operators in the area by offering a better price per ton than the larger companies do. He has become highly respected in the community because the local mining companies pay above union scale to their workers providing a better standard of living," Stella reported.

A familiar loud vibration entered everyone's ears as the Firebird Naci drove pulled into the drive. Barbara jumped up from her seat and ran out the door to greet him.

"I don't like it," Bill quipped.

"Get used to it; he seems like a good boy," Stella commanded with a stern look on her face indicating that she'd better never hear of any trouble from Bill. "She is getting to the age, Bill when she is going to do what she wants whether you like it or not. Remember that you taught her to be independent. Besides, I like Naci so don't you do anything to spoil it for Barbara." As tough as Bill was, he respected his mother and heeded her wishes.

Barbara met Naci at the end of the walk. She jumped into his arms and wrapped her arms around the strong column of his neck. Both legs wrapped around his midsection forcing him to support her body weight with his grip on her firm ass. Barbara gave Naci a soft, wet, lustful kiss. Her tongue lashed between the seam of his lips. The slow hunching of her pubic bone against his lower stomach teased his swelling hardness.

She whipped her tongue back into her moist cave and slowly released her wrestler's grip with her legs lowering her hunching pelvic bone down and over his aching bulge.

"We can't have you walking in with a boner; Bill would flip out."

"You're right," He gasped as his young hormones raged.

"Let's go in and play setback," she toyed with his wanting desire. Her deep brown eyes begged, "I want you inside me, but you must play it my way."

"No, no, l want more," Naci pleaded as he tried to hold onto Barbara's ass, but he lost his grip to gravity.

Barbara shot a glance at his midsection and smiled, "We better give it a minute."

After a few minutes of conversation, Barbara grabbed his hand and led the way into the kitchen. She stayed close in front of Naci to hide his discomfort until Naci sat down across from Stella. Barbara took her place at the end of the table to be Bill's partner.

"Hold on a minute," Bill announced. "Naci you sit at the end of the table; I want to be your partner. I want to know more about you, and one way is to see how you think."

Barbara shot a devilish look at Naci, then announced, "Don't worry, Bill, he is a great partner." She turned slightly toward Naci so Bill could not see her expression. She rubbed her tongue around her lips indicating to Naci that he was in for a good time after the card game. Her right foot was crawling up his pant legs. Stella noticed her teasing, and gave a slight grin.

"Barbara Ann, cut the crap, and let's start the game," Bill snapped as he handed Stella the shuffled deck to cut.

Three hours of continuous play ended up with an even score.

"Well, I've had enough," Stella announced. "My bottom side is tired."

"Yep, me too." Bill followed. "Naci, you did well. We'll do this again."

Barbara tapped Naci on the leg with her foot then jolted her head to the door indicating it was time to leave. "Good night, everyone; we are going for a ride."

"Be in early Barbara," Stella suggested.

"Ok, Mom, we will."

The rumble of the 365-horse engine came to life when Naci turned the key. He placed the gear shift into reverse and slowly let out on the clutch taking command of the General Motor's power plant. Once out on the street, Naci placed the standard transmission into first gear and revved the 400-cubic engine up before popping the clutch leaving two black marks on the street about one hundred feet long.

CHAPTER 3

The green Firebird came to a sudden stop just as Naci pulled up to Rack's 396 Chevelle.

"Well, well, what have we here, Naci and his little green bird," Rack sarcastically commended. "I hope you can handle the little green bird better than what's sitting in your passenger seat."

"What's that supposed to mean?" Naci demanded as he slowly opened the driver's door and exited the car.

"Now, hold on Naci, no sense getting all riled up over a rumor."

Naci closed the Firebirds driver door, walked up to Rack's Chevelle, and placed both hands on the lower frame of the open driver's window. He began to rock the car with his sheer body strength, demonstrating his intention to bring the rumor to a halt.

"Now, like I said Naci, no sense getting all worked up about a silly little thing like what we heard."

"And what might that be?" Naci demanded.

"You know, how you can't satisfy Barbara Ann."

"She's with me and not you Rack. That should speak for itself."

"Yea, yeah, let's go down to Salmon Run. I hear someone painted off a quarter mile drag; I want to bury that bird once and for all." Rack challenged.

"Sounds good; besides, you have an advantage," Naci added.

"Oh yea, what's that?" Rack quizzed.

"Since you can't seem to keep a girl, or at least get one to ride around with you, you have a one hundred ten-pound advantage," Naci laughed as he jumped back into the Firebird. He pulled out onto the street then mashed down on the fuel peddle that left his mark on the street.

Word spread like wildfire of the grudge run. The local law enforcement didn't try to stop them. Salmon Run is a section of roadway completely safe from the public. It kept dozens of muscle cars off the main roads. In fact, it drew muscle cars, taking the grudge runs off of Hughes Bridge just south of town and Marlinton Straight, which was about twenty miles north of Richwood.

Naci and Rack stopped at the Amoco station on Main Street to top off their gas tanks with premium white blend consisting of 98 octane. By the time they arrived at Salmon Run, a large had crowd gathered at the starting line. Dozens of pickups positioned to view the grudge run with their rear bed full of lawn chairs pointed towards the starting line. The knoll above the starting- line was occupied by locals sitting on blankets.

The two GM cars lined up at the freshly painted start line. Salmon Run was a perfect location for grudge runs. It was a section of old US 19 that was made obsolete due to the construction of the Summersville Dam back in the 1960's. The road was long enough past the quarter mile mark to give plenty of room to stop once the race was complete.

Naci smiled at Barbara and exited the Firebird. He walked back to the rear of the car and opened the trunk. The young dragster opened his tool bag, removed a wrench, and opened his side pipes to expedite the exhaust that provided more horsepower. He returned to the trunk and retrieved a gallon of bleach. Naci poured the contents over the rear tires then quickly returned to the driver's seat. He placed the Firebird into reverse, revved the engine, and released the clutch burning off the liquid. He did the same in forward returning to the starting line. The crowd cheered in excitement.

The crowd appointed a start flagman who was in place in front of the two muscle cars. The crowd was silent, and engines were idling as the start man raised his hand. He checked the position of both front tires to the painted mark. He indicated for Rack to pull up and then commanded,

"On the mark," He raised his hand, and then five seconds later dropped it shouting, "Go!"

Both muscle cars released 700 horses of raw engine, smoking all four rear tires, which filled the night air. Rubber dominated everyone's nostrils. The two cars made a clean straight hole shot. Both ran neck and neck throughout the quarter mile. When they crossed the finish line, the Firebird was ahead by a half of a car length.

Both cars came to a stop. Rack spun his Chevelle around then pulled it up to Naci's Firebird so that they were door to door.

"Now, everyone knows a stock Firebird can't outrun a 396 Chevelle," Rack complained.

"Hey, I bought this car used, and no one mentioned anything about a modified engine," Naci defended with a smirk.

Barbara interrupted, "Hey, Rack, we won; you lost so just go back to The Smoke House, play pool with your buddies, and when you get tired of playing with them, go play with yourself. We have more important things to do than to sit here arguing with you." Barbara grabbed Naci by the neck, pulled it forcibly, and gave him a long deep kiss. She broke the kiss off and leaned her hot upper body down to give Rack a good look through the driver's window. With a sexy voice, she teased, "Hey, Rack, been getting any lately? Naci sure has, and believe me, I'm satisfied." Rack placed the Muncie transmission into first gear and peeled rubber as he pulled out.

The Firebird pulled up to the locked gate. Naci turned to Barbara Ann and gave her a long kiss. Their tongues intertwined with passion. Naci caressed her cheek with tender affection; his teenage hormones began to escalate. Barbara pulled away from their passionate kiss and cried, "Naci, get that damn gate open, I want you. Do you realize it's been two weeks since our last romp?"

"I know but you must understand it's football season, and I must conserve my strength?" Naci defended.

Barbara shot a stern look at Naci then nodded her head several times towards the gate, indicating that she didn't want to talk; she just wanted to make love.

In one swift motion, Naci was out of the car and unlocked the gate. Barbara advanced the bird forward, which allowed Naci to close and lock the iron entrance. He jumped into the passenger's seat as Barbara placed the car into gear. They drove up to the top of the mountain. The view of the town below was magnificent. The lights twinkled as the wind swayed the oak trees giving the impression that they were on a timer.

They both exited the car and met at the rear; Naci opened the truck and retrieved a blanket. When he spun around, his lips met Barbara's. Naci gently sucked on her lower lip demanding Barbara surrender to his teenage lust. She gasped for air due to her raging hormones, which caused her body to tingle from her lips down to her needy groin. Naci tossed the blanket on top of the trunk without a second thought, and then unnoticed, it slowly slid off the car landing on the ground. Naci moved to the coil of her neck while he used his arms of steel to pick Barbara up and softly place her on the edge of the trunk. Barbara spread her long slender legs to surrender her near virginity to the man she loved. Naci pushed his bulge against her groin and placed both hands on her bottom to keep her from sliding as he hunched her pubic bone giving temporary relief to his desires. Naci continued to ravish her unique kissing style, as her tongue slid in and out with a cadence-like method as if she pleaded, "Please get that thing out of your pants and make me happy." In and out, her tongue commanded. He softly grabbed the bottom of her t shirt and in one quick motion pulled it over her head breaking the kissing cadence.

"Now, we're getting somewhere," She barked with a devilish expression. Her eyes begged Naci to disrobe.

Barbara leaned forward to unclasp her bra, which gave freedom to the most perfect mounds a seventeen-year-old could have. She leaned back and smiled; her melons bounced when she threw her bra aside. The warm fall night air stimulated her pink nipples, but when Naci touched them, they grew needy and hardened. Their lips met again as she grabbed Naci's belt and unhooked it, unsnapped his pants, and placed her curious hand on his zipper. In one quick motion, she pulled the zipper to the bottom giving relief to his swelled member. She broke the kiss; the pulse in her love channel escalated to a hot moist throbbing. Barbara needed to feel him inside her.

"Now, that's what I'm looking for, something to satisfy my wet box," Barbara shouted. She relieved his shaft from its constraints. Naci shoved both pants and undershorts to the ground. Instinct led him to unfasten Barbara's cut offs; his fingers trembled with anticipation.

Barbara smiled, pushed his fingers out of the way, and offered, "Gosh, Naci, you're fumbling is tugging on my shorts; it's rubbing my button, and I'm going to spew." She unfastened the brass button then raised her sweet bottom to make Naci's task of removing them easier. In one lustful motion, he removed both her shorts and panties releasing the sweet scent of her delicious love canal. Naci instinctively lowered his head to absorb the fragrance of her honey pot. He slowly kissed her inner thighs with a slow loving passion that Barbara taught him. She placed her hands on the back of Naci's head and guided his tongue to her needy spot. His hungry tongue found the folds of her youth. "Oh my goodness, Naci, yes, yes that's it." He guided his tongue from the bottom of her slit to the top until he reached her love button. He paused, then gave it a gentle suck. "Mnnn, that's the spot; caress it so tenderly. Oh, that's so good!" Barbara begged over and over as she lightly hunched. Her loins demanded more. He could sense her erotic desires, so Naci increased his speed and depth, which escalated her hunching. Naci repeatedly moved his tongue up and down until she began to quiver. "Hold on for a second, Naci; I'm about to explode. Please stop." She demanded. Naci wasted no time pulling up, wiping his soaked lips. His hands made it to her taut nipples and firm breasts. He played with them trying to replace the joy he just lost. Barbara leaned her head back and held her upper body with her arms wedged against the rear window of the car. Her deep breaths indicated near organism.

"Hold on, Naci, don't make a move," She could feel her treasure vibrate. Her pink flesh begged for more.

"Go ahead, splurge; I'm sure you're good for more tonight." Naci pleaded with desperation; he needed to see her satisfied.

"Yes, but the first one of the night with you is always special, and I want to lead up to it several times."

His raging hormones disagreed.

There she was in the moonlight; head leaned back taking deep breaths holding off her first delight of the night. Naci watched her enjoy one of life's amazing natural happenings. Her plump breasts were heaving with every breath she took. Her taut nipples pleaded for attention, and her sweet-smelling love box begged for Naci to return. He could see her start to quiver, then it subsided. Heavy breathing dominated by both brought them to the edge of sheer delight. Barbara raised up and purred, "I almost came, but I didn't." Her expression told Naci to get back to work; she needed him to continue. "Now, bring me back to uncontrollable waves of pleasure."

Naci wasted no time and placed his member into her juicy love box. It felt so warm and moist; he was in second heaven. He began to hunch along with her in perfect rhythm. They kept a steady pace looking each other in the eyes as they wallowed in their lust. Barbara's tongue added a new level of pleasure as it protruded slightly out of the corner of her mouth while her heavy breathing escalated. Her deep brown eyes begged for this to go on as her hips hunched with every creamy stroke. The two teenagers pawed and grunted like wild animals in the wilderness.

"Oh, Naci, my rapture is on the way," Barbara pleaded. "Please, stop-stop."

Naci did as asked and stopped his stroke but left his flesh buried in its reward. Each heart beat could be felt in their groins. Her eyes closed; she concentrated on not climaxing while Naci moaned for the pleasure to continue.

"I know this is hard on you, but I want my first delight to last a long time," the horny vixen pleaded. Her love canal began to spasm sending little pulses of madness to Naci's aching member.

Naci began to hunch out of pure need; he was only human. He slowly moved in and out just a few inches; it helped his uncontrollable desire. Barbara pulled her bottom back trying to prevent her from uncoiling her spunk. Naci grabbed her ass and started to pile drive her creamy split with a hammer like cadence. He ignored her plea to stop.

"Stop, Naci, I'm enjoying this way too much. Please stop—oh, oh my" Barbara dug in with her hips to meet his rhythm. "Oh, shit, I love this sensation.

Don't-don't you dare stop." The desire, the hunger for more exploded on her face. Her lustful lips formed a perfect circle out of pure need with escalated breaths. Her demanding eyes begged for more.

She fell in cadence with him and continued to enjoy the ecstasy. Her core relieved itself of the sweet scent and continued to produce love juices. Heavy breaths took command. Sweat began to flow from both bodies due to the warm, fall night.

"Naaaci- I'm going to peak—ooooh, here I go, what a feeling," Barbara announced with a soft tone. She grabbed Naci around the neck. He experienced her joy as she climaxed. She stiffened then shivered, the sudden hard jerks and then light ones, the flow of love juice, and the sweet aroma. Naci joined her as the ecstasy of the human lust exploded to quivering satisfaction. Both held onto each other as he rubbed the base of his stiff shaft on the outside of her and expended hot, wet glory. Her eyes looked up at Naci to thank him for the euphoric pleasure. She leaned her head back and closed her eyes as their bodies returned to normal. The night was now quiet with an occasional cricket calling for its mate. Minutes passed as their heartbeats returned to normal. Naci leaned forward and kissed Barbara; their lips touched, jaws moving in perfect unison displaying their love.

Silence continued to dominate until an unfamiliar screech was heard. Both Naci and Barbara brought their attention to the noise. On top of the Firebird, a solid, black Raven landed and looked straight at them. Unaffected by the previous events, the Raven seemed extremely interested in them. Unafraid, it walked from the front of the roof to the rear to get a closer look.

Barbara gave Naci a quick glance, as to say, "What the hell?" She raised her left hand and offered her index finger. The Raven stopped, examined the extended offering, then stepped onto her finger. She brought her new friend closer and looked into the Raven eyes.

It was completely quiet for the next few minutes. The Raven never questioned its fear of the humans. It jerked its head from side to side to investigate its new friends. Stunned Naci tried to place his hand on the Ravens head; it gave out a cry and flew away.

"Did you see that?" Barbara asked. "I wonder why it wasn't afraid?"

"I don't know, but that's the strangest thing I have ever seen."

"I just don't understand why the Raven showed interest in us and why wasn't it afraid?"

"I haven't the slightest idea," Naci observed as he softly caressed her cheek. He stared at Barbara as she watched the Raven fly away. The love and affection Naci felt stirred his youth. He could sense the hormones reacting.

Barbara placed both arms around Naci's neck and gave him a wet, lustful kiss. She teased Naci until his shaft responded, pulled back, and smiled then jumped off the trunk and ran around to the front of the car. Naci tried to follow but forgot his pants were down around his ankles and almost fell. He wasted no time, removed his garments, and caught up with Barbara. She observed the view and placed Naci's arms around her waist. The city lights twinkled in the shadow of darkness; headlights moved as cars navigated the streets as if they were lost. He began to kiss her on the back of her neck using his chin to push back her long, black hair to expose her soft skin. He outlined the shell of her ear with kisses. He walked his lips up and down the base of her neck. The warmth of his touch and his soft and tender kindness gave Barbara an emotional high. She knew that Naci loved her. It was clear by the way he continued to adorn her with affection. Barbara adjusted her head to give a long, luscious kiss using her tongue to deliver her message to Naci. His Phallus began to swell giving new meaning to her desires. This continued until she couldn't wait any longer. She spun around, placed her arms around Naci's neck, and gave one slight jump until he caught her naked ass with both hands. Her wet cave begged for his swelled crown. She found his shaft and guided it to her glory. The joy returned as fast as it did the first romp. The off balanced position they were in caused Naci to lean and fall backwards onto the hood of the Firebird. They landed between the two hood scoops, which were common on his model. Barbara took command and worked her hips up and down to give luscious pleasure to both. She grabbed both hood scoops with her hands and humped herself to delight. After her crescendo, she pulled off Naci and offered to change positions so he could enjoy his climax. He agreed, and this time, she sat at the edge of the front right fender that gave a perfect height for Naci to deliver pleasure to both. She leaned back on her elbows, raised up her hips and cried out, "Hurry, Naci, I want you buried deep inside of me." He wasted no time; Naci split her pink flesh with a commanding cadence and delivered erotic pleasure to her. He raised up on his toes and found her G-spot.

Naci didn't need to be told twice; he hammered her with every ounce of strength he could muster. Her wetness continued as if she hadn't fornicated for months. Her eyes gleamed with sheer delight while he drove her to the point of no return. She grabbed her plump, vibrating melons using her fingers lightly to massage her nipples. Sweat dripped from Naci to Barbara's lower stomach. This continued until his jism started to flow. Barbara could tell the exact moment that he uncoiled his spunk. Naci arched his back with an uncontrollable moan then collapsed into her arms in total exhaustion. Barbara dug her nails into his hips and cried, "Oh my God, what a night."

After a few minutes, Naci rose up from Barbara's breasts with a smile and began to speak. The Raven landed on the car's roof.

"How about that, Barbara? I think your new friend likes watching us make love."

"I can't believe that it's not afraid of us."

"Yeah, I know, since the Raven seems to like you; I think you now have a nickname," Exclaimed Naci. "I'll call you Raven. That way, I'll never forget this night. How's that sound to you?"

"Raven, I like it. Yes, Raven."

"Next weekend, we'll come back and see if the Raven is still around."

The following weekend the couple returned, and to their surprise, the Raven greeted them. They took feed up on the mountain to help the bird through the winter. In fact, they never told anyone about the bird or their special spot. They called the spot Raven's Hideaway.

CHAPTER 4

THREE YEARS LATER

"Suhh," Bill instructed with his fingers across his lips. He tapped Barbara on the shoulder and pointed down to the shelterbelt. "Get your rifle ready; he's feeding just below us about one hundred feet."

Barbara raised her 308 and placed the eight-point buck in her scope. The woods were clear with hardly any brush between her and the deer. In fact, it was standing in a small, pine grove. The wind was in the hunter's favor; the deer had no clue that he was about to become roast and stew meat. She gently squeezed the trigger, and the two-hundred-pound deer dropped to the snowy ground. It was a clean kill right through the jugular vein in the neck.

"Atta-girl," Bill yelled. "I knew you could do it." He could not have been happier if it was his kill. "Let's go down for a closer look."

When they arrived at the fallen deer, Barbara took the end of the rifle barrel and poked it in the ribs, making sure that it was dead. "I believe that he's dead," Barbara announced then pulled out her hunting knife and began to gut the future meals. After removal of all organs, Barbara placed her hunting knife back in its sheath.

"Help me put him on my back, Bill, and I'll carry him back to the truck."

"Hell, Barbara Ann, I'll carry him," Bill demanded knowing that the deer was too heavy.

"Nope, you have always preached that he who kills the deer, must carry it out to the truck."

"Okay, have it your way," Bill concluded.

This time, she was in a bit of a bind, with her personal defense training and young age the dead buck proved to be too much for her to carry. Barbara made it about half a mile before she tired out. Bill laughed as usual and helped her pull the dear instead of carrying it. Once back to the house, they drug it up to the large, oak tree in the back yard.

Bill tied the hemp rope onto the deer's antlers with a stern yank. "I'm glad you came home for Thanksgiving break instead of working on campus this year," Bill said in a grateful tone. "Mom and I sure miss you since you started attending West Virginia University. It has been hard on her the past two years since you all left for college. Hell, we even miss old Naci."

Barbara took the loose end and threw it up and over the lower branch. "Yes, I know, but we are trying to finish by working our way through instead of taking out student loans."

"Is he working during the break?" Bill asked.

"Yes, with our apartment rent and tuition, he must work. His job recovering gas well leases as an independent agent keeps him pretty busy. The only time that this client could meet with him was during Thanksgiving because his work has him traveling out of the country most of the year. Naci is meeting some pretty important people due to the work he does." Barbara explained.

"Mom and I worry about you going to school and working. Are you sure that you're happy?" Bill asked.

"Yes, with your help and Uncle Dave's along with Naci's dad and us working, we will be fine," Barbara explained. Bill and Barbara pulled on the rope until the deer hung high enough to keep the dogs and coyotes from making a quick meal of it. Bill tied the rope around the base of the tree.

"Let me ask you one more thing, Barbara Ann."

She turned away suspecting that Bill was going to ask what he had wanted to know since he raised her from a baby. Her birth mother, Bill's sister, sold Barbara Ann when she was just a few days old to a family in South Carolina. When Bill and Stella found out, they drove to the foster parents and brought her home where she remained until she left for college. Bill had been like a father and big brother all in one to Barbara Ann. She couldn't keep anything from him; she just simply loved him too much.

"Yes, go ahead; I know what you're about to ask." Barbara surmised.

"Are you and Naci ever going to get married?"

A tear formed in her left eye, then one in the other. Her fore head drawled, showing pain. The tears began to flow as she bowed her head and held it with her hands. Bill walked up to her and placed his arms around her not saying a word. Five or so minutes passed then Barbara broke the silence.

"We want different things out of life; Naci wants to see the world, travel, and experience different things. I want to stay in West Virginia and work in the mining industry. I've tried to explain to him that coal is energy, and this country needs the coal industry no matter what the Liberals and EPA say. Besides, I don't want to leave you and Mom."

Bill looked Barbara in the eye and proclaimed, "Don't worry about Mom and me; it's your future that you should think about. Did you talk to Naci's parents about this?"

"Yes, they need him in the family business. I've tried to convince Naci to stay, but so far, he hasn't changed his mind." Barbara confessed.

"Let's not give up hope; we will all try and convince him," Bill added. "Never give up on him, Barbara Ann; he is a good man. No matter what happens, he will always be there for you."

"I hope you're right, Bill. I don't know what I'd do without him. We see eye to eye on most things except our future. He seems set on travel, moving beyond what West Virginia has to offer. I know one thing, if Naci doesn't see the world when we graduate, he will be miserable."

"Let's not get all worked up just yet; we still have a year and a half," Bill noted.

"That's right. Let's go in the house and eat. We can worry about it later," Barbara Ann smiled and wrapped her arm around Bill's waist as they returned to the house enjoying the time together.

The whole family was gathered around the table, food loaded on the dining room table and hands folded for prayer. Barbara Ann delivered meal time grace then the room erupted with joy and happiness.

Bill filled his plate full of the usual Thanksgiving foods, turkey, mashed potatoes, gravy, stuffing, cranberry sauce, sweet potato casserole, and green beans. "You've outdone yourself this year, mom," Bill exclaimed; he devoured the food on his plate as all followed suit. The day ended on a high note. After all the dishes were done, everyone sat around the table and enjoyed each other's company catching up on the latest news and events.

CHAPTER 5

APARTMENT IN MORGANTOWN. ONE YEAR LATER.

The apartment door closed with a distinctive click.

"Raven, is that you?" Naci yelled as he lit the candles.

"Yes, it's me, how are you---?" Raven stopped in her tracks with a grin on her face. "Wow, candle lit dinner? You must have missed me."

"You have no idea," Naci confessed as he lit the last candle.

She hesitated, moved her head slightly and noticed the soft music in the background. It was Jack Jones's Impossible Dreams. Raven threw her car keys on the coffee table as she hurried to greet Naci. Their lips met as if they had been apart for months. A long, loving kiss proved to Barbara how much she had missed the true love of her life. Naci responded with equal passion, and the kiss ended with a long hug needed by both.

"Something smells delicious," Raven commented. "What are we having?"

"Your favorite, fresh trout, twice baked potato, and asparagus followed by sweet German Chocolate Cake," Naci proudly remarked.

"Wow, I should go away more often," Raven commented as Naci motioned for her to sit. He pulled the chair out; Raven moved into position, and he helped her slide the chair up to the table. He unfolded a napkin and placed it on her lap. Next, he poured two glass of Asti Spumante and handed one to Raven. "Here's to our happiness," Naci held the glass up to Raven's, and with a slight ting, the two glasses met. They each took a sip as they looked each other in the eyes. "You know, Raven, during the day my heart is filled with love, and my dreams at night are only of you," Naci confessed. Raven's eyes filled with love and appreciation. Naci smiled then escaped to the kitchen. Raven took a deep breath then a small sip of wine. "This is really something, I'm getting the royal treatment," Raven thought.

Naci returned from the kitchen with two perfectly loaded steaming dinner plates. "This is simply delicious looking," Raven observed as Naci placed the plate in front of her. He sat his plate down across from hers.

"Please, indulge," Naci suggested as he took his seat and unfolded his napkin.

Raven took her first bite and savored the fresh trout seasoned with lemon juice and light pepper. "Mm, this is delicious Naci, how thoughtful of you to prepare a welcome home dinner." Raven placed her left hand out on the table for him to hold.

Naci responded and smiled while he held his glass up gesturing a toast. Raven followed suit and placed her glass up to his. "May our relationship never change, never end, and when we are sitting across the table twenty years from now enjoying the same meal, may it be with the same amount of love that we cherish today," Naci toasted then gave his glass a soft tap to the side of Raven's. They both looked deep into one another's eyes as they sipped the wine. "You know, Raven, I cherish every minute that we're together. My love for you is like an addiction. I can't help myself; you are the center of my world."

Raven placed her glass on the table, smiled, and took her hand away from his to resume eating. A long silence followed as her eyes began to tear up. After a few minutes, Raven broke the silence and vowed, "You know that I love you Naci with all my heart, but this and a hundred more candle lit meals will not change how we differ."

Naci interrupted, "What are you getting at, Raven?"

"Hell, you know exactly what I mean, our future," Raven spoke with a harsh tone. "My mind is made up; why can't you see it my way? All that I'm asking is that we take it slow after graduation, stay here, and work in the coal fields. You know mom isn't getting any younger."

"We've been over this time and time again; let's not get into this tonight. Let's just enjoy each other and live for the moment," Naci commented as he looked her deep into her soft brown eyes and smiled.

"No, no, you're not going to do this to me again."

"What?"

"You know what I mean; you slide this issue under the covers and change the subject every time I bring it up."

"Under the covers is where we do our best work," Naci returned with a smile as he held his wine glass up mocking a toast, then he took a drink.

"Damn it, Naci, I'm tired of talking about this. For once, take me seriously. Why can't you just agree to stay here for a few short years after we finish college and enjoy time with our families?"

Naci sat across from Raven with a completely changed demeanor; he looked deep into her eyes with a grimace on his face that she had not seen before. It scared her. Raven saw something for the first time that she hadn't noticed before, a side of Naci that she wasn't sure she wanted to know. He looked cold, emotionless, and like it was killing him to talk about this subject. The cold silence lasted for what seemed like an eternity. Raven was afraid to make a sound; her voice was locked, her mind racing with all kinds of thoughts. "Why doesn't he confide in me? What is so secretive that he can't tell me?" Then Naci broke the silence and confided, "Look Raven, my love," he leaned over the table and placed the palm of his hand on her left cheek. "My Barbie," His voice began to quiver, and his eyes began to tear. "I can't begin to explain how this subject has hurt me; it is like a knife in my heart. I am convinced that our love for each other is pure. Neither you nor anyone else on planet earth will ever convince me that we are not made for each other. It is like God has a plan for us, to do great things, but not here."

Raven grabbed both of Naci's hands, holding them as if this was the last time that she would touch him like he was slipping into a deep pool of water never to be seen again. "No, no, Naci don't talk like that; we can work this out, somehow, some way. We will make it work; trust me. I don't want to lose you." Tears flowed from her eyes and down her soft cheeks. With a scared quiver in her voice, Raven began to absorb what was happening, and her temper began to take control, "Damn it, Naci, I don't want to go on without you. Do you understand?" She pulled her hand back, picked up her wine glass, and threw it against the wall. Wine painted the wall, and glass peppered the floor. "I must have you in my life; I don't want it any other way." Raven forcibly stated while she pounded her hands onto the table shaking the contents to the floor. "How in the hell can you throw away eight years?"

"I'm not throwing away our relationship. Let me explain; just calm down. We will get through this," Naci pleaded.

Raven took a deep breath and then noticed the song playing on the stereo, Andy Williams's "Can't Get Used to Living Without You."

"Ah shit, turn that damned music off," Raven shouted.

Naci obliged and flipped the switch; silence fell over the room.

"All right, start explaining," Raven demanded with a look on her face that Naci hadn't seen before. For the first time, they both discovered a serious flaw in their relationship. They both knew it but hadn't confronted it in this way before. The broken wine glass shattered about, the wine still running down the wall. The half-eaten dinner Naci just prepared sat under the lit candles. Raven looked at Naci with anticipation while waiting for his explanation. Her heart raced, not from fear but anger. What in the world could explain why he was acting this way? Naci continued to do what he did best. He stood up from the table, walked around, and gently grasped both Raven's hands. She resisted, but that didn't deter him. When Naci felt the resistance, he stroked the back of her right hand while he gently rubbed her head. He knew not to force the issue.

"You know, Raven, we are a perfect match. We respect each other in every way possible. You and I are meant to be together. From the very first time I saw you, I knew we were meant for each other. That means that what we have now is solid. Our love grew stronger as we got older, which means our love is everlasting. We have shared so much together. Your family is very special to you, and I grew to understand why. Watching you and them together made me realize how special you are. You have become a great person, and I want the very best for you. I wouldn't risk this for anything. I truly love you and want to spend every possible minute with you."

She looked up as forgiving tear filled brown eyes. He gave a gentle pull that asked Raven to stand up. He tenderly put his arms around her waist and took his right hand to rub her back. She turned her head and laid it on his chest. Naci whispered, "I love you more than anything or anyone in this whole world."

Raven took a deep breath and returned the jester.

"Naci, I do love you, but you must understand my position on this. I don't want us to part ways, and in the same token, I don't want to leave Mom; she is getting older and needs me," Raven explained.

Naci knew that he must be careful how he responded; he certainly didn't want to upset Raven because of how strongly she believed in staying.

"Just explain to me why you don't want to stay?" Raven asked. "Don't beat around the bush, Naci; tell me why you want to leave."

The room fell silent. Naci's strategy didn't work, and he knew it. Raven didn't buy the stall technique. Sure, she believed that he loved her deeply, but now, he didn't have a choice but to confide in her.

"Okay, I will tell you the whole truth and the reason why I can't stay after we graduate," Naci confessed as he gently pulled her away from the hug and softly placed his hands on Raven's shoulders. He looked her dead in the eyes.

Raven saw the seriousness that Naci displayed. Her heart began to race with uncertainly and fear. Her hands felt balmy and cold. Raven held her composure while waiting for him to continue.

"You've met my parents and grandparents." Naci started to explain with anxiety. He knew that by telling her the truth, he was putting her life in danger, but if he didn't, she could be gone forever.

"Yes."

"You must promise not to tell a soul," Naci demanded with a firm conviction.

Raven swallowed then answered, "I promise."

"First, our last name isn't Fennell."

Raven looked shocked and confused as anger began to build. A thousand thoughts flowed through her mind. After a minute, Raven drawled her fist back and smacked Naci in the jaw. She followed with a solid hit to the stomach that slightly bent him over.

"Then, what the hell is it?" She demanded with her body in the attack mode that was drilled into her by her uncle.

Naci knew that he deserved it, but none the less, he didn't expect such a violent reaction. He rubbed his jaw and stomach at the same time. He looked Raven in the eye then smiled.

"I knew you would be upset, and Lord knows, I've wanted to tell you a thousand times before, but the family discouraged it. They are going to be upset when I tell them."

"Naci, or whatever you name is, quit stalling," Raven demanded as she grabbed his shirt collar and gave it a hard pull while she drove her knee into his crotch.

Naci moaned and folded up in the middle. The pain shot up to his ribs. If she had been any other person, Naci would have beaten her to a pulp.

After Naci finally stopped coughing, he started to explain only to be interrupted by Raven's phone. She glanced at it lying on the table after the third ring. She quickly grabbed it and answered it.

After a few seconds, Naci could see the life drain out of her. When the conversation ended, she laid the phone back on the table and looked at Naci then began to cry.

"What's wrong, Raven?" Naci asked.

"Mom died a few minutes ago," Raven quivered then fell into his arms sobbing.

"Oh, honey, I'm so sorry,"

They both held each other and cried.

★　★　★

The funeral was held a Walker Memorial Cemetery. The weather was cool with clear skies. Reverend Baker conducted the service reflecting on Mrs. Beirne's life without her loving husband, who left this earth thirty years prior. Her struggles and triumphs raising ten children and Barbara were nothing short of monumental. No government assistance was accepted or considered. The Beirne Family had too much pride and dignity. Every sibling, their families, and life-long friends and coworkers of the elementary school attended. Community leaders either attended or sent their regards.

"May God have a special place in heaven for Stella. She was the glue that held the family together after the tragic death of her late husband, John. She lived a life of hardship and somehow provided for her ten children by cooking day after day at the Summersville Grade School. Most remarkably, she gave up her summer vacation to cook for the various events at the Memorial Park. Her dedication to her family and community is sure to put a smile on our Lord's face as he meets her coming through the pearly gates. Friends, please remember Stella Beirne as a child and shepherd of God, who will be remembered for years to come in our hearts. Let us pray," the Reverend commanded.

"Lord, as you look upon your kingdom with all your wisdom, please make a special note for the kindness and selflessness that Stella has given to her family and to those of us who personally knew her. Thank you for all the times that we sat with her listening to her stories and to all of her kind words about her family and friends. Please make certain that she has a special place in heaven to rest, Lord knows she deserves it. We have sent to you, God, a precious gift; please welcome her. Thank you, Lord, for the beautiful day that you have provided, and please watch over all of us, and grant us safe travels back to our homes. Amen."

The attendees began to break up with children running back to the cars that they came in. Reverend Baker was consoling the family as others began to walk to their cars. Raven and Bill stood at the casket's side giving a last good bye. Although Stella was getting old, it was still hard to say goodbye. Naci stood back leaving the family to grieve together. He felt alone at the funeral; family and friends noted that he was not at Barbara Ann's side due to her request. Naci hadn't spoken to Raven in three days.

After about fifteen minutes, the family began to disperse. Naci stood firm and watched Bill and Raven leave together in Bill's car. Alone, he walked down to the grave and placed his left hand on Stella's casket in the same place her hands were crossed inside. His head bowed.

"How can I ever get used to the idea that you are gone? I love you and miss you tremendously. Your warm smile that you gave me a thousand times, I will truly miss. I can honestly say that you were an inspiration to me for several years as I grew older. I thank you for letting me into your heart and your home. Thank you for believing in me and trusting me with Barbie. Also, Stella, thank you for keeping my secret and not telling her. May God find you as good of a friend and confidant as I have; rest in peace, my good friend. Oh, one more thing, I'll see you in seventy or eighty years," Naci quavered under his breath with his head bowed over her casket. A single tear dropped from his eye and landed on her casket.

★ ★ ★

Naci pulled into the driveway of the home place where everyone gathered after the funeral. When he stepped out of the car, Bill met him in the driveway alone.

"Barbara Ann asked me to stop you before you came in. She would like for you to leave for a few days. Now look, Naci, I haven't had a chance to find out why, but I will. Then, I'll talk with her. Something is bothering her. At first, I thought that it was Mom's death, but now, I'm confused. Give it a few days, and I will call," Bill explained.

"Okay, I'll wait, but please tell Barbie that I love her and understand," Naci returned.

Bill put his arm around Naci's neck and pulled down placing Naci's fore head against his. Naci smiled at Bill and gave him several pats on the back. The two separated and Bill stood looking at Naci as he closed the door and started the car's engine.

The Firebird backed out of the drive and down Irish Corner. Naci didn't see Raven standing at the living room window crying.

Bill returned to the house where he found Raven standing at the living room window. "All right, Barbara Ann, what is this all about? Naci is a good man. Asking him not to come in is not like you; what's wrong?"

Bill put his arms around her shoulders and led her to the couch. Barbara wiped the tears from her eyes and sat down.

"The past few months, Naci has changed; he seems different. I noticed that he began to withdraw. At first, I thought it might be another woman because he traveled and was gone a lot. I'm still not sure, but one thing I do know is that his love and devotion to me is as strong as ever; that's what has me confused. Deep down inside of me, I know that he loves me; I just know it. Just before you called to tell me about Mom, he was starting to open up. He confessed to me that his name was different. We never talked about it again. On the ride down here from Morgantown, we were silent. Bill, I just don't know," Barbara explained.

"I know one thing, Barbara Ann, until you and Naci talk, you can only speculate. Give it a few days then talk to him; find out the truth. You owe your relationship that much."

"I know, Bill. I love you," Barbara wept as she laid her head down on his shoulder. He held her hand and caressed her head.

★ ★ ★

Two weeks passed, and Naci hadn't heard from Raven. His work and studies had taken a back seat to her absence. The agony of loneliness dominated his mind. With each passing day, the pain in his heart was increasing substantially. His head ached, and his appetite vanished. Even still, he respected Raven enough not to call.

Four weeks later, Naci was near depression. He hadn't slept or eaten for three days. His work and studies had stopped. Naci resorted to driving day and night; he didn't know what state he was in. He drove until the Firebird was near empty then stopped for gas. Still, he promised not to call. Near total exhaustion, Naci pulled into a Holiday Inn. He opened the door to his room; it felt cold, maybe because he was so tired. After a hot shower, he slid into bed and instantly fell into deep sleep. An hour later, his cell phone rang, but it fell on deaf ears. The screen indicated that it was Raven calling.

★ ★ ★

The maid unlocked room 402, entered the bathroom to clean, and noticed Naci's clothes lying on the floor. She exited the bathroom and went to the bed where he was still asleep. She could see Naci on his back, head turned with both arms out from his side. The bathroom light penetrated the darkness just enough to show the maid his hard body. She stood frozen not because she hadn't seen a man naked, but it had been awhile. The sheet only covered his one leg and groin. For a moment, she dreamed of what it would be like to make love to a man again; her loin began to throb; her heart beat came alive, and her mind felt a shower of goodness. She knew she'd better return to her work before her lust exploded.

"Hey, Mister, you need to get up," the maid shouted and shook the bed. She walked to the window and opened the curtain. Bright Florida sunshine poured in over Naci's face. He moaned and turned over.

"Are you staying another night?" she quizzed.

"Huh?" Naci moaned. The deep sleep seemed to have his eyelids glued shut.

"You must either pay for another night or get up?"

Naci sat up in bed and asked, "What time is it?"

"Noon," the maid responded.

"Thank you," Naci declared as he stood up in front of her. He forgot that he wasn't wearing any clothes and walked over to the window. "Nice day, isn't it."

The maid stood without answering; she just stared. Her lust and desire returned; only this time, she knew what she wanted, and it wasn't the job that she was paid to do. Naci stood with the fourth-floor window at his back and smiled still not aware of his nakedness. With electricity sparking in her body, the maid flipped the door latch to the lock position. Naci still half asleep and not quite aware of the situation smiled as she approached him with a seductive grin. Her arctic blue eyes glazed with lust and indicated that she was pleased Naci was placed in this room by the front desk. Naci was now more awake and noticed the lustful look that she displayed. Underneath the maid uniform was a voluptuous twenty-eight-year-old woman who didn't have a wedding ring on. She wasted no time letting Naci know exactly what she wanted. Her wicked eyes stole Naci's attention as she placed both arms around his waist and delivered a deep, long, wet kiss. Her style was different than Raven's. Her tongue action was much less than he was accustomed; a void seemed to exist, so Naci filled it with his. This was just the right move to elevate her mood. She wasted no time using her fingers to explore his back. As the passion flourished, she worked both hands down to the cheeks of his derriere giving notice to him that she meant business.

Naci felt the hormones begin to rage inside his loins. His male Alpha started to erupt with escalated breathing. A natural moment broke the lustful kissing as Naci picked her up and gently placed her onto the king-sized bed. He hesitated to admire the beauty hidden beneath the maid's uniform. She moaned when she placed her arms above her head to tease her victim like a black widow spider luring its prey into her web. Her ash blond hair flowed over her shoulders; her face of an angle hid the upcoming action of the devil. The horny maid patted the bed to her right indicating that she wanted to take charge and for Naci to heed her command. Seeing him on the bed made her body tingle from head to toe. She unfastened her top snap and unzipped her maids dress. In one swift movement, she pulled the dress up and over her head revealing her soft but firm breasts hidden in a black, lace bra. Her natural blond hair floated down and covered her face, a quick sweep with both hands gently placed her hair back into its natural position. She loved the freedom of near nakedness. She straddled her victim giving Naci a front row seat to her luscious body. The sword of his desire grew by the second as it rubbed the back side of her ass. She knew his needs and wanted to satisfy him, so she became motivated to fornicate. The maid stood up and removed her panties and wasted no time finding his pleasure rod. When she was about halfway down on it, Naci could feel her gratitude by the amount of sweetness that flowed from her pleasure valley. It flowed like a river of warm honey that gave Naci immediate sensuality. When he was completely penetrated, she began to work her magic. The desire and satisfaction on her face told Naci that it had been a while since she was with a man. With her eyes closed, she absorbed all the pleasure her hips delivered. Her movements on top indicated that she received deep pleasure with each stroke. Naci's hands were busy caressing her firm, taut breasts through her bra. This gave her additional pleasure. With one easy snap, her straps swung around to the front. Naci grabbed the center of her bra and flung it across the room. This freed her perfect globes, bouncing with joy. He placed his open palms over them to help stimulate her taut, brown berries. After a few strokes, the maid groaned with delight.

"Jesus, I'm going to cum!" The vixen whispered; her blushed expression showed her joy. The bottom of each stroke gave an extra pelvic hunch that delivered the nectar of her soul. She placed both hands on Naci's shoulders and gave one last hard hunch. Then it happened; she drawled her hips up almost to the point his member escaped the warmth of her love box. She held her hips high and began to quiver; the river of pleasure began to flow down on Naci's stomach. Her spasms continued for at least thirty seconds.

"Holy shit, what a ride! It's been a long time," the maid confessed. She sat on his shaft not wanting to dismount. Her breaths in tiny pants, she realized her curvaceous hips were hungry and needed attention. She began to gently hunch back and forth; the motion gave her pleasure. With her back arched and eyes closed, she concentrated on the sweet goodness nature ingrained into her genes. The second flow of sweet nectar of her orgasm added to the bliss. By now, Naci couldn't control his rapture. After a few seconds, she collapsed onto the bed beside him. Satisfied the maid quivered for about five seconds while she admired Naci. The expression on her satisfied face showed Naci her delight and appreciation for his performance. He touched her face and gently wiped away the tears. He knew that they were tears of thankfulness. Her flush subsided as her heart beat returned to normal. The maid's emotions began to flourish as she smiled at Naci. She leaned over and kissed his forehead.

"Guess you'll need to change the sheets now," Naci laughed.

The maid smiled, "Hi, my name is Lynn. What's yours?"

Naci looked her in the eye, raised up on his left elbow, placed his right palm on her sweaty cheek, and announced, "We'd better jump into the shower and get you cleaned up."

"Oh, no, you don't get off that easy. Tell me your name."

Naci stood up and held out his hand. Lynn accepted, and he helped her up and followed her into the bathroom where she turned on the water and gathered clean towels.

"Look at the register at the front desk, and you can find out my name."

The hot shower felt good to Naci. He lathered up a washcloth and began to wash Lynn's back. He rubbed her starting with her shoulders and worked his way down. When he reached her milky bottom, he caressed her perfect tush much slower. He rubbed each side from the outside to the inside and down her crack. When he softly pushed the washcloth between her cheeks, Lynn hunched her hip back and slightly spread her legs. He began a cadence of this very motion knowing that it gave pleasure to her. Naci could see her free hand begin to rub her love button. Next, he pulled Lynn to his stomach and began to wash her luscious breasts. With each soapy stroke, he rubbed her begging nipple. Naci caressed one nipple then the other. He could see her wet head turn to her right, and she angled it up. Her lips began to move in and out; her eyes were closed as she absorbed the pleasure that he gave to her.

"Oh, fuck, don't stop; I'm past the point of no return," Lynn sobbed in a low, voluptuous voice. She increased the rubbing between her legs, and Naci continued to caress her breasts.

"Oh, oh, I'm spent, "Lynn whispered as her body fell limp. Naci held her until the last quiver subsided. Once the climax ended, they finished washing each other.

Naci stepped out of the shower and wrapped a towel around his waist. Lynn smiled as she stepped out of the tub shower. Naci could now see her luscious body. He held a towel around her back then wrapped it in front. Lynn grabbed an extra one from the rack as they left the bathroom.

"You are quite something, Lynn," Naci complimented.

"You're not so bad yourself."

"It has been years since I enjoyed sex like this. Thank you." Lynn said in a sensual tone.

"I'm glad that you enjoyed it."

Naci finished drying himself then started to dress.

"Well, big guy, do you think you'll be in town long?"

"I don't really know. It depends."

"On work or how horny you'll be in few hours?" Lynn remarked with a smile.

"I think you're a tease, or are you offering me a reason to stay?"

"I get off at six. Why don't you stop by and find out?"

Naci picked up his back pack, slung it over his shoulder, and looked at Lynn. She returned a confident smile that triggered something in his mind. They both drew together and kissed.

"I don't know what else to say," Lynn confessed.

"Same here, Lynn."

"Maybe we've said enough," Lynn suggested.

Naci stopped, thought for a second, then said, "I may just take you up on your offer. I don't think we've said enough."

Lynn smiled at Naci then gave him a wink.

Naci nodded as he left the room, turned down the hall, and never looked back. He pulled his cell phone out to check messages and grumbled, "Damn, it's dead."

The day felt good. Naci observed the clear, blue skies and warm Florida breeze as he stopped at the car door. The sun massaged his face as he placed his sunglasses on the bridge of his nose.

"I may just hang around in Florida," Naci mumbled to himself as he opened the car door and slid into the bucket seat. He plugged in his phone to charge and thought, "Damn, I'm hungry."

The Firebird turned into the parking lot of Jerry's Barbeque. When Naci entered, he noticed the young waitress behind the counter.

"What will you have?" she asked.

"What's good?" Naci asked.

"Well, just about everything, but I'll tell you what I like."

"Okay."

"I like the pulled pork platter with extra sauce, corn on the cob, and cole slaw," the waitress promoted.

Naci smiled, which was something that he hadn't done very much lately, "Sounds good to me."

He pulled out his phone and turned it on. After a few minutes, the screen lit up, which indicated a missed call. Naci saw that it was Raven and noticed that she called over fourteen hours ago. His face drew a long, stale expression. At first, he felt a warm glow in his heart. Then it dawned on him, "She left me hanging for over a month, so I think I will let her wait too." He returned the phone to his pocket.

The meal was every bit as good as the waitress claimed. Naci asked for the bill and decided to call his parents to let them know where he was.

"Hello, Dad," Naci announced.

"Yes, I'm fine. I'm in Florida."

"How long? Oh, I don't know. Can you get along without me for a few weeks?" Naci asked.

Naci held the phone listening to his father for at least five minutes. He explained the family business is growing, and Naci is needed. In fact, his father suggested that he take a leave of absence from college.

"Yes, taking a few months off from school is fine. Could you call the university and tell them?"

"Thanks, and I'll see you in a few weeks."

"Hold on, son," his father mused. "What about Raven have you convinced her to work for us and travel yet?"

"No, I don't think we are going to work out. She hasn't called for over a month. I've tried to convince her, but as you know, her mom passed away a month ago, and she has shut me out of her life."

"Don't give up on her son. She is good for you, and from what you have told me, she would make a good fit."

"I know; never give up. Okay, I'll see what I can do, goodbye."

CHAPTER 6

"**B**arbara Ann, let's go to the Stonewall Jackson Grill and get some lunch," Bill said as he was coming into the kitchen. "Hell, you need to get out of the house; it'll do you some good."

Barbara looked at Bill, smiled, then added, "Okay, Dr. Beirne, I'll let you take me as long as you're paying."

"Sounds good to me," Bill approved, "Now, get ready."

Bill opened the diner door for Barbara then stepped in and waited to be seated.

"Follow me," the hostess commanded. "Is a window seat okay?"

"That's fine," Bill returned as he took his place in the booth.

Barbara nodded her approval as she slid into the seat across from Bill.

The waiter showed up and took their order of baked steak and gravy. Everyone knows that this is the specialty of the house, so naturally, that is what is ordered.

Bill smiled and looked Barbara in the eyes, and she did the same. He spoke, "Barbara Ann, you know as you go through life many things can and will happen to you. Some will be planned; some will not. You must always be prepared, and mostly, be prepared for the unplanned events. They usually happen when you least expect them, and those are the ones that could be the most important. I've been very fortunate during my lifetime and have made the right decisions because I always had a plan. Occasionally surprises came up, but I managed to make the right choices."

Bill took both hands and reached under his shirt collar and pulled a thick neck chain up and over his head. Hooked on the lower end of the loop was St. Christopher's cross. He placed it in his right hand as he smiled and looked at it. Then without a word, he raised his head up to meet Barbara's eyes. Bill motioned for her to bow her head as he gently placed the cross around her head. He then helped Barbara to pull her coal black hair through the chain. Bill took the suspended cross and placed it into her right hand then closed her fingers to form a tight fist. He took both his hands and placed them over her clenched fist, saying "Barbara Ann, I don't want you ever to remove this cross from your body no matter what. It will always take care of you so please never forget this conversation. It has served me well, and it's time for it to do the same for you. Now, look me in the eye and promise to never, under no circumstance, take the cross off, promise?"

Barbara smiled with deep emotion, "I promise." Bill smiled and removed his hands and watched his niece carefully place the cross under her shirt. He then pulled a small notebook out of his shirt pocket and handed it to Barbara Ann. "What's this?" She asked while looking at the notepad.

"There is a list of clues on the pages. They don't make much sense now, but in time, they will. When you figure out the final clue, it will give you the location of a very important manual that I've written. Once you find it, put it in a safe location, and most importantly, don't tell anyone, promise?"

"I promise. I don't understand, but this will be between you and me," Barbara Ann promised.

Bill looked at Barbara and smiled. She returned the smile with a heavy heart.

Bill asked, "Well, it's been over three months, and you haven't called Naci back Barbara Ann. You kept him in the dark for a month, and when he called you, what happened?"

"I wanted to see him, but he was in Florida and not ready to return. Naci needed time to sort things out. I'm afraid that I screwed up by shutting him out after mom's death. We talk from time to time when needed. He quit school to work for his family full time. He's doing what he wanted to do all along."

"Did you ever find out what his name is?" Bill asked.

"I've asked, but Naci explained that as long as we are apart, there's no sense in going down that road."

"How do you feel about him?"

"Damn, Bill, I still love him, but now, he's the one who's shutting me out. A piece of my heart has been ripped out of me," Raven explained in a hopeless tone.

Bill placed both his hands on the table with his palms up. Barbara followed by placing her hands on top of Bill's to bring comfort to her in time of need. They looked each other in the eyes, and Raven could see the pain Bill had for her, his eyes began to tear. Raven saw this and began to cry as her emotions took command. She had hurt the most important people left in her life, and now, she could see the pain that it had brought to Bill. Unexpectedly, a loud crack filled the air. It made a sound familiar to Raven's ears. She couldn't believe what she saw. The large plate glass window next to their booth shattered into a hundred pieces. She closed her eyes and lowered her head to avoid the flying glass. Barbara also felt Bill's grip relax and pull away with the force of a tandem truck. When the glass stopped flying, she opened her eyes to witness the horror of what had just happened. Bill was lying on the diner floor with a bullet through his skull.

"Oh my God, Bill!" Raven screamed as she fell to the floor to comfort him. She placed his blood-soaked head into her lap and screamed, "Somebody, call 911."

The tears began to flow as she held Bill. The patrons screamed as they ran out the back door. Raven knew deep down that Bill was gone. A thousand thoughts ran through her head.

"Why did this happen, and who would do this?" Raven cried and cried until the ambulance and police arrived. Suddenly, Raven realized that she lost her mom, Bill, and Naci all in four months. The anger began to build. Once the paramedics took over, Raven went outside. A natural thing began to happen. She put her sorrow aside, and with an unusually clear head, she wanted to find the killer and ravish hell on him. She knew from Bill's training and stories of his experience in Viet Nam to look at the angle the kill shot came from. She looked across route nineteen. Beaver Creek was beside the road, then a stand of trees, and after that an open field.

Raven thought, "There's no good place for a sniper." She looked to her right, and up on a mountain, she realized that the mountain was the only place that he could have taken the shot. "Now, I know where. I still need to know why. I will not rest until I find out who and why they did this." Raven growled under breath.

Raven jumped into Bill's truck, drove south, and turned left into the Peck farm in hopes to find the sniper. She hiked through the woods until she reached the top of the mountain above the Stonewall Jackson Grill and then scouted until she came to the only place the sniper had a clear angle for the kill shot. She saw a blanket and one empty shell casing. Raven picked it up and smelled it. She sat on the ground just above the blanket to think. Raven could see the imprint of the sniper on the blanket. She could see the tripod imprint in the soil. She sat thinking about what happened. "How did the sniper know that we would show up at the Stonewall Grill, and how did he know to be at this exact spot?" Raven thought. "Why would they want Bill dead and not me?"

Raven sat on the mountain and studied until the police arrived.

"Took you guys long enough to get up here," Raven scolded.

The officers nodded knowing that she was right. It took them too long to figure out that the shot had to come from this spot.

"You will need to go back to the diner and talk to Detective Reed," the officer demanded.

"Tell Detective Reed that if he wants to talk to me, he'll need to look me up. I have a killer to find," Raven announced as she took off through the woods.

Raven pulled Bill's truck into the driveway and turned off the engine. Bill's wife came running out to meet Raven.

"Are you all right, Barbara?" she asked. Her eyes were red and swelled from crying since the police called. Beth managed to respond.

"Yes, I'm fine. How are you?" She returned with tears forming.

"I can't believe that he's gone," Beth sobbed, and Raven hugged her.

After a few minutes, Raven pulled back and asked, "Beth, did Bill talk on his cell phone this morning? Did anyone call him?"

Beth thought for a minute then returned, "Yes, I believe he received a couple of calls, but that's not important now. I must tell you what I just found out."

"Go on; what are you talking about, Beth?" Raven asked.

"Bill had a secret; he didn't work on construction full time. The only time he drilled was on local jobs. When he traveled out of town, he worked at another job. I'm not sure what he did, but I found plane tickets for several flights during a couple of week job when he was supposed to be drilling. The out of town drilling jobs were always in one location. When they were completed, he came home. He never traveled to multiple sites while on the road," Beth explained. "There's one more thing; Bill gave me an envelope several years ago to keep, and he told me to open it only upon his death." Beth handed the opened envelope to Raven, and she read: "The Lion's roar is not at you, but his breath stinks; he could be your friend. Watch out for the Preacher; his gospel does not speak the truth. Rothman digs coal, but he looks the other way." Raven looked mysteriously at Beth, "What the hell does all this mean?"

"I don't have a clue," Beth answered with a worried look. "Barbara Ann, do you see the phone number at the bottom of the page?"

"Yes," Raven returned after looking down and repeating the number out loud.

"Do you by any chance recognize it?"

"No, should I?"

"It's the bank president's personal phone number. I called this afternoon, and he informed me that Bill had set up a bank account in my name," Beth explained with a tremble in her voice.

Raven looked at Beth with a look of confusion, "And…"

"The account has a balance of over three million, four hundred thousand dollars."

Raven's expression changed; a dead serious look formed with her brow drawled. She asked, "Where did he get that amount of money?"

"I don't know. I don't know," Beth kept repeating with tears running down her cheeks. "How could he keep this amount of money hidden from me, and why hadn't he mentioned it before?"

"I don't know Beth, but I'm going to find out about the money and who did this to Bill if it's the last thing I do; I swear," Raven committed. "I'll be back. I need to find his cell phone."

"Bill left it on the kitchen table. Follow me, and we'll look at it," Beth motioned for Raven to follow her back to the house. Beth picked up the phone and looked at all the recent calls. She scrolled down and recognized every one of them. "I don't see any unusual numbers. I know all these listed."

Raven motioned for Beth to give her the phone. She went to the text and began to scroll and found only one contact.

Lion: What's your 20?
Bill: Home.
Lion: Meet me at the courthouse tonight at 10.
Bill: Will do.

Raven looked at the time on the phone. "This text came in this morning at nine, and it is now three. I guess I need to be at the courthouse tonight."

"Now, Barbara Ann you should notify the police and let them in on this," Beth advised.

"Hell, they would be the last ones I'd call," Raven scorned then continued to look through the phone for clues. "I don't see any more texts or voice mail; he didn't use the phone much."

Raven hugged Beth as the two stood in the kitchen thinking about how their lives changed this afternoon.

"I'm going to lie down for a while," Beth announced as she patted Barbara on the back.

"That's a good idea. I think I will too."

★ ★ ★

Raven's eyes opened as she turned over on the bed to stretch. She noticed the light coming from the kitchen. She got up, exited the bedroom, and walked down the hall to the kitchen door way. Beth was sitting at the table reading a novel. Raven went back to the bedroom and found her phone lying on the bed. She checked the time, 8:50.

She entered the kitchen and grabbed an apple out of the fruit bowl. Beth looked up, "Barbara Ann, I wish you would let law enforcement handle this."

"You know what I think of that idea. I'm taking Bill's Dodge."

"Okay, but I wish that you'd change your mind," Beth pleaded.

Raven picked up Bill's cell phone and walked out the kitchen door into the darkness. She thought that if Lion showed up tonight, he's probably not the killer because he wouldn't know anything about what happened this afternoon. Besides, the letter read, "The Lion's roar is not at you, but his breath stinks." The engine started flawlessly as Raven released the switch. She fastened her seat belt and pulled out of the driveway.

Raven pulled into the abandoned lot across from the courthouse and turned off the head lights. She glanced at her watch and noted the time, 9:30. She then opened the console and pulled out Bill's Glock. When she picked up the handgun, she felt a silencer. She installed it on the Glock's barrel. Raven checked the two clips and chamber for shells. She then exited the truck and walked down Main Street until she met the stair well leading up to the second floor of the radio station. She used to clean the doctor's office located on the same floor and still had the keys. She opened the door and quietly made her way up to Dr. Brown's office. Raven remembered that there was a stairway that led to the roof so she decided that it would be a good location to monitor the upcoming event. Once in place, Raven looked at her watch; it was 9:55.

At precisely 10 PM a strange car pulled up in front of the courthouse and turned out its headlights. As the car came up the street, Raven noticed only one occupant. The driver left the engine running. She could see him through the windshield. He picked up his cell phone and began to type. A few seconds later, Bills phone quacked indicating that a text arrived.

Lion: I see your truck, but not u-what gives?

Bill: I didn't like the surprise at noon.

Lion: I could pretend I don't know, but you're smarter than that.

Bill: Now u tell me-what gives?

Lion: I told the Preacher that if he missed, I'd have hell to pay.

Raven was confused because the letter stated that the Lion was their friend. She grabbed the Glock and opened fire on the car. She aimed through the windshield and drained the clip. She then ran down to the street, and to her surprise, the car was still there. When she opened the door, she understood why. Her excellent marksmanship drove six shells into his legs. Raven placed the fully loaded Glock on his temple and threatened, "If you want to continue to breathe, tell me who the Preacher is and where can I find him." The driver's breathing was at panic mode; with the interior light on she could see why; he was pushing down on his femoral artery trying to stop the bleeding. Raven pulled out her phone and called 911 and told Lion, "I'll either see you in the hospital or hell; now talk."

Raven took out her phone and snapped a photo of the Lion, then continued to interrogate him, "Who are you?" The Lion cried with pain then announced,

"The Preacher is second in command. I take orders from him. I swear to God that I knew nothing about the sniper attack this afternoon."

"Then who is the Preacher, and who does he take orders from?" Raven screamed. Starting to faint, the Lion grabbed Raven by the arm and whispered, "The Big……" He passed out. Blood began to flow from his leg. Raven pulled her sweatshirt off and wrapped it around his leg and tied the two arms together. The make shift bandage seemed to work. She checked his pulse then slammed the car door and ran across the street to Bill's truck. She started the motor and pulled out onto Main Street. Raven took a deep breath and thought, "Damn, that felt good, at least I got some revenge."

The gossip was flying the next morning around town. In the local barber shop located across the street from the courthouse, all three barbers were talking about the past day's events.

The owner of the shop and elderly barber commented to his favorite customer, "Man, the two shooting yesterday was exciting; it surprised everyone. Nothing like this ever happened before in Summersville that I can remember. How about you Big R?"

"You're right, Bob. I never heard such a thing," Big R returned as he took a puff on his cigar. There was a smoking ordinance, but it wasn't enforced.

Bob swung the chair around when he finished so Big R could see himself in the mirror. He observed, "That looks better." Big R approved and nodded his head.

Big R was a pillar of the community. He made his fortune in coal as a mine owner, and everyone liked him because of his generosity. The R stands for Roy, but due to his long standing community charity, everyone called him Big R. He was Bob's first customer some forty years ago. He got up from the barber chair, handed the elder a twenty, and motioned that he didn't want change. Big R exited the shop, crossed the street, and drove off in the same green Ford pickup that he had owned for twenty years.

CHAPTER 7

Raven pulled the Dodge into the hospital parking lot the next afternoon. She entered the main doors carrying a bouquet of flowers and walked up to the information desk. "The gentleman with the gunshot wounds brought in last night, is he taking visitors?" she asked. "Yes, but who are you? I'm Barbara Anderson, my cousin Jenny asked me to deliver these flowers. I don't know him personally but could you see that he gets these for her if I'm not allowed to visit?" Raven asked. The receptionist looked at Raven and asked, "Honey, don't I know you from High School?" Raven returned with a friendly jester, "I'm sorry, but I don't think so. Then again, my memory isn't what it should be." The inexperienced receptionist looked at the patient roster, smiled, and announced, "Hell, deliver the flowers up to room 207. We're a little shorthanded today." Raven thanked her and proceeded to the elevator. The door opened with a ding, and Raven stepped into the hall. She asked for directions and was guided to room 207.

Raven entered the room and laid the flowers on the counter next to the sink. She stood looking at the Lion and said, "You better water these." The Lion turned over to see who his visitor was. "Damn, you have the nerve to show up here. Do you realize that I could call the police?"

"Yes, but you won't and for good reason. You probably are tired of answering questions, and if you drag me into this, it will only cause all those big, bad cops to show up again. The last thing that you want is more attention," Raven returned.

"Go on, and ask me what I was doing at the courthouse last night. Oh, and by the way, I'm sorry Bill's life ended the way it did. He was like a brother to me, and I would have never allowed something like this to happen if I could have warned him," the Lion explained.

"Hell, you expect me to believe you? Last night you alleged that you worked for the Preacher," Raven shouted then realized where she was.

"I don't know how much you know about his job, but…" Raven interrupted, "Bill's wife just discovered that when he worked out of town, he wasn't drilling like we thought."

"Okay then, you know next to nothing," the Lion stated then motioned for Raven to take a seat. "Bill was a contract killer and has been for several years, in fact, ever since he was discharged from the army forty years ago."

With fire in her eye, Raven grabbed the back of the chair and pulled it over to the edge of the bed,

"Tell me everything you know, and I might let you live."

Unfazed and a little annoyed by Raven's threats, the Lion spoke up, "Bill always claimed that you would make a great hit man, excuse the pun."

"You bet, and my first kill is the son of a bitch who killed him," Raven exclaimed with a vengeance in her eyes. "You're not making any sense. If you work for the Preacher, how did you know Bill so well?" Raven asked, paused, and looked the Lion in the eyes. She stood up, walked over to the bed, placed her hand on his throat, and began to squeeze. He grabbed Raven's wrist and growled with pain saying, "I know you have the advantage, but I'm your only source of information for now." Raven held fast; the unshaved stubble pierced her palm. She squeezed and shoved her hand with commanding force just before she let go of his throat. The Lion shot a quick glance at Raven then grabbed his throat to massage the pain away. She walked away from the bed to look out the window. After a short pause, Raven turned, looked the Lion in the eye, and commanded, "Talk."

"Okay, listen carefully. There are two organizations that you need to be aware of. One is good, but the other evil. The Preacher is the kingpin for the Roth. He is the one who took out Bill. The other group is led by The Panther who as far as I know is the head of the Rock Foundation. He is the one who Bill and I work for, not the Preacher. Now, this has nothing to do with the mob or organized drug crime. There is an industry, as we call it, or a movement to clean up America's legal, business, and political landscape. The Rock Foundation goes back for decades before World War II; it is driven by the political right. The

Roth has been around since the early seventies, and their views are the opposite. Their ideology is driven by the political left. Both are heavily funded, and they stop at nothing to accomplish their objectives," the Lion explained. The Lion paused then simply stated, "America is at war with itself."

"So, why did the Preacher take out Bill? He shouldn't be much of a threat after forty years," Raven asked.

"The Roth has offered a bounty for years; every top Roth agent has been assigned to kill him because Bill is a Legend who the Roth named "the Myth." He has single-handedly picked off the Roth's key personnel over the years. His skill level was second to none. I've seen him make a kill shot as far as a thousand yards. Sniper wasn't the only way he worked though; he was excellent at hand to hand fighting. He alone stalled their growth, and no one could take him out. Once they found out who he was and where he lived, it was only a matter of time," the Lion remarked while he shook his head in disbelief. "Damn, I'll miss the Myth."

"Why would you miss him? He worked for the Panther," Raven asked.

"I'm a double agent. Bill and I served together in Nam," the Lion responded.

"Funny, Bill never mentioned you," Raven asked.

"Did Bill talk about any of this?" The Lion asked. Raven knew that he had a good point. She began to understand the scope of this situation. Her mind raced with a thousand thoughts. "So, what you've told me is that this man called Preacher is Bill's assassin and the leader of the Roth?"

"Well, not exactly, the main man for the Roth is not the Preacher, although he's the main field operative. He is not the one who calls the shots."

"Who is? He must be the one ultimately responsible, right?" Raven asked.

"You're going to be surprised when I tell you," the Lion returned as he stared at the distant wall of his hospital room.

"Hey, Lion, or whoever you are, who the hell is the leader of the Roth? I want to start with him and work my way down to the Preacher," Raven scolded with an aggravated tone.

The Lion adjusted his automatic bed, lifting his upper body, then continued, "His name is Roy Rothman, AKA the Big R."

"I don't believe it, what an ass,.I'm going to make him wish that he'd never met me," Raven screamed with hate. "I'll make him wish that he wasn't born." Her face turned red with anger.

"Now, hold on, missy. I know that Bill taught you better. If you go off halfcocked, you're likely to end up like your uncle. For now, you are in way over your head. You're a baby in the woods, Raven. You need help. Besides, the Rock Foundation doesn't take lightly one of its own being assassinated," the Lion made a strong point. "You must put together a plan, run surveillance, and size up your target. Besides, the Roth doesn't know your sudden interest. You have the advantage, so don't blow it. Raven, do not go rogue. You need proper training. If you go rogue, you'll open a can of worms that only the Myth could have closed, and you're nowhere as good as he was."

Raven stared at the floor; her attitude turned callous. She wanted to cross the Rubicon but knew her inexperience could lead to her demise.

"Hold on a minute, you mean to tell me that the Big R and Bill lived in the same town and didn't know each other after all these years? Come on," Raven ramped. "This doesn't make any fucking sense."

"Just proves how good your uncle was. Roth belonged to the same church as Bill."

"If Bill knew the Big R, why didn't he take him out?" Raven quizzed.

"He and Bill were drinking buddies, so naturally, Bill extracted information from him. Hell, he is worth more alive than dead. Somehow the Roth found out that Bill was the Myth, and the rest is history."

Raven stood with her back to the Lion staring out the window and thought, "The son of a bitch makes sense. My question is, who snitched on Bill?"

Raven scalded a gaze to the Lion. His quick eye caught her expression. She took two slow steps to his bed and bent her head down, took her left hand, and pulled her long black hair over her left shoulder. Raven lowered her head down to his ear and whispered, "Okay, Lion, you live for now, but by God, if I discover any of this is not true, I'll hunt you down and ravish pain upon you that will make what I did to you last night seem like a scratch." Raven straightened up, went to the door, turned to Lion, and announced, "I meant every word. In the past four months, I have lost the three most important people in my life, and I don't have a damn thing to lose. If I find out that you set Uncle Bill up, you're dead meat." Raven disappeared into the elevator leaving the Lion worried for the first time in his life.

CHAPTER 8

The dawn light began to edge through Raven's bedroom window. Minutes passed, and the red glow of the horizon dominated the sky. Raven watched the sun rise every morning since her uncle's death. The conversation that she had two days ago with the Lion was all she thought about. She knew the Lion was right, going this alone was suicide. The Roth would hunt her down and make an example out of her. "Oh, shit, I haven't told Naci what happened," Raven thought, and she picked up her phone to check the time. "Damn, 6:30 is a little too early to call. I'll take a run then call," Raven concluded.

The run and shower felt good to Raven; it was a great way to relieve stress. Five miles in the hilly terrain of West Virginia Mountains equated to about ten miles on the beach. Raven pulled the last brush stroke through her long, black hair then picked up her phone. It seemed like an eternity before it began to ring. A distinctive click sounded then a familiar voice was heard, one she truly missed. It felt like heaven to her just to know that in a minutes notice she could call Naci, and he would answer.

"Hello, Naci," Raven gushed.

"Is that you, Raven? It's so good to hear your voice," Naci returned with an upbeat tone.

"How do I begin, Naci? It's Bill; he was murdered two days ago," Raven cried, tears began to flow not only from the thoughts of her uncle's death but to hear Naci's voice, the only true love she had ever known. A long silence commanded the conversation.

"I can't believe it, my God. Are you okay?"

"I'm okay, but I really need you right now. Can you get away?" Raven pleaded with a quiver in her voice.

"Of course, I'll book the next flight into Charleston. Don't worry; I won't let you down."

"God, it will be so good to have you here, and Naci, I'm so sorry for the way that I've treated you the past four months. Can you forgive me?"

"Raven, I will always forgive you. I have never stopped loving you."

Raven started crying uncontrollably. The events she had faced the past few months proved too much to hold it in any longer. "I'm sorry, Naci. I just need you so much; please hurry."

"I will," the phone went silent. Naci stood in disbelief. "The Myth is dead." Naci dialed number one on his speed dial.

"Naci, make it short. I'm busy," The voice demanded on the other end.

"The Myth is dead." A long silence followed, "Are you positive?"

"Raven just called." The phone went silent then disconnected.

This changed the whole strategic landscape between the Foundation and Roth. Roth had always struggled to keep key personnel because the Myth hunted them down. This leveled the playing field; the Roth now had the motivation to recruit top agents.

A knock on the motel door caused Naci to jump up from his stupor. He was half asleep from the long flights. He arrived two hours prior from St. Petersburg, Russia. He knew that it would be Raven, but he still hesitated, not sure how things would go. Did she truly miss and love him or was it just sympathy that Raven was seeking? Naci flipped the latch back, reached for the handle, and opened the door. There she stood more beautiful than he remembered. Her long, black hair seemed fuller, and her face filled with hope that radiated her abundant natural beauty. Her eyes begged to see Naci, and her lips yearned for the sweetness of his soft gentle kiss. "Damn, Naci, don't just stand there; invite me in." Raven commanded with a smile. Naci stepped back and gave her entry then shut the door. She turned, placed both arms around his neck with her eyes closed, and delivered a passionate kiss so powerful that Naci couldn't resist. He responded with the love and passion that the two deserved. Raven pressed her firm breasts upon Naci's chest not to deliver a message of need but to express the loneliness that she had endured during the past several months. The kiss was so powerful, so sincere. Raven wanted, no, needed to show Naci that she was wrong to shut him out of her life. She needed to hear him say "I love you" in person. She pulled her lips away and stared him in the eyes. With both her hands cradled on his face, she longed to hold and caress him. Raven pleaded, "Oh, Naci, I have missed you. I need to hear you say 'I love you, Raven.' I truly am sorry, and I love you so very much."

Naci looked at Raven and returned a kiss so passionate that she knew deep down that he had forgiven her. The passion continued until neither could breathe. Their lips tore apart as they both gasped for air. Naci pushed her long hair back exposing her sensual neck, and Naci began to kiss it with more passion than ever. She rubbed her hands up and down his back to show her needy love. Due to the mounting passion, her loins were on fire. Oh, how she has missed his naked body next to hers. Raven's love flowed from her heart. Naci sensed this and fulfilled her wish with his swelling member. Raven fully understood what she desired, grabbed his t shirt to remove, but it resisted. Frustrated, she ripped it from his chest. She pushed back and looked at his solid muscular chest. She dropped her handbag and shed her overcoat. She kicked off her heels, unfastened her skirt, and grabbed the top of her blouse and ripped all the buttons shedding it from her needy body. She pushed Naci back onto the bed where he uncontrollably fell on his back. Raven reached into her hand bag and exposed a switchblade and clicked it open. Naci's eyes began to show concern until he saw her place it under the front side of her bra and cut it. The sharp edge of the switch blade exposed her round breasts giving them the freedom that they needed. Her pink nipples sprang to life. She then slowly slid the razor-sharp blade down her side, under her panties, and cut each side exposing the sexy round of her small belly. She leaned over and cut Naci's shorts off, which gave freedom to his aching bulge. Raven threw the knife at the wall where it stuck. She climbed on the bed and placed his beast inside of her. She reacted like a starved love addict who hadn't had sex in years. The hot pleasure flowed from her loins up to her luscious breasts. She began to hump and hunch with fever passion. Four or five humps in, she stopped and gave a loud moan, "Jesus, I'm going off," and the love juice began to flow. The sweet scent of her cunt filled Naci's nostrils. His desire to climax heightened. He grabbed her arms and in one swift motion reversed positions. He then began to deliver pleasure upon her. Like Raven, he exploded his passion. He fell on top of her. Their eyes met, something they haven't done in months. She placed her arms around his neck and thought how wonderful his naked body felt next to hers. Raven adored every second that Naci laid on top of her, his hard body pressing down on her side. She lifted up her left leg inviting him to replace the void with his right leg. Naci could hear his heart beating when he laid his head against her right breast. Her neck cradled his head, which gave her a sense of security that she missed. The room filled with the scent of passionate sex. The only noise was the traffic on route nineteen. Raven placed her left hand on Naci's right cheek and began to caress it. She wanted to touch him in every affectionate way possible. She had an overwhelming need to express her love for him. She never wanted to go without him again. Raven knew for sure that she was addicted to Naci and could not go another minute without him.

"What are you thinking?" Raven asked in a quiet tone. She wanted to scream out "I love you," but she knew Naci, and a slow method was the best.

"How good you are in bed." He knew that she couldn't see his face. "Or how about this?" Naci raised up on one elbow so he could see her face, "I love you very much, and if you shut me out again, I'll…" Raven placed her hand on his lips and whispered, "Just shut up, and don't say it. I will never leave you again, but you must promise one thing."

"What?"

'You will never stop loving me no matter what."

Naci nodded then gently delivered a kiss to Raven to show her how much he loved her. Raven responded with a slow, passionate kiss. She deliberately slowed Naci down to prevent this kiss from becoming a heated, lustful sex romp. She drew her head back breaking their lips apart. Her pulse raced not with sexual tension but with passion. Her body trembled with happiness. Raven thanked the Lord with all her heart that she was back with him. Naci couldn't control the passion pouring from his heart. A tiny pause in their emotions gave them an opportunity to look deep into each other's eyes. A deep, ingrained love bloomed with a small tear that ran down each other's cheeks. This very moment gave birth to a powerful and renewed love that both so desperately needed.

Nothing was mentioned about the past few day's events. Raven didn't want to think about anything but her and Naci. She wanted this to be their time together with no distractions or interruptions. Naci sensed this and kept the conversations romantic. They engaged in a gentler, softer intimacy that provided a chance to explore their love instead of their sexual lust. They caressed each other and talked about their feelings into the night. The hours drifted by until sleep dominated both Raven and Naci. They found peace with one another on this magical night.

CHAPTER 9

Naci woke up rested and whole again. Raven was back in his life. She knew her life was different, not because of losing her uncle but because she realized that Naci was her true love. She realized that she should have stood by him and faced the truth about his past. So what if he had lied to her about his name and family secret? Naci was only protecting his family. Raven knew that she was wrong, and now, Naci was back in her life. She was finally ready to talk.

"Hey, sleepy head, are you going to sleep all day?" Naci began to tickle her side. "Don't you know that I hate that," Raven cried. She pretended to act sleepy then turned over and slapped Naci on the butt. "Ouch, that hurt… No, it felt good. Do it again," Naci laughed then pointed to his behind. "You're so funny," Raven returned as she jumped out of bed. Let's take a shower and grab something to eat. I'm starved." Raven started the shower, gathered the towels, and stepped in. Naci followed, and both washed each other and enjoyed the long hot shower.

When Naci finished washing Raven's back, he tapped her on the shoulder and motioned for her to turn around. He noticed the cross hanging on the chain around her neck. Naci started to ask where she got it but noticed a 308-empty shell cartridge hanging on the same neck chain as the cross. He acted as if it had always been there, not asking why she started wearing it. Naci suspected that the empty cartridge was her uncle's kill shot.

They pulled into the Greek Restaurant where the valet attendant opened Raven's door. "How are you today?"

"Fine, thank you."

The restaurant was of normal décor, including tile floors, stucco walls, and tile roof. The host smiled and directed the couple to a table. "Is this satisfactory?" Raven nodded as Naci held her chair. The waiter brought ice water and filled their glasses.

"Would you like to see the wine list?" he offered.

"That's not necessary; just bring a bottle of Chianti," Raven directed.

The waiter did as he was told. He returned with the wine and took their order. "May I suggest pasta with pistou sauce and house bread?"

Raven disagreed, "Not the pistou sauce, too much garlic. Do you have puttanesca sauce?"

"Of course," the waiter answered then stepped over to Naci.

"Just make it the same."

The low volume music made it possible to carry a normal conversation. Two other tables were filled, and the occupants seemed content.

"Naci, we have a lot to talk about. I know that last night was special, and I appreciate you not bringing anything else up except our relationship. I really do," Raven commented. Naci looked at her with bright eyes not offering to interrupt. This is one quality Raven liked about Naci; he didn't speak his mind until it was the right time.

"Since Uncle Bill's funeral, I have found a lot out about him. He had a secret; he was a paid assassin who worked for The Rock Foundation. Have you heard of them, Naci?"

"Yes, I have Raven."

"Okay, before we get into all that, I think you need to be honest with me," Raven stated. "Let's start where we left off several months ago in our apartment in Morgantown. What is your name?"

Naci smiled at Raven and gave her a sincere look then explained, "Okay, here it goes. Our last name is not Fennell; it is Vacara." Raven's forehead drawled slightly. She wasn't sure, but she thought that it sounded familiar. Naci picked up on her facial expression. "Maybe this will help; my parents, John and Pauline Vacara were American Hero's in WWII."

Nodding her head up and down, it came to Raven. "I heard that they retired to a tropical island that is heavily guarded."

"They made several enemies in their time." Naci returned. "They didn't retire. They are a vital component of the Rock Foundation, and yes, among other locations, we have a tropical island."

Raven looked at Naci puzzled. She was not quite mad that he held this from her all these years, but she was partially proud that he was part of a famous family. "So, tell me then; who are the people you lived with all these years?"

"My parents wanted me to have a normal life, so they relocated me here in Summersville with Foundation agents."

"So, you never knew your parents?"

"I wouldn't exactly say that. I visited several times a month flying from my grandmother's compound near Clarksburg," Naci explained. "I actually know the real John and Pauline better than the agents."

"Now, explain the Rock Foundation," Raven said after she had regained her concentration.

"My grandmother, Amelia founded the Rock Foundation," Naci informed Raven. "The Foundation intended to act as a financial watch dog of Congress and to fight the inhumane treatment of humankind all over the world. The goals have changed since those days. Now, the sole purpose is to fight the ideology of the liberals in America. They have way too much influence in this country. Their cause is led by a group of Progressives called The Roth. But I want to make it clear; The Roth has absolutely nothing to do with the Rothschild family. I'll tell you more about them later."

Raven looked disturbed. She growled, "They're led by the Big R Rothman, a pillar of our community, what a piece of shit. He had the whole town around his little finger with all the donations and charity events. What a front and Summersville was the perfect all American small town."

"Yes, and his front as coal operator is ironic because all liberals hate fossil fuels, especially coal. They claim that it contributes to climate change," Naci laughed. He went on to explain more. "He is funded by Wall Street billionaires who say that they believe in green energy. The liberals who are in control of Congress and the White House dole out billions of dollars to these select Wall Street cronies who own failed solar and wind corporations. Most have sold them to the Chinese and any other nation who will pay the price. Our government has brainwashed the middle class into believing that the future of American energy is now with wind and solar, but the technology isn't economically feasible. They are driving up the debt with these programs and others. Also, they are stripping Americans out of the civil liberties while they pay higher and higher taxes to fund green energy along with social programs such as the war on poverty and socialized medicine to name a few. These programs, along with almost every program designed to serve and protect the people, is bankrupting our country through mismanaged and unaccountable leaderships."

"Yes, all conservative Americans know this but have allowed these progressives to take control of Washington," Raven noted. "It's time to drain the swamp called the Washington Establishment." A silence followed that gave the two lovers time to digest the previous conversation. Raven's demeanor began to change as she began to think of the implications of all this and how it affected her life. "Who is the Preacher? He is the son of a bitch who killed Bill." Raven asked with tears in her eyes.

"He's a top Roth operative and Big R's right-hand man. He works mostly in Virginia and D.C. He stays close to politicians to receive information to feed back to the Big R."

"So, he's in the swamp too?"

Naci nodded his head yes.

"I swear to God that I will not rest until I see his dead, sorry ass lying on the ground in front of me," Raven ranted with a look on her face that Naci had not seen before.

"In fact, we want to bring you into the Foundation and train you to be one of our operatives," Naci announced with confidence that she would agree. The unfortunate timing of her uncle's death was the turning point in Raven's life.

Raven looked up from a cold stare and with confidence replied, "I live for the day that I can bring these bastards to justice and justify revenge to Uncle Bill's death."

"Okay, good, but first we need to train you at Wolf Summit, the headquarters for the Rock Foundation," Naci explained.

"I'm ready. Let's go," Raven said with a smile. She stared at her plate; her thoughts were a million miles away. How good it felt to her to have Naci back into her life, and now, she had a plan to avenge her uncle's death. "What did you say about Wolf Summit?"

"It's the Rock Foundation's headquarters here on the East Coast. Intelligence from all over the world comes in and is processed there. The compound is well guarded, and one of our top operatives will train you. With your background and skill set, the training period will be a short one.

Suddenly, the food tasted better, the day seemed brighter, and Raven finally had hope that she could avenge her uncle's death. "When do we start?"

Naci smiled and picked up his cell phone, pressed speed dial, and began to speak. "Hello, yes it's me.

She is one hundred percent on board." A long pause and smile on Naci's face indicated that the recipient gave their approval. "Fine, I will bring her up in a few hours." Naci pressed the off button and laid his phone to rest on the table. "Looks like you are going to become a Foundation operative."

Raven smiled and asked, "Are you parents involved with the Foundation?"

"Yes, both of them are very much a part of the Foundation. In fact, they are at Wolf Summit now. After you are fully trained and when the time is right, you will learn of their involvement."

Raven smiled and finished her lunch. The music seemed softer to Raven, the words of the love songs began to mean something to her. She turned her head as if it made the sound clearer and smiled.

"What's making you smile?" Naci asked with a warm glow and warm sensation.

"Oh, how life throws a curve but somehow things work out," Raven answered as she looked deep into his eyes. "My God, how fortunate I am to have you back in my life." A small tear trickled down her left cheek.

Naci stood up, placed a hundred-dollar bill next to the check, and offered his hand to Raven. She took it and followed him out to the car.

Naci turned the rental car off route 50 onto the paved road. He drove until he came to a large iron gate. It looked as if it had been constructed at the turn of the century, built twice as strong as it needed to be. Naci pushed the speaker button and assured the attendant that he was authorized to enter. The massive gates swung open leaving a channel to enter. Once inside the compound, the grounds resembled the Biltmore in Asheville NC. Large oak trees filled the landscape nestled on the rolling fields giving summer shade to those who might need it. Carefully planted flowers along the drive gave Wolf Summit a distinct beauty.

The doorbell sang a familiar song that brought back childhood memories. An elderly man opened the door and greeted the duo with a smile. "Hello, my man, Naci," the gentleman greeted.

Naci offered his hand, "How in the hell are you, Ethan?" The two hands met with a powerful clasp, and once again, the two tried to out squeeze one another.

Ethan broke first then rubbed his aching hand. "Yes, my best friend, you have become a man."

"Ethan, I would like to introduce Raven. She is very special to me, and I would appreciate if you give her your best attention."

Ethan nodded and stepped aside to allow entry. "Everyone is in the conference room working."

"Thanks, old friend, I can take it from here," Naci informed.

Naci and Raven entered the room, and a blanket of silence fell. Raven's eyes met Amelia's with a look of curiosity. Raven didn't flinch until Amelia gave a slight smile. She walked over with her hand out, "You must be Raven. I've heard a lot about you, and I must say it was all was good."

"I the same, except Naci didn't mention how beautiful you are," Raven complimented as she shot Naci a stern look.

"Uh, okay, Raven I would like you to meet my real parents. John and Pauline walked over to Raven and greeted her. After warm handshakes, John asked, "Can I get you a cup of coffee?" Raven nodded yes.

Amelia turned the conversation over to a more serious tone, "All of us here at the Rock Foundation are truly sorry for the loss of your uncle. He was truly a one man 'Myth.' His contributions will never be equaled, and the knowledge of the Roth that he provided is irreplaceable.

Raven swallowed hard and fought back the tears.

"I understand that you want to become an operative?"

Raven nodded yes then replied, "I want nothing more than to pay back the hell that the Big R gave me when he ordered uncle Bill's death. I want to pull the trigger to end his life."

"Yes, and you will be given that opportunity, but you must understand that it's not the time for the Big R to die. You are not trained. If you were to go rogue and try to terminate him now, you would sign your death certificate," John Vacara informed. "If a Roth agent didn't kill you, we would. Everyone needs him alive."

"I don't understand why you would allow the one person who is responsible for the death of your best agent to live?" Raven asked.

"The Roth is funded by someone in Congress, and we need to find out who. It's that simple," Pauline explained. "So, please don't go off and ruin years of work. We need you to be strong and smart. Killing someone is not to be taken lightly. Not only do you need to be trained on how to kill but also we need to train your mind to accept why you kill. If you don't receive the proper training years, later you could be eaten up with guilt, which may lead to your demise."

Raven nodded in agreement then asked, "I do have one question; who is the Panther?"

Everyone looked surprised when she asked. The room was dead silent. Amelia cleared her throat then asked, "Where have you heard the name Panther?"

"You have an agent named the Lion. I incapacitated him and then delivered flowers to his room while he was in the hospital. Let's just say that after I delivered them, I convinced him that it was in his best interest to talk. He told me about the Rock Foundation and the Roth," Raven explained.

"It looks like you will be easy to train," Naci commented. "You're way ahead of most. To extract information from a veteran agent without training is impressive."

"It wasn't hard. I was holding Uncle Bills hands when he was murdered. That gave me all the motivation that I needed to persuade the Lion to talk. I grew up with Bill. He spent countless hours training me in martial arts and how to shoot. The most important lesson that he taught me was to pick a cause, a damn good cause, and engage in it with all my heart. That's why I'm here, to avenge his death; this is my priority," Raven raged with a look of vengeance that Naci had never seen before.

The room fell silent again. Everyone processed the situation for the next few seconds until Raven commented, "Can the Lion be trusted? I delivered a moderate amount of pain to the Lion and extracted information from him. You know why I'm committed to becoming an agent, but do you know this of every single operative who works for the Foundation?'

Amelia looked pleasantly surprised and commented, "I can see Raven is not only going to be easy to train, but she is going to make an excellent operative. The Lion has been with us as long as your uncle. As far as I know, he has never once questioned his loyalty to the Foundation. Of course, over the years, I have seen agents who completely surprised me. Only family can be trusted, Raven."

"Once you are trained to our satisfaction, you will be sent out in the field to perform certain tasks for us; this will be part of your ongoing training. Some jobs will be meaningless, while others will be sensitive. We will guide you every step of the way," John explained.

"Will I work with Naci?"

"No, and the reason is that you two have an emotional connection. Do you understand?"

"Yes."

"Good." Amelia agreed, "Let's get her in the system and start her training now."

"You still haven't answered my question," Raven persisted.

Amelia returned with a stern voice, "The identity of the Panther is information that you don't need to know."

Raven smiled and returned, "I will make it one of my top priorities to find out who the Panther is."

Everyone one in the room stood silent, each thinking the same, until Amelia announced, "Raven says what she means and will be a formidable agent." Amelia strolled over to Raven and stood toe to toe with her, "Watch what you ask for. You may not want it."

"I have always found a way to get what I want, and if I don't like what I find, you will never hear me complain. I will just deal with it," Raven returned with a confident tone. "Don't misunderstand what I meant, I appreciate the opportunity, but my final goal is to terminate the Big R."

"You know that I've been on this earth eighty plus years, and I don't believe that I've meet a new operative with this much spunk. John, take her under your wing and see that she gets trained, but not with your special skills. She may just be her uncle's replacement," Amelia quipped with a slight grin as she left the room.

Raven was taken back by the confidence Amelia had in her, but she caught what Amelia revealed to John, "What does she mean by special skills?"

Naci shot a quick glance at his father and commented, "What Amelia meant was to skip the Nazi torture procedures."

What Raven didn't know was that John had the most advanced mind in the world because of his genes, special training, drugs, and a Nazi operation to the base of his skull, which made him the world's foremost mentalist. To stay alive, John needed a special serum applied periodically into a tube at the base of his skull.

CHAPTER 10

The plane landed with a slight bump as the wheels touched the surface of the runway. One could see the heat waves rising from the hot, sticky asphalt. Raven's heart was in her throat. When she swallowed, a slight pain followed almost as if she had indigestion. She knew that Naci waited patiently for the past six months while she was in training. The pilot spun the craft around to point the exit door towards the private landing gate. The jet engines began to throttle down with a loud whine. Raven stood up and walked to the front of the plane at the same time as the co- pilot unlatched the door. Naci pushed up the steps to welcome Raven to her first visit to the Vacara Island. Raven gave the pilot a nod of thanks just before she stepped out of the plane. She turned her attention from the pilot and towards the steps. Her eyes lit up when she saw Naci.

Her momentum never slowed until she reached her lover's outstretched arms.

Smiling, Raven hugged Naci as if they had been separated for years. She began to kiss his neck and cheeks then stopped long enough to say, "Oh God, Naci, how I've missed you."

Naci returned to his love, "Six months without you seemed like an eternity. No contact by phone or email was almost unbearable. The only thing kept me from storming Wolf Summit to see you was my commitment to the Rock Foundation."

Raven closed her eyes to concentrate on the euphoria in her mind. Having Naci in her arms meant the world to her. Minutes passed then she felt Naci's heart rate begin to escalate. Raven knew that something was different, call it a gut feeling, but something wasn't quite right. Naci seemed to stiffen up; his muscles began to spasm.

"Come on, Naci, we must not be late," a female voice filled Raven's ears.

She opened her eyes to find the most radiant, glowing woman she had ever seen. Her full body brunette hair bounced as she walked, and when she stopped, not a hair was out of place. Her jaw line offered a chiseled look, and her green eyes announced that she was a woman who always got what she wanted. Her voluptuous body could only be matched by a Playboy model. The overwhelmingly sensuous look could only be outdone by her attitude. Raven found out later that she had enough attitude for the both of them.

Raven pushed back from Naci, then growled with a stern tone, "Why, Naci, don't let the cat take your tongue. Who is this gorgeous woman?"

Naci couldn't make his mouth work. His silence added to the tension.

Impatient, Raven advanced towards the stunning woman with her hand out, "Hello, my name is Raven. Who might you be?"

She offered her hand as well then replied, "Hi, my name is Jill, Jill Carter. I'm Naci's partner."

Raven kept her composure. She looked at Naci and said, "How nice to have such a qualified partner. Is she good at everything she does?"

Naci now on the defensive and able to speak returned with a sharp tongue, "Yes, Raven, she is the best partner I've ever had."

Jill spoke up and informed, "Raven, I'm the lucky one. Naci has helped me out of more than one jam. He's got my back."

"I'm sure that he's good at covering your back, and I bet his most contributing attribute is his ability to keep Foundation information from leaking out," Raven gestured in a less than cordial tone. "He certainly kept you a secret." Raven realized that Naci came on board full time with the Foundation just about the same time that she shut him out of her life. "Shit, I may have driven him into her arms," she thought.

Jill turned toward Naci and announced, "Come on, big guy. We have a briefing to attend." Then she turned to Raven, "I'll have him back before you know it."

Raven, fit to be tied, dictated, "What the hell, Naci? I didn't expect to be cast aside in less than five minutes after I got here."

Naci looked at Raven and explained, "I'm sorry, honey. I don't have any control over these meetings, and I certainly didn't know what time you would be landing."

Raven was stunned by his casual tone. After all, they had been lovers for years. She had it in her mind that she was the only woman in Naci's life. She never dreamed that it could be any other way. "Damn- damn, I may have a problem with this," Raven grunted under her breath. She could feel the hot flash climbing up her spine.

Just then a car pulled up, and the driver exited the vehicle, opened the rear door, and stated, "Miss Raven, would you please get in?" He opened the door with a smile and asked how her flight was.

Raven was still concerned with recent events and didn't hear the driver. She only knew one thing; she was pissed at herself and Naci.

"If you please," the driver pleaded. "Mr. John Vacara wants to see you asap."

Raven shook her head. She was so in disbelief with the presence of Jill in Naci's life that she didn't see the car pull up. "Miss Raven, are you ok?" The driver asked.

"What did you say?" Raven barked at the driver.

"I'm here to pick you up. Mr. John wants to see you."

Raven entered the car using her left hand to slam the door shut as she sat down in the back seat.

★ ★ ★

Raven entered the Mediterranean style house overlooking the Caribbean. The front hall was massive extending well above the second-floor ceiling height. The natural stone walls and tile floor produced a cool environment, and the house was kept at a comfortable temperature by several air conditioning units. It felt cool to Raven's face as she walked into the home.

"Welcome, my dear Raven, how was your flight down here?" John Vacara asked as he held out his arm offering a hug. Raven returned with a delightful smile. She had always found Naci's dad intriguing and polite.

Naci's mother, Pauline, entered the foyer from the kitchen wiping her hands on the apron around her waist. "How nice to see you, Raven."

Raven smiled and offered a hug to Pauline, which she happily accepted.

I'm so glad to see you two. How nice it must be to live here on the island."

"Yes, this is the perfect environment. I just love swimming in the ocean. Will you join me in the morning, Raven?" Pauline asked.

"Yes, I will," Raven returned with a calm tone. She was starting to feel better. Raven began to calm down now that she was in the Vacara's presence. She knew that they meant business, and the focus of her mission was to become the best agent that the Foundation had ever had.

"The driver will deliver your luggage to your room. Let's go to the kitchen and have a drink," John suggested.

Raven swirled the drink in her glass, watching the ice cubes spin around, then tipped it up and took a drink. The rum and Coke felt good to Raven. She felt as if the weight of the world that was on her shoulders was slowly subsiding. The Foundation training brought to her attention the urgency of their mission. Her escalated training schedule didn't lower her results; she scored higher than any previous agent including Bill. Wolf Summit instructors already called her another myth; only she could turn the early rumors into a long-lived legend with her assignments in the future.

"Follow us," John motioned as he opened the communication room door allowing the two women to enter first. The room was quite large with computer stations all around the exterior walls and windows above bringing in the glow of the blue colored water of the Caribbean. Raven noted that all the computers were on, but not all the stations were occupied. "Where are the personnel who man the computers?"

"Today is an off day. John and I monitor the stations. Everyone needs a day off," Pauline explained. "You and I need to work on the physiological implications of becoming an assassin."

"Yes, I think I'm mentally ready, but I appreciate all the training you can provide to help me deal with it now and for the future," Raven returned.

John and Pauline coached Raven for the next six hours on their personal experiences and how they dealt with the physiological pressure of being a paid assassin. The real-life stories from the days of Nazism and throughout the cold war days helped Raven understand it was necessary to complete the mission, even at the cost of human life.

"Look at the time," John announced. "Raven needs to get her sleep. We have a lot to go over tomorrow. You will understand our mission starting with the communication room in the morning."

"How long do you think it will be before I go out in the field?" Raven asked.

"Sooner than you think, Raven," Pauline announced. "The final decision will be Amelia's, with our recommendation. In fact, you handled this first session with complete concentration and dedication. John and I are very pleased with the results tonight especially after the surprise you witnessed when you landed."

Raven shot a quick stare at both Pauline and John as she was reminded of the day's events. She had blocked Jill and Naci out of her mind during the training. "If I'm going to survive as an agent, I can't let anything upset me. If I did, it could cost me my life. I had a tremendous amount of training from Bill, so I'm ahead of the game."

"You weren't the least bit concerned when you found out Jill was his partner?" Pauline asked.

Raven looked at Pauline and laughed, "I was until I saw the two of you. I know that you and John experienced the very same thing with a beauty named Nadia. You two are still together."

Surprised, John and Pauline asked, "My God, Raven, where are you getting your intelligence from?"

Raven smiled then answered, "Once I learned of the Rock Foundation, I spent hundreds of hours researching its past. Most information came from Washington archives and public libraries. They have a tremendous amount of information stored on microfilm from newspapers and recently unclassified documents. John Vacara was quite famous during the war. I believe your code name was Cat Man. Also, some of your trainers were more than eager to give me information. Bill taught me how to extract intelligence from people."

"So, Naci's partner Jill doesn't bother you in the least?" Pauline quizzed again.

"No, because my focus is on getting the son of a bitch who assassinated Bill. I can't accomplish this if I worry about those two. Don't get me wrong, I love Naci very much, but my mind is made up; becoming an operative is much more important. If Naci and Jill become involved, I will know it and deal with it. I don't know where Jill stands with this organization or how valuable she is, but I'm certainly not afraid of her."

Pauline and John agreed, "It's been a long day. Let's get some sleep."

Raven nodded in agreement, left the communications room, and walked up the stairs to her room. She saw her luggage sitting at the foot of the bed. The ceiling fan was on medium creating a gentle breeze over the bed. Soft background music was playing, which helped her to relax. Raven took a deep breath, which brought her attention to how tired she was and how much she had been looking forward to a relaxing shower. Raven removed her blouse then her skirt exposing her nearly flawless body. She opened the bathroom door, walked over to the shower, and turned on the water. The stone lined, door-less shower walls gave way to the rain drop shower head protruding from the ceiling. Raven removed her under garments and stepped into the cool falling water. It felt good after such a grueling day. She closed her eyes and let the stress flow down the drain. She stood not moving a muscle and focused on a relaxation technique in her mind. The object was to picture a recent event or to envision a future physical feat. Her mind was captivated with her favorite vision, terminating the Preacher and watching him suffer from the hell that she would ravish upon him for the death of her uncle. She was so absorbed with the visualization that Raven didn't notice Naci standing behind her in the shower. He placed both hands on her deltoids and began to caress her long sensual neck. He massaged her traps and the base of her neck. The rubbing motion aided her with her visualization. Raven covered his hands with hers as if to help him. Naci knew that she was into visualization to help accomplish her goals. After a few minutes, Raven whispered under breath, "Yes, you son of a bitch. I have satisfied my revenge. May you rot in hell."

Then Raven came back to reality and was startled by Naci's presence. She turned and smiled at him. Her long, black hair pressed down on her head and neck giving her a sensual look. The drops of water ran down her forehead across her smiling cheeks. She placed her arms around his neck and delivered a soft, loving kiss. After ten short seconds, Raven pulled her head back and moaned, "God, have I ever missed you, Naci."

"I have waited six long months for this moment, Raven. I love you," Naci returned.

They washed each other then stepped out of the shower and wrapped towels around themselves.

Raven was toweling off her long hair when Naci said, "Let me explain my occasional partner, Jill." Raven interrupted and placed her finger over his lips shaking her head no. "Naci, you don't have to explain Jill. We both have a job to do, and I trust you with her. I want this job for my revenge and your happiness. Believe me, Naci, I'm happy to be here, and the time that we get together will have to do. I have a lot to learn and a long road to reach my goal. Your parents made it, and their relationship survived, so will ours. Now, get that towel off, and ravish me."

Raven felt cold. She began to shiver. She suddenly opened her eyes. Cold water was flowing out of the shower head. Raven quickly turned off the shower and grabbed a towel.

★ ★ ★

The next morning Amelia walked around her desk and placed Raven's folder in front of her as she sat down. "When will Raven be ready to go on her own?"

"I think Raven is ready for an assignment," Pauline recommended.

"Yes, I agree. It has been six months since she arrived, and she has done remarkably well," John said.

"Good, I have a teaser. We analyzed a mid-sized company in Charlotte, and they have done the necessary steps. Let's send her in to collect," Amelia directed. "In fact, rent her an apartment in Charlotte. If she proves worthy, we will buy her a water front home on Lake Norman. We will have years of work on the east coast. Also, Charlotte has an international airport that will give her a logistical advantage," Amelia directed.

Pauline exited the room. She found Raven on the front porch admiring the ocean. "Raven, Amelia wants to talk to you." Raven could sense that this would be the day that she was finished with months of training. Raven fought back a smile. Her heart raced; endorphins flowed to every corner of her brain. They stood before Amelia who was now seated at her desk.

"It has been brought to my attention that you are ready to go solo. Raven, do you know deep down in your heart that you are ready? Before you answer, make sure that you are ready both mentally and physically."

A long silence fell on the room. Amelia looked Raven in the eyes and asked, "Are you ready for your first assignment?"

Raven smiled and quickly answered, "Yes."

"Good, John and Pauline will brief you. Good luck and God's speed." Amelia got up from her desk and left the room.

John took control of the meeting and began to explain the method that she would be exposed to for all the operations. "First, we only communicate by text." John handed her an iPhone. Your assignment will almost always be delivered by a brown envelope, usually located in the local airport locker or the destination airport."

Raven nodded with each command.

"Second, you are never to come here or to Wolf Summit. If you're in trouble, it could jeopardize the whole program."

"Yes, I got it."

"Third, never, and I repeat, never, go rogue. If you do, it can only be rectified by death."

Raven knew this and shot a stern look at both John and Pauline then agreed, "Of course."

"Fourth, do not attempt to terminate the Preacher or Big R without our acknowledgment. If for some unlikely event you are in the same room with Rothman, do not terminate. If you were to kill him, it would ruin our master plan. We need him alive for now, and I promise you will deliver the kill shot."

Raven reluctantly shook her head in agreement, "I promise to wait until you give the order to terminate them."

"Okay, good, here is a sample directive that you will find in the brown envelope. Study it on your return flight to Charlotte. The real envelope will be in locker number 51 at the airport."

"Thank you, and I promise that you will not be disappointed," Raven walked over to John and Pauline and gave each a long hug.

"The driver will give you a lift to the air strip." John directed.

"I'll need to pack a few things and say good bye to Naci."

"No time for all that, Raven. Your bag is packed and on the plane. Naci and Jill flew out about 15 minutes ago on assignment," Pauline answered.

Raven was a little taken back by the sense of urgency of this conversation, but she didn't quiver. She simply smiled and exited the room.

On the plane, Raven suddenly realized that Naci hadn't come to her room last night or tried to talk to her. She began to get mad not, at the possibility that Naci could have fallen in love with Jill, but with the fact that he didn't even try to contact her. A small tear ran down her left cheek. "Christ, what have I done? I didn't make an effort to contact Naci last night. He may have thought that I was tired and didn't want to bother me," Raven thought. "My damn obsession with revenge of Bill's death may drive a wedge between Naci and me."

CHAPTER 11

Raven located the lockers at the Charlotte Douglass International Airport. She stood in front of number 51 not trying to open it. She was having second thoughts and beginning to doubt herself. Raven reached out with her left hand to grasp the pad lock. She held it tightly while she thought, "Now if I open the door and accept the challenge, there is no turning back."

Raven closed her eyes and took a deep breath. With one swift, confident motion, she opened her eyes and unlocked number 51. To her surprise, there was only a leather shoulder bag in the locker. She looked both directions then placed the leather bag on her shoulder, walked over to a seat, and opened it. She removed the brown envelope, opened it, and began to read.

Raven Anderson – Job # 817249

Location- Harrisburg NC-North East of Charlotte

Purpose- Deliver Solution to Galvan Enterprises (owners LW and David Priest.)

Days to complete- three

Bid- 17,000

Raven pulled out the Solution and read it completely. When she finished, she phoned Galvan Enterprises and scheduled an appointment. Raven convinced Galvan that she represented a new metal fabricator and wanted to do business. They eagerly accepted an early appointment for the following day.

Raven pulled up to Galvan Enterprise's main office. She turned off the engine and stared. The building was old and run down. A foul stench began to irritate her nose to the point that it caused her to place a handkerchief over her nostrils. She walked to the side of the building to look for the source of the odor. The galvanizing tank was the culprit. The 850 degree Zink produced a heavy odor that floated out from under the shed. When Raven turned, she noticed the telephone cable box. She disconnected the main line. She briskly walked to the office and entered hoping that the smell would dissipate once she was inside.

"Yes, can I help you?" the receptionist asked.

"My name is Raven Anderson, and I'm here to see LW and a David Priest."

"Yes, you may go in. Both just stepped into LW's office," she commented as she pointed to the center office door.

Raven walked over to the door and took a deep breath. She turned the door knob and entered the office. Her beauty captured both LW and David Priest's attention.

"Well, good morning, Miss Anderson. Come in; come in," LW smiled and shot a condescending glance to his partner David Priest.

Raven smiled and glanced at David Priest. He returned the gesture with a smile. LW pulled a chair out from the conference table and motioned for her to sit. Once all three were seated, LW asked, "Now, how can we be of help?"

Raven opened her brief case and handed both men a copy of the Solution.

"What have we here?" LW commented.

Both business men stared at each other after they had read a couple of pages. Outraged, David Priest laid the folder down on the table, "What the hell is this crap? They want us to pay one hundred thousand dollars to whom?"

Raven smiled; she knew that this was an easy way to make a living. She explained, "You see, gentlemen, the way we see it is you can either pay or face dire consequences."

"You have got to be kidding. We're not going to shell out a hundred grand just because somebody called the Panther said so," LW replied.

"Judge Wilcox dismissed the charges in federal court last month," David Priest returned in a stern voice.

Raven smiled and with her head nodded to the conference table, "May I suggest that you finish reading the Solution."

Both did as they were told.

"This is simply outrageous. You're suggesting that we pay another fifty grand to three charities," LW exclaimed with a nervous tone. "Miss Anderson, I must ask you to leave before we call the Sheriff."

Raven shot a stern look at the two executives. Slowly, she got up from her seat and backed herself to the door. "I think that I'd better explain a couple of things." With both hands behind her back, Raven locked the conference room door.

The distinctive click brought LW to his feet, "Now, see here," LW exclaimed with a hostile tone.

"Sit down," Raven ordered.

Mr. Priest reached for the phone and discovered it was inoperable. He feverishly pounded on the disconnect buttons in hopes to somehow make it functional. "The damn phone is disconnected LW."

LW dropped his right hand down towards the row of drawers on the desk. Raven quickly reached inside her business suit and produced a 9mm Glock with a silencer.

"I wouldn't reach into any of those drawers, gentlemen. In fact, everyone, calm down and listen to what I have to say. We hacked into your primitive computer network and discovered withdrawals on several occasions that total one hundred thousand dollars. Now, we thought that certainly seemed odd since Judge Wilcox just dismissed a case that you two were involved in. About a year ago, a small child was hit by a car that you two were in; LW you were driving. As you well know, she lived, but she is crippled for the rest of her life. Another funny thing about all this is that your insurance company did the very same thing and wrote Judge Wilcox a sizeable refund check. There was no media coverage. In fact, the parents contacted the local newspaper and tv stations, but nobody was interested. Gentlemen, the Panther is very interested. That's why I'm here," Raven explained.

LW glanced at his partner with deep concern. Beads of sweat began to form on his forehead. David Priest's mouth began to move, but no words were coming out. Both men were in disarray.

"Gentlemen, let me help you gather your thoughts," Raven offered. Her endorphins began to flow. The sense of taking control felt good and bringing justice to this girl's family did make a difference. "First, LW, you're going to sit in front of your computer and spit out four checks as the Solution dictates. While he's doing that, Mr. Priest, look on page twelve of the Solution. You will notice a trust fund has been set up. Your company will deposit ten thousand dollars per month into this fund, and The Panther will see to it her family receives the money."

"What if we don't or can't afford to make the monthly deposit?"

Raven thought for a minute, leaned over the desk, and slammed the butt of the Glock down on David Priest's left hand then she quickly took her free hand and covered his mouth. The pain caused him to growl with clenched teeth. He grabbed his broken hand and placed it on his lap. LW glanced over his shoulder when he heard crunching bones. In fear for his safety, his typing speed increased.

"With clenched teeth, David Priest screamed, "Damn it, LW, she broke my hand; do something."

"I am. I'm writing the checks so just be quiet before someone hears you."

"Now, where were we? Oh yes, to answer your question, miss a payment and find out," Raven warned with a cold, ruthless look. "Besides, you're good for it. Remember? We hacked your system."

The printer began to print. When finished, LW handed the checks to pointing to an extra check made out to her.

"LW, I can see you're the smart one," Raven smiled with a slight grin. "Now, a couple of other things, don't make me come back. If you miss a payment or if any of these checks don't cash, the next visit will make this one seem like a kindergarten party." Raven held open her leather case and directed, "Gentlemen, please place your cell phones in here."

The two did as they were told and placed their phones in Raven's leather case. She removed a roll of gray duct tape and instructed LW to tape David Priest's hands behind his back and secure them to the chair. Raven then did the same to LW. Just before she exited the office, she placed tape over their mouths.

"No, no, not on the mustache." David cried. Raven smiled as she applied the tape.

She closed her briefcase, smiled, walked over to the door, and unlocked it.

"By the way, don't call the Judge. I'll be paying him a visit real soon. I don't think that you will want to be mixed up with him anymore."

Raven returned her car onto the beltway, pulled out her phone, and hit the voice to text button.

Raven: Galvan, job successful.
Panther: Excellent, any trouble?
Raven: None.
Panther: Go to your apartment another job is waiting.
Raven: K

CHAPTER 12

Raven opened her apartment door and placed her suitcase by the closet door. She walked over to the floor to ceiling windows and looked out. The twenty-fifth floor view was spectacular. The down town Charlotte skyline was beautiful. Tall, glass covered buildings reflected the evening sun that cast a red glow over the whole area. It looked as if a photographer used special lighting to create such a grand view.

"The Foundation certainly knows how to welcome an agent," Raven thought. The one bedroom unit was very accommodating. She liked the location just off the beltway.

Raven opened the brown envelope and pulled out the Final Solution, "Now we're talking," Raven thought as a slight grin began to form.

Raven Anderson - Job # 817250

Location - Ballantine. NC

Purpose - Deliver Final Solution to Judge Wilcox

Days to complete - Five

Bid - Forty-five thousand

Also, she found a blueprint of the apartment with a note attached that read, "Please find the switch under the granite counters in front of the sink. Push it." Raven found the switch, did as directed, and the top folded aside. A complete arsenal rose up that exposed a full line of hand guns and high-powered long guns that included extra clips and ammunition. All were displayed for her choosing. Raven stood and admired the collection of weaponry.

"So much for cooking," she thought.

The rookie assassin smiled as she pulled her suitcase into the huge bedroom. The bedroom was larger than the living room and kitchen together. Raven thought, "They must want me to spend a lot of time in here."

She threw the folder onto the bed and removed her business jacket. Raven opened the closet door and discovered that it was full of that same jacket only in different styles and colors. "The Foundation knows how to dress a girl," she thought.

Raven removed the rest of her clothing and walked into the bathroom to shower. The hot water felt good to her as she stood thinking about the day's events, "I think that I'm going to like this life style. These jobs will prepare me for my ultimate goal, to terminate the Preacher."

Raven slid nude under the covers and drifted off to sleep.

RAVEN AND THE PANTHER

The next day, Raven followed her GPS to Judge Wilcox's address. She drove around the neighborhood several times to familiarize herself with the location. His house was typical mini-mansion style. She parked across the street and studied the home's blueprint provided in the envelope. Once she memorized the layout, she read the complete Solution, which explained why the Panther chose to execute Judge Wilcox. At 7:30 PM, he pulled up in his Bentley, opened the garage door, and drove in. He exited the car and walked around the back of the vehicle then over to the interior door and disappeared into the house.

Raven thought, "I could pull in and terminate him as he walked behind the car….No, bad idea. I'm too close, and someone in the neighborhood might see me." She turned and looked up on the hill across from his house. "Of course, a high-powered rifle is the preferred choice. That way, I have time to escape. This plan is ingenious. I will leave the same paraphernalia that the Preacher did when he terminated uncle Bill. This way it will look like he could have done it."

The next morning, Raven drove up on the hill above the Judge's house and scouted the area. She found the perfect spot, a natural bench level that gave the perfect angle to the Judge's driveway. Raven stayed all day to make sure that no one used this area for bird watching or hiking. At precisely 7:30 PM, the judge did as before pulled into his garage, exited the car, and walked the same path around the rear of the vehicle and to enter the house. Raven thought, "It looks like tomorrow evening is the one, old man."

Raven pulled out her iPhone and began to text.

Raven: Looks like tomorrow evening is the kill – long range the best.

Panther: Ok, make sure you're not conspicuous and move quickly once kill is complete.

Raven: Got it.

The next afternoon Raven placed herself in position. She was apprehensive, a little nervous and excited all at the same time. Her heart rate was at an elevated level and proved to Raven that this type of lifestyle could be dangerous to her emotional health. Weeks of mental training by John and Pauline was put to the test at this precise moment. This type of event would change a small part of the world for the better. Raven glanced at her watch and was surprised by how quickly time passed by.

An hour later at 7:15, the familiar Bentley turned into the Judge's driveway. Raven was in position, looked through the rifle scope, and witnessed something that she wasn't expecting. She completely calmed down; all the apprehension disappeared. Her heat rate calmed to a rhythm below normal. Raven slid into a zone of total concentration; the world was tuned out except for what she saw in the scope. The judge did as usual; he stepped out of the car, closed the driver's door, and turned towards the rear of the car. Raven placed the cross hair on his skull. She followed him to the left rear tail light then gently pulled the trigger; the sniper rifle gave a distinctive kick and produced a muffled thump. She followed the trajectory of the kill shot and saw it penetrate the Judge's forehead. Blood exploded onto the rear of the car and floor. He instantly collapsed to the concrete floor, no life left in his body. All the apprehension left Raven's body.

She felt satisfied now that her first kill was completed. No remorse or doubt was in her mind as she watched the Judge lay lifeless on the garage floor. Raven now knew without a single regret that she was on her way to inflict revenge for her uncle's death. A pool of blood appeared below his fractured head. The surrounding sounds of life began to penetrate Raven's ears again; the wind picked up in the tree tops above, and the sound of a lawn mower in the distance grew louder. Satisfied that the Judge is terminated, Raven exited the bench and returned to her car.

The drive back to her apartment went without a hitch. There was no traffic congestion, and she even caught all the green traffic signals. She pulled into the parking garage below her apartment, picked up her iPhone, and began to text.

Raven: Termination complete.
Panther: Good and u?
Raven: Fine, ready for another assignment.
Panther: Take a day or so. Will be in contact.

Raven was in the elevator and just about to exit when her phone dinged. She looked at the screen and noticed a text.

Naci: Congratulations.
Raven: Thanks.

The phone was silent the rest of the evening. This bothered Raven even more than the kill.

CHAPTER 13

FIVE YEARS LATER

Raven pulled into the PNN parking garage in her Ford Super Duty and looked at the dash clock – 8 PM. She adjusted the climate control turning it down a couple of degrees. Hot summer nights in Jacksonville, Florida could be unforgiving. The parking garage was well lit, with no noticeable activity. Her cell phone announced an incoming text.

Panther: Are u on site, level 4?
Raven: Y.
Panther: Have u read the packet?
Raven: Y
Panther: Here is a photo of the subject.
Raven-Got it!

Panther: See the elevator doors?

Raven: Y.

Panther: Ur subject should be there any minute.

Raven: -K

Raven opened the center console and retrieved a Springfield .45 caliber semi-automatic with a silencer. She dropped the clip to make sure that it was loaded and returned the clip into the handle. She then loaded a shell into the chamber with a distinct click. Suddenly, the elevator doors opened and out stepped the subject. Raven dropped the Super Duty into drive and pulled up to the subject rolling the passenger window down.

"Mr. Holt, please get in," Raven said.

"What, who are you?" Mr. Holt asked.

"If you want to live, you will get in. Now, hurry," Raven commanded.

Mr. Holt hesitated with a confused look. He glanced at Raven then out at the parking garage. Raven raised the 45 caliber to persuade Mr. Holt that time was of the essence and she was serious. The fear poured over his face. He opened the passenger door and jumped in. Raven dropped the shift into drive, mashed the fuel peddle, then advised, "Better buckle up."

"Who are you?" Mr. Holt asked with a nervous tone as he snapped the buckle.

Raven placed the hand gun in the space between the right front seat and center console then turned her full attention to getting Mr. Holt who was out of harm's way and delivered to the correct agent. She turned out of the parking garage using the full 800 foot-pounds of torque that the Ford diesel engine provided.

"Let's just say that I'm the best and only friend you have right now."

"I don't understand," Mr. Holt cried. "I haven't harmed anyone or done anything wrong. This is outrageous. I demand an explanation." Mr. Holt now realized the seriousness of the situation, and fear began to dominate him. He held the briefcase up against his chest with crossed arms. Small beads of sweat began to form on his forehead.

Raven looked in the driver's right-side mirror, turned the blinker on, and turned onto the on ramp to Interstate 10 West. "I haven't been told why you're the mark, but I'd guess that it's got something to do with what's either in your head or in the brief case that you're carrying. Mr. Holt, sit back. We have about a five-and-a-half-hour drive."

"Where are you taking me?"

Raven looked at Mr. Holt with a curious look then answered, "Federal Court in Atlanta, Georgia. You mean that you don't know what this is about?"

"Not a clue."

"Bullshit, you've been transferring DOJ money to the DNC," Raven shouted with a stern look.

"What's DOJ money?" Holt asked.

"Don't play dumb with me. It's money collected from fines. For instance, if a car company doesn't meet Federal Emission Standards, the Feds take them to court, and the Federal Judge rules in favor of the government. If the accused pays the fine up front, they get a cash discount. The money is deposited into the Department of Justice's account; then the DOJ transfers the bulk of the money to the Democratic National Committee. Last year alone, the DOJ collected some fifteen billion dollars. So, don't play dumb with me. You have proof and are going to testify."

The hostage asked, "How do you find out such things? They told me that I would be completely protected."

"Well, Mr. Holt, shit happens, and things don't always go to plan. Your protection was murdered three hours ago; that's why I'm moving you to a safe house."

"I didn't agree to all this. They said that it would not be a big deal," Holt argued.

"Well, Mr. Holt, you've been played for a sucker," Raven said.

Raven shot a quick glance at her hostage then turned back and focused on the highway. She pressed the navigation button on the steering wheel. The navigation responded.

"What do you want, Raven?" The woman's voice asked.

"How far to the next rest area, Susan?"

"One minute please."

A few seconds later the speaker came alive, "Approximately 65 miles."

"Thank you, Susan," Raven said.

After about an hour, Raven turned the F-350 off to a rest stop and brought the Super Duty to a halt.

"Why did we stop?" Mr. Holt asked with a worried look on his face.

Raven exited the truck, walked around to the passenger's door, and opened it, "Do you need to visit the little boy's room?"

Holt shook his head no. Raven grabbed his right arm and pulled.

"What are you doing?" Holt asked.

"Let's just say that I'm taking no chances with you. Mr. Holt, you need to get in the back seat and lie down. You are too much of a target to ride up front." She tightened her grip on his arm so he wouldn't run and helped him into the rear seat. He was much too valuable to get into a foot race with him; although, he would be no match for her speed.

Raven pulled back onto Interstate and pushed the speed limit by five miles over. Driving conditions were perfect, light traffic and clear skies. She drove for several hours without incident.

Suddenly Raven's iPhone signaled a text.

Panther: 20?
Raven: 1 hr. out.
Panther: Will forward drop location – Plans changed.
Raven-: K

The glow of the Atlanta lights began to show up on the horizon. The long, uneventful trip started to wear on Raven. Her eyelids felt as though they were tied to lead weights, and her head began to nod. "Goodness, I need a wake me up," Raven thought.

Suddenly, Susan lit up with a warning alarm, "A heavy object approaching at ninety miles per hour; proceed with caution."

A dark van pulled up alongside Raven's truck to pass, except it deliberately banged into the side of her truck with a loud scraping noise that caused the pickup to veer off the interstate. The sheer weight of Raven's truck was no match for the attacking van. She held the wheel straight.

"Warning, warning, make appropriate decisions to avoid conflict," Susan advised. "Raven, please be careful."

"Well, that's more like it," Raven laughed as she regained control of the Super Duty.

"No matter what, Mr. Holt, stay down," Raven commanded as she briefly looked over her shoulder.

Raven mashed the fuel and took the Ford up to 95 miles per hour putting her well ahead. She steered back onto the right-hand lane, glanced into the side mirror, and located the van two lengths back in the left-hand lane. Raven lowered the driver's window, retrieved her 45 caliber hand gun, then slammed on the brakes. The van's driver didn't pick up on this amateur move. When the van unexpectedly caught up with Raven, she simply shot out the van's right front tire.

"Dumb asses," Raven commented as she watched the van pass her, lose control, and flip on its side sliding down the concrete highway creating sparks and a loud screeching sound. When she passed the disabled van, Raven rolled down the right rear window, pointed the 45 pistol towards the now exposed gas tank, and squeezed the trigger. She floored the F 350 as the gas tank erupted, killing all occupants. Raven dialed 911 and reported the accident.

"Are you all right, Mr. Holt?" Raven asked as she slowed back down to the speed limit.

"Yes, I'm fine," he answered.

Fifteen minutes passed, she picked up her phone and began to text.

Raven: I'm in Atlanta - encountered agents - all is good.
Panther: New drop - Embassy Suites — Room 201
   4700 Southport Rd
   Atlanta Ga 30337
Raven: Got it!
Panther: Take Holt to room. Two agents will knock
   on door then call out, "Delivery from Panther
   Deli." Turn Holt over to them, then catch shuttle

to Airport. Go to locker for next job. This one is high priority.

Raven: K

"Business is good," Raven thought to herself.

"Looks like Mr. Holt, you're going to the Embassy Suites," Raven reported.

"Susan, did you intercept the text?"

"Yes, Raven I will program the navigation system."

"Thank you, Susan."

"My pleasure, Raven."

Forty-five minutes later, Raven and Mr. Holt entered room 201 in the Embassy Suits. "Not a bad room," Raven said. "Smile," Raven snapped the picture then sent it.

"It's been a pleasure, Mr. Holt."

Just then, there was a knock on the door; the two agents announced their presence. Raven, gun in hand, checked the peep hole, opened the door, smiled then left.

Raven turned the combination on locker number 51 at Atlanta International Airport, opened the door, and retrieved the envelope and suitcase.

"Let's see where I'm off to tonight." Raven opened the envelope and read the instructions.

Raven – Next job

Budget – $75,000

Location – Dallas, TX

2 days to complete

Target – Judge Wilford

Level – Terminate

Reason - Record indicates constant leniency to convicted rapists and drug traffic. Subject is now jeopardizing his high office and judicial system.

Raven continued to read the solution proving his derelict of duty to the high office that he swore to defend.

As always Raven, be careful. Your flight leaves at midnight; text to indicate your decision.
—Panther

Raven read the complete solution absorbing all factual information that it contained. When finished, she closed the document and took out her iPhone and began to text.

Raven: Consider Wilford terminated.
Panther: Contract considered valid and official with this text.

★　★　★

Raven woke up rested. She stretched with her arms extended above her head. She threw back the covers revealing her naked body. The scent of the previous night's sleep filled her nostrils then escaped into the room. Raven smiled when she remembered her dream. She moved her hand down to the glory of her crotch and felt the wet sweetness escaping her love canal. A warm quiver began to escalate giving her mild pleasure. She gently rubbed her love button until she experienced a mild, delightful organism. She slapped her wet pussy to add additional pleasure. She then worked magic with her finger. Her pink womanly center pulsated and tingled with delight. Raven continued until the sensation drained from her body. "Damn, it feels good to cum," Raven thought as it gave instant relief to her sexual tension. "What a good way to start the day," she pondered. Raven glanced at the room clock, 10:02. She realized how hungry she was. She entered the bathroom and started the shower. She placed a Glock under a bath towel on the towel rack. The warm water flowing over her body felt good. She arched her back and leaned her head back to give way to the warm shower. The beads of water soothed her face and massaged her scalp; she turned around to let the warmth caress her back. The shower gave her a great start to the day.

Raven got dressed and was combing her hair when she looked at the door and saw the envelope lying on the floor. She walked over to the door, stooped over, and picked up the envelope. It was something unusual; it felt heavy to Raven. She placed the comb on the dresser and opened the envelope. She found the bill for the night's stay and a Morgan silver dollar dated 1921. Raven didn't scare easily, but this deeply concerned her. She wondered who placed it in the envelope. Raven looked up when she heard the sound of a key being inserted into the door. She retrieved her handgun, then hid in the closet. A small, metal device pushed into the open space that the door bar allowed. The perpetrator gave the metal device a quick jerk, and the safety lock released. He slowly entered the room looking at the open bathroom door. Just as he entered the bathroom door, Raven attacked him from behind with one effortless jump. She wrapped her powerful legs around his neck and rode him to the floor. His firearm slid across the bathroom floor. Out of desperation and because his oxygen supply was diminishing, he begged for freedom. Raven needed information, so she slowly relaxed her thighs and let the small Chinese killer gasp for air.

"Who the hell are you?" Raven demanded.

With his hands gripping her thigh, he just laughed. Raven applied pressure again, then whacked the top of his head with the handle of her gun. She said, "Do you have amnesia?" She then placed the gun barrel to his exposed skull.

"Please, please, no job worth losing life. Please forgive?"

"Who paid you?"

"No want trouble. I talk now."

Raven knew that this was an act. He was a well-paid assassin who would kill her in an instant given a chance. "Who paid you, damn it?"

He used his core and threw his right leg up and back in an attempt to drive his foot into Raven's skull. She reacted and leaned her head to the side. At the same instance, a muffled shot entered his foot causing severe pain.

"Grrrr," the assistant moaned.

"Talk, you bastard," Raven commanded as she shot his kneecap. Again, blood speckled the walls.

"Arggg." He grabbed his knee. "Okay, okay, I talk now. Some Chinese man said you were the one who killed my brother last night at Club Shameless. He said he saw the murder, and a rich, beautiful woman did it. He told me the hotel and room you were staying in. He said you were pissed. The supply of cocaine came up short, so you kill him."

"Did you place a silver dollar in my bill last night and slide it under my door?"

The Chinese man screamed, "What silver dollar?"

Raven knew that he was telling the truth. She relaxed her thighs and jumped up. The assassin quickly reached for his backup weapon. She ended his miserable life. Raven patted him down for additional information but came up blank. He carried nothing that indicated his identity. She knew that he wasn't an ordinary thug. She quickly re-showered, dressed, and left the room. Raven placed her bag into the car, checked her Glock, then placed it back into the holster. She walked into the lobby of the Hilton and walked up to the front desk.

"How may I help you?" the attendant asked.

"Who placed my bill under my door?"

"The night clerk. Is there something wrong?"

"Is he or she still on duty?" Raven asked.

"No, he left about two hours ago."

Raven looked past the attendant and noticed the signage indicating the clerk on duty last night. "I need Jason Smith's address and photo ID. Before you say, 'I can't give it to you,' I want you to take a good look under my jacket." Raven opened her lapel showing the attendant her Glock. "I'm not afraid to use this; I promise. So please, save me the trouble and your life, and give me your's and his address." The clerk reluctantly printed off the information and handed it to Raven. "Please don't tell anyone that I did this." Raven took the paper from him and said, "Don't contact Mr. Smith or anyone. This information better be correct, or I'll make good on my promise."

Raven drove the rented Lincoln LX to northern Dallas from the Dallas-Fort Worth airport Hilton. The upscale Reserve of Southlake supported an average home price of one million plus. The brick wall surrounded the subdivision displayed bronze letters that read, "Shady Oaks." Houses located in this subdivision had seven to ten acre lots. The homes were made of stone or brick and about twenty years old. Shady Oaks was a meticulously maintained neighborhood with the latest home security systems to discourage the average burglar. Raven had infiltrated dozens of similar neighborhoods and getting inside was usually not a problem. Raven drove until the navigation indicated the Wilford address. She pulled out an iPad device developed for the Foundation. Raven connected directly to Wolf Summit satellite. She now had live coverage of her location. Raven placed her arm out of the driver's window and confirmed the movement on her screen. She memorized the location of the Wilford home in perspective to the other homes. She decided to drive around and scope the rear of the property looking for alternative entries to the property beside the front drive.

The evening sun dropped lower and lower by the minute, and driving west became particularly aggravating. Raven turned right on Elm Street eliminating the blazing sun in her face. She drove several hundred feet, and on the right, she noticed a narrow roadway. She estimated that this was directly behind the Judge's home. The narrow lane gave way to a cell tower, something that she wasn't expecting. She turned off the engine and slowly exited the Lincoln. She stood, looking from left to right, giving her ears a complete scope of the area noting any out of the ordinary noises. After a minute or so, Raven walked around to the rear hatch and opened it. She quickly opened her travel bag and retrieved a flak jacket. Once in place, she loaded the pouches with two automatic 9mm, Nighthawks, and four loaded clips. She then placed a ball cap on her head and pulled the bill down to disguise her face. She quietly made her way down a small slope onto the back of the Judge's property. She could see the back of his stone mansion several hundred feet to the south. The darkness began to dominate providing Raven a natural camouflage.

She continued to walk towards the house as her eyes continually adjusted for the diminishing daylight. An owl began to hoot, and a nearby fenced dog barked, both providing an excellent sound barrier, which covered the sound of Raven's footsteps in the dry woods. She advanced all the way up to the back door of the Wilford home. She carefully checked the rear door and each of the side windows looking for any signs of life inside the house. She saw the cook preparing the evening meal indicating that the judge was at home or would be shortly. Raven slowly turned the rear doorknob, and to her surprise, it was unlocked. She opened it about six inches then stopped. A few minutes passed, and no apparent alarms sounded, which indicated that there was no alarm or it was not activated.

Raven entered the back porch and effortlessly made her way to the kitchen where the cook had her back to the assassin. With one quick blow to the back of the head with the butt of a Nighthawk, the cook dropped to the floor. Raven quickly spotted the kitchen phone and disconnected it. Next, she silently made her way into the dining room. The table was set with elegant china and polished silver. Suddenly, Raven could hear small footsteps running in the next room. Raven quickly slid up against the wall next to the living room door. In seconds, the swinging door opened with the enthusiasm of a small child. Raven raised her gun not expecting a child, then quickly holstered the

Nighthawk. She grabbed the small girl with a hand over her mouth and ran back into the kitchen.

On the way in, Raven noticed a door and opened it. The room resembled a bedroom, which was most likely occupied by the cook. Raven dropped to one knee at the edge of the bed and gently slid the young girl under it. She pulled the extra blanket that was folded at the foot of the bed down over the side that she had placed the child under to give her more time to escape without being seen. Raven exited the bedroom and house without incident. She returned to the rental car and drove off.

"Damn child, where'd she come from?" Raven thought as she navigated the Lincoln back to the street. She pulled across the street in front of Judge Wilford's home to wait. In about fifteen minutes, the familiar sound of sirens filled the air as two police cars pulled into the drive. The four officers entered the house. Thirty minutes passed then the front door opened, and to her surprise, all four officers exited and drove away not noticing that Raven was sitting across the street.

Raven slowly pulled out into the street and drove to the next corner and turned right. The street took a steep incline for about two hundred feet then leveled off for the next home's drive. She turned the rental car around and drove down the slope heading back towards the Wilford home. She pulled over to watch from a distance. An hour later, a black limo pulled up to the front door. Raven raised a pair of binoculars and verified the occupant was Judge Wilford. He entered his home without any suspicion of Raven's surveillance.

Two hours went by, a taxi pulled into the Wilford drive and beeped its horn. Five minutes later, the front door opened, and a middle-aged woman and a small girl exited. The small girl turned around and waved to Judge Wilford who returned the jester. Both entered the cab. The brake lights lit up indicating that the driver placed the transmission into drive. With headlights on, the cab drove to the street then headed north.

"Thank God, the girl is gone," Raven thought to herself.

Raven slid lower in the driver's seat to prepare for a long wait. She knew from experience that her subjects differed in preparation time for bed. Some read, others showered or watched tv before going to sleep. She needed to give the Judge time. It was a peaceful evening at Shady Oaks. Elderly couples took evening strolls, and an occasional jogger went by. Outdoor activity was kept to a minimum at best due to the size of the estates. Most families had their outdoor recreation contained within their property. Tennis courts, swimming pools, archery, and some of the younger occupants even owned obstacle courses, climbing walls, and golf cages.

An hour later, her phone pinged indicating a text.

Panther: 20
Raven: Across street from Judge's home.
Panther: B on alert - 2 cartel kingpins may show up!
Raven: K
Panther: Ur Plan.?
Raven: Enter and terminate in two hrs.
Panther: Good.

Just then, a car pulled up to the Judge's home. Raven put the phone down and picked up her night vision binoculars. Two Hispanic men exited their car and entered the home without notice to the owner.

Raven: The pins just arrived.

Panther: Abort."

Raven: Negative, will set up as cartel hit.

Two minutes pass.

Panther: Ok, photograph cartel and send. May be reward.

Raven: 10-4

Panther: B careful.

Raven: I left a mess in room 402, Dallas Hilton North. Please take care of it.

Panther: A dead body?

Raven: Yes, Chinese man-professional.

Panther: Same as gone. You're already popular.

Raven: I know, will text in 30.

Raven laid the phone on the console, closed her eyes, and took a deep breath. She knew that they would be armed, which changed the dynamics. As always, her job required a deep mental state to motivate her actions. Two minutes passed, she put on a pair of thin black cotton gloves then opened the driver's door and began her descent to the Judge's home.

Raven slowly opened the unlocked front door with her left hand while the right supported a 9mm Nighthawk. Once inside, she retrieved the second Nighthawk from the flak jacket. A light and voices from the study indicated the termination point. She moved slowly taking every step with caution. Suddenly, a movement caught her left eye. She looked down, and to her surprise, a cat walked in front of her not paying any attention to Raven.

"Son of a bitch must be blind," Raven thought.

She continued to the study. The door was ajar just enough so Raven could see the contents of the room.

From the shadows of the hall, Raven observed all three men and could listen to the trio.

"What do you expect, miracles? You haven't given me the time necessary to make arrangements for your brother's release, Carlos," The judge explained.

"I know, that's not why I wanted to meet with you. My American friend…" Carlos gestured with a smile.

"Then what do you want," The judge questioned with a curious tone.

"You're a Federal Judge; is this not true?" Carlos asked followed by a serious look and then a taunting laugh.

The judge nodded indicating yes. The tension in the room built as the conversation began to turn. Raven could sense the mood change. She knew her element of surprise was diminishing by the second. She decided to make her move.

Raven stepped up to the partially opened study door. With her left foot, she forcibly shoved the door open. The movement of the swinging door caught all three by surprise. With the speed of a cougar, she entered the room with both handguns pointed. The Kingpins didn't have time to retrieve their weapons.

"What the fuck, Judge? I thought we could trust each other?" Carlos questioned with an angered tone.

"I don't know, Carlos," The Judge quipped with a surprised look on his face. "Who are you?" The judge demanded in a nervous tone as he looked at Raven.

Raven was clearly in charge and didn't answer. She moved to the Judge's side staying in the clear of him so to face the Mexican's who were agitated. The mounting anger that they displayed indicated this could explode at any second. Raven took no chances and terminated the two with both index fingers. The silencers bellowed a faint noise that didn't escape the study. Two bloody shells, blood, and bone fragments hit the wall behind the Mexicans. The thud of two falling bodies could be heard only by the Judge and Raven.

The Judge stood frozen in disbelief after Raven's stone-cold assassinations.

"Damn, woman, who the hell are you?" The infuriated Judge demanded.

Raven quickly moved to the side of the desk where the two Mexicans once stood. She holstered one of her guns while keeping the other trained on the Judge. She dropped to one knee and reached under the coat of Carlo's jacket and pulled out his 9 mm Glock. Raven stood up, released the safety, and pointed it at the Judge.

"No, no, don't do it, please," he cried. "Look, I have money. How much?"

With one soft squeeze of the trigger, the Judge fell to the floor. Part of his skull and face were plastered on the wall just below his framed law degree. Raven quickly placed the Glock in the dead hand of Carlos. She then returned to the Judge and placed both of her guns in his hands. Raven photographed the results and sent them to The Panther.

She looked through the study door into the hall and didn't see anyone. Raven quickly exited the home returning to the rental car. Her phone indicated an incoming text.

Panther: Received the proof. Good job. I will keep
    you posted on the two Kingpins. I like the way
    u left the murder scene, no Foundation evidence.
Raven: K.
Panther: Take few days off, you deserve it.
Raven: If it's all the same, I'd rather keep working.

Half an hour passed then her phone lit up.

Panther: Go to Wolf Summit. Amelia needs you.

Raven: Thank you. Does a Morgan silver dollar dated 1921 mean anything?

A few minutes passed then her screen lit up.

Panther: Congratulations you just reached international fame.

Raven: Can't be good for The Foundation.

Panther: It was bound to happen.

Raven: Who is or are they?

Panther: He is known as Morgan.

Raven: Why would the assassin who I terminated behind Mike's bar have a Morgan silver dollar in his pocket?

Panther: He was rogue, definitely not Morgan's style to ambush. If and when you encounter Morgan, you'll meet him face to face.

Raven: Thanks for the intel. Morgan left his or her calling card in my motel bill this morning, then one of their thugs showed up.

Panther: Keep a sharp head. Morgan is relentless.

Raven: K.

Raven parked her car in front of the clerk's apartment located in a suburban area of Dallas. She entered the door and took the stairs to the second floor. Raven knocked on Mr. Smith's door, and to her surprise, he yelled, "Door's open." Raven pulled her handgun with her right hand and used her left to open the door. She shoved it open quickly and stepped aside to use the hall as a barrier. Mr. Smith was lying on the couch but quickly sat up due to the odd entrance. Raven, satisfied that he wasn't an immediate threat, entered the apartment looking both directions.

"Who are you?" Jason asked with a nervous tone, not knowing why such a beautiful woman would be interested in him, let alone carrying a handgun. Raven checked his bedroom and bathroom for possible adversaries, then returned to the living room.

"You placed a silver dollar into my bill at the Hilton last night. Who gave it to you?"

Jason stood up and faced Raven. His confidence began to build, now that he realized that he was bigger than her. He smiled and said, "You are quite good looking. Why would you want to know who gave me the silver dollar? What is worth to you?"

Raven looked him dead in the eyes and said, "I don't have time for this shit." She grabbed him in the crouch, placed the other hand on his throat, and squeezed with both hands giving him a taste of her world. His demeanor instantly changed. Jason began to realize that he was in trouble.

"I don't know his name. He gave me a hundred-dollar bill and told me to put the coin into your bill; that's all."

Raven released her grip, stepped back, and asked, "What did he look like?"

"I didn't notice that much, tall, middle-aged Chinese man with dark hair."

"Was he well dressed?" Raven asked.

"Just the usual, collared shirt, slacks, and a jacket."

"Did he walk with a limp, have any scars, or noticeable traits like speech impediment or body actions?"

"Nope just normal - all Chinese kind of guy."

Raven was satisfied that he couldn't be of any more help, so she turned and walked to the door. She turned and said, "Don't discuss this with anyone. If we ever cross paths again, I'll know you were lying just now, and I will kill you, understand? I will terminate you, no questions asked. Just make sure that you don't get involved with this matter anymore if you value your life." Jason rubbed his neck trying to sooth the pain Raven had caused. She moved like a cat, quick and silent, as she left his apartment and glided down the stairwell.

Raven exited the building.

CHAPTER 14

The receptionist picked up the desk phone, dialed, and began to speak, "Mr. Hunt, your three o'clock appointment, Raven Anderson, is here to see you."

Mr. Hunt snapped, "Send her in." Clearly, Mr. Hunt was in a foul mood. The receptionist returned the receiver to its cradle and cursed, "I'm fucked."

Raven nodded a jester of thanks to the naïve receptionist, then turned with confidence to enter Mr. Hunt's office. Her nostrils irritated, she could smell the sharp stench of newly laid carpet. The first impression of the richly decorated office didn't impress Raven. Questionable to her observers, just like her reason to be in Mr. Hunt's office, Raven Anderson gave new meaning to "I'm fucked."

"Mr. Hunt, I think you know why I'm here," Raven announced with a demanding voice as she placed her briefcase on the table adjacent to his desk. She removed two bound data reports. She stepped over to Mr. Hunt's desk, handed him his copy labeled "The Solution," and shot an intimidating look at him.

"One month ago, the Panther contacted you and discussed the outcome of your trial. One week later, you received this report with the recommendations noted on page twelve. As of three days ago, you have not held up to your obligations that were agreed upon."

Raven removed her iPhone from her pocket and accessed the Panthers online bank account. She said, "You have five minutes to make the agreed electronic deposit."

Mr. Hunt looked at Raven just long enough to stir her curiosity; his eyes drawled with a wrinkled forehead, showing deep resentment. He stared just long enough to push her patience then proceeded to type feverishly to complete the electronic fund's transfer.

"Ding." Raven's phone sounded. She quickly slid her finger over the screen until she saw the posting. "Perfect, the transaction is complete." Raven smiled as she continued manipulating her phone until she logged out then announced, "Now, look on page fourteen, item 5. It states that you will produce three checks payable to the listed charities. Do you have them?"

Mr. Hunt shot Raven a stern look then announced, "I'm tired of this bull shit. I don't like it."

"I'm sure that you understand the consequences, Mr. Hunt. They are detailed on the last page."

His eyebrows drawled down at Raven. With a high pitched but weak voice, he professed, "What if I don't give you the checks?"

Raven turned her phone sideways, located Panther's text string, and using both thumbs, began to text, "He left me no…"

"Okay, okay, I'll take care of it," Mr. Hunt responded with a weakened voice. He picked up the phone and instructed his secretary to print three checks to the charities indicated in The Solution. Word on the street is that The Panther means business, and although this is his first exposure, Mr. Hunt was a practical man. "What the hell does the Panther have against me? I was cleared of all charges."

"I don't question the reason. I just fulfill the contract," Raven snapped, as she returned her phone to her pocket.

Pointing his right index finger at Raven, Mr. Hunt threatened, "Let me tell you sister; I didn't like the way his people came in here without my approval, pried into my ledgers, and examined my tax returns. On second thought, what if I don't give you the three checks?" Mr. Hunt proposed with a slight grin. "Besides, I already paid all I'm going to towards this outrageous audit. I don't think that you will execute the conditions on the last page." His sudden confidence gained momentum.

Annoyed, Raven's eyes scanned around the office. She noticed the floor to ceiling office windows, show casing the Atlanta skyline. Buildings covered the foreground, and suburbia circled for miles like waves in a pond produced by a rock thrown in. The busy streets and sidewalks produced an urgency that could be felt in Mr. Hunt's office. Raven stared out the window, which made her appreciate Charlotte, a much smaller city. Time seemed to slip away during her visit to Mr. Hunt's office. "Even Charlotte sometimes is too busy," Raven thought. "I can't wait to spend some time at my mountain cabin." Her cabin provided a calm and relaxing hideaway from the high level of stress that her job produced.

Raven's patience began to run thin. With all the ways her life had changed during the past year, Raven stayed in a half-pissed mood. She advanced towards Mr. Hunt with a demanding tone, "I have a flight to catch, and I don't have much time." The look on her face told him that she wasn't kidding. Raven returned to her briefcase and removed a 9-mm handgun, inserted the fully loaded clip with a loud click, and loaded the first shell into the chamber. She slowly raised the firearm and pointed the laser dot on his forehead. This distinctive noise along with staring down the barrel of her gun got Mr. Hunt's undivided attention.

"Now, if you would like to find out how bad of a mood I'm in, don't produce the three checks," Raven said.

The office doorknob began to twist alerting Raven that someone was about to enter. She placed her gun behind her folded arm as his secretary entered the room. Mrs. Jones scornfully looked at Raven.

"Place the checks on my desk, and take the rest of the day off with pay." Mr. Hunt scuffed.

She hesitated, but then smiled as the rare news was absorbed. "Thank you, Mr. Hunt. Will that be all?"

"Yes."

Mrs. Jones wasted no time exiting the office. The door closed with a click, which gave Raven reason to relax her grip on the handgun. She extended her hand out, and he reluctantly surrendered possession of the checks. Raven placed the checks and hand gun into the brief case, shut the lid, and with a smile, slid it off the table resting it on her thigh.

"Now, that is the most practical thing you've done since you transferred the money," Raven announced with a smile.

"How do I know that you won't be back for more?"

"You don't. Make sure that you read page eight in The Solution. We expect you to send to us the names of political hacks who are funding your business to launder money back to them for personal gain."

"If I need to return, it will be neither pleasant or for money," Raven informed on her way out of the office. "I could be the nastiest person you've ever met. Just make sure that these checks clear and you hold up your end of the bargain." Raven closed the door to exit the building.

Raven opened her iPhone to favorites and pressed the top name, Naci. "Hi hon, how's your day going?" Raven asked as she entered the elevator.

"My day is great," Naci commented then asked, "Any problems with this morning's appointment?"

"None, went just fine?"

"Good, listen, I'm up here at the cabin and thought maybe you could drive up tonight for a romantic dinner?"

"That sounds wonderful, Naci," Raven returned, with a smile on her face, although he couldn't see it. The excited tone of her voice made Naci feel good. She listened to Naci with her full attention. The look on her face showed the world that she loved Naci. She loved him almost as much as her work.

"Okay, good, I'll meet you this evening on the ridge. Yes, I would love that. I'll have a cozy fire built; it makes for a good ending to a long work day. I love you, bye!"

Her stride, a replica of a world class model's, caused her thick, long, coal black hair to bounce with each step. Raven's beauty radiated as if she were audition-ing for a starring role in a Hollywood movie. The cold, sensual look in her eyes drew attention from her observers. Raven's lips, thick with passion, were adored by every female who noticed. Her business suit was hand tailored to her exact measurements, which complemented her athletic build, but one could argue, it displayed her sexuality.

The neatly dressed door attendant smiled at Raven as he opened the door. The street noises of downtown Atlanta aggravated Raven. She was more comfortable with the solitude the mountains offered. "Would you like a cab?" The door attendant asked as he noticed the fifty-dollar bill that Raven placed in his gloved hand when she walked through the door.

"Yes," Raven answered. The ecstatic man rushed to the street and instantly waved a cab to the curb. He opened the rear door of the cab with a smile, "Have a great day." Raven nodded as she entered the cab. The driver started the meter, looked in his door mirror, then abruptly pulled out into traffic, "Where to, lady?"

"Atlanta International Airport, and please make it as quickly as possible. I have a flight to Chicago in two hours."

The cab driver looked into his rear-view mirror at Raven, gave a slight smile, and pressed on the gas pedal.

★ ★ ★

The 747 roared down the runway causing all the passengers to lean back in their seats. The huge craft vibrated and groaned with each revolution of the massive jet engines. Lift off reduced the noise to a low-keyed scream as the plane turned its nose straight up, conveying all the torque the 747 could muster until it reached correct altitude.

Now satisfied that the pilot brought the huge plane past the critical point of the flight, Raven opened the newly acquired briefcase to examine the next case. The sound of both latches gave a distinctive tandem click. She carefully opened the lid and stared at the single document labeled, "The Only Solution."

"Dumb son-of-a-bitch," Raven thought as she opened the document exposing the first page, "Mr. Peterson, sole owner of Peterson Manufacturing, hasn't cooperated with the conditions of the Solution thus has left no other options and must be terminated," The Panther signed using his or her distinctive signature. Raven had never met or spoken to The Panther. She continued to read the contents of The Only Solution, which described the complete turn of events and her reason for the devastating task at hand. Mr. Peterson was heavily involved in the liberal political view. The political party that he donated to fundamentally wanted to change this country and promote social justice. The swamp in Washington was a group of elitist politicians, accepting donations from foreign financiers who wanted to destroy America. Raven fully under-stood the implications of this ideology and was eager to do her part. This radical movement had changed her life forever, caused her extreme personal loss, and she was completely dedicated to putting an end to the madness.

An hour later, Raven was in front of locker number 52 at O'Hare International Airport. She placed the contents into her brief case, walked to the curb, and entered the first available taxi.

The cab pulled up to the address that she gave the driver. He glanced at the meter, looked up into the rear view mirror with his hand open over his shoulder, and said, "It will be 22.75, please." In anticipation of the amount, Raven handed him thirty dollars and said, "Keep the change." She never tipped cabbies heavily. In Raven's mind, sitting on your ass isn't the hardest living to make. The cabbie shot an unappreciative look into the rear-view mirror, not knowing who Raven was, how she thought, or what she was capable of doing.

She stood in front of the thirty-story marble fronted sky scrapper and noticed the stainless-steel letters that read, "Peterson Enterprises-Founded 1970." With a deep breath, she pushed the massive door open and entered. She made it over to the directory and confirmed what she already knew; his office was located on the top floor. Raven entered the elevator and pushed the lighted number 10 as the doors closed. Once in the elevator, she could not help but notice the handsome man five years her senior staring at her with a smile. She turned towards the lone occupant and smiled. He returned the gesture and solicited, "Here on business or pleasure?" The elevator door opened, and Raven stepped out never speaking.

The hallway was extremely crowded as she walked towards the ladies' room. Once inside, she entered a stall and placed the brief case on the commode seat. Raven pinned her long, black hair up and covered it with a blond wig. She then reversed her business jacket after she strapped on a shoulder holster. Raven picked up the handgun and marveled to herself, "A Super Scout .45 caliber, the Panther went all out on this one." She dropped the clip from the handle to check for ammunition then loaded the first shell into the chamber. Raven picked up the folder marked The Only Solution and exited the restroom.

★ ★ ★

The elevator doors opened after the light indicated 30. The occupants exited including Raven. She flowed with the crowd until she came to the receptionist for Mr. Peterson.

"May I help you?" the middle-aged woman asked.

"Yes, I have an appointment with Mr. Peterson."

"Name?"

"Raven Anderson."

The receptionist typed with fever speed on her laptop then glanced up over her glasses at Raven. She gave the impression of disapproval, which most likely she did with all good-looking women who did business with Mr. Peterson. An alert on the computer screen stole the receptionist's attention from Raven.

"He will see you now."

Raven smiled and returned, "I'm sorry that you don't approve," The receptionist shot a displeased look in response to Raven's remark.

Raven entered Mr. Peterson's office. Her eyes met his as she mentally prepared for the task at hand.

"Well, well, what have we here?" Mr. Peterson quipped as he stood up and met Raven in front of his desk, offering his hand. "Mr. Johnson never told me that you were so attractive."

Raven met Mr. Peterson and handed him The Only Solution.

"What's this?" Mr. Peterson asked with a pleasant tone as he took the folder from Raven's hand. His half-assed smirk indicated his iniquitous thoughts as he undressed her with his eyes. Used to this behavior, Raven returned a slight smile. She used her voluptuous sensuality and looked him in the eye. His facial expression began to light up, which indicated his heightened sexual desire. Raven saw his hunger and for a brief moment, toyed with the idea of leading him on, but she realized that her time was short. She placed her left hand under the folder that he held and raised it. Her facial expression indicated to Mr. Peterson the urgent matter at hand. He moaned in a song-like cadence with a slight head jester. Suddenly, he noticed Raven's serious look and looked down at the document. His demeanor instantly changed when he read the front cover. He fully understood the outcome. His overweight frame showed signs of panic. His hands trembled as each breath he took became deeper and harder to accomplish. His eyes moved side to side as he read the cover several times. Raven had seen this reaction before. She pulled the .45 from the hidden holster to scramble his thoughts before he tried to defend himself.

He looked down at the handgun. Beads of sweat formed on his forehead as he tried to think. His mind drew a blank to any physical activity. He pleaded, "I have money, lots of money, just name your price."

Raven stepped back, retrieved her iPhone and with swift fingers began to type. She placed her iPhone on his desk with an account number on the screen. "Deposit one hundred thousand dollars into this account."

"Yes, yes, this is very reasonable," he snapped with a grateful attitude. He stepped back to his leather chair, sat down with a thump, and began to type on his laptop.

Raven's phone broadcasted the familiar ding when the transfer was completed. She picked up the phone, logged out, and brought up another account number. Raven handed the phone to him.

"Deposit fifty thousand into this account," Raven directed.

He looked at the screen then boasted, "St. Jude's, very commendable."

Mr. Peterson did not hesitate. He typed, and in a few seconds, Raven's phone indicated that the transaction was completed with a confirmation email.

"Well, that should square things up, doesn't it?" he desperately asked. His expression deepened with every second. Raven stared at him with her dark brown eyes drilling fear into his soul.

"Don't just stand there woman. What else do you want?" He demanded in a disrespectable tone.

"Let's go for a drive."

Mr. Peterson looked confused. Panic returned and overtook his mood. He reached for his intercom button.

Raven waved the handgun in disapproval and said, "I have a feeling that your secretary knows not to disturb you when there are female visitors. We will take your private elevator to the parking garage."

The door opened to his private parking stall. Raven quickly glanced about for anyone who could identify her. She shot out the security camera with her handgun. Her years of experience taught her to keep a silencer attached to her handgun. The low muffle of the .45 and the glass hitting the concrete gave Mr. Peterson a dose of reality. His usually high spirit vanished.

"My, what a nice car, you certainly have an exquisite taste for luxury."

The familiar double tweak indicated both front doors were now unlocked. Raven opened the passenger door with her gloved hand. Mr. Peterson opened the driver's door and entered the car the same time as Raven.

With trembling hands on the steering wheel, Mr. Peterson asked, "Where to?"

"You're going to hell, but first, I have a question, and if answered correctly, it could save your life."

"Yes, yes, what's the question?" Peterson begged.

"Who in Congress is funding your business? I know for a fact that your so-called government contracts are overpaid bribes. You overbid contracts and donate half the contract amount to someone in Congress. Now, damn it, who is it?" Raven demanded.

"I don't have a clue what you're talking about," Peterson cried.

"You must think that I'm pretty stupid to believe an answer like that," Raven said as she looked away from Peterson, checking the parking building for anyone who could recognize Raven as she stepped out of Peterson's car. "Your time just expired."

He snapped his head toward the passenger's seat and blubbered in a nervous tone, "I'm sorry, what was that?" Raven turned back to Peterson, handed him a white handkerchief and instructed him to hold it up to read the fine print. Mr. Peterson did as told. He struggled to read the message, so Raven grabbed the upper edge and held it up to the top of his forehead. With the handkerchief in the perfect spot, Raven squeezed the trigger. The handkerchief floated to his lap after doing an excellent job of keeping Raven clean. She photographed the results then returned to Mr. Peterson's office. She stopped at his desk and retrieved a thumb drive from his lap top. Raven stopped in front of the mirror by his door and unbuttoned the top two buttons before she opened his office door. Raven walked by the secretary and shot her a sultry look and announced, "Mr. Peterson wishes not to be disturbed; he will let you know when he is available. He's taking a shower if you know what I mean."

She looked up over her glasses with disapproval and grumbled under her breath, "Another one of his damn paid escorts. Why do I continue to work here?"

Raven entered the elevator keeping her back to the door as it closed. She returned to the bathroom on the tenth floor and resumed her identity before leaving the building to catch her returning flight to Charlotte.

The drive up to the Mountains took longer than the plane ride from Chicago to Charlotte. The Ridge, as she called it, sat on a mountain spur overlooking a thirty-mile open view. The cordillera of the Blue Ridge Mountain system extended from the back side of her property to the front view across the Yadkin Valley. On clear nights, she often sat on the deck observing the commercial planes traveling to and from Charlotte. Beyond the altitude of the planes, one could see the island universe with billions of stars. The cabin pointed east providing some of the most spectacular sunrises the Blue Ridge Mountains offered.

Raven switched off the Jaguar's lights when she pulled up to the cabin. She could smell the seasoned oak burning in the fireplace. Raven wanted to sneak into the cabin to surprise Naci. She softly closed the car door. A voice came out from the shadows of the dust to dawn light high above the barn door.

Raven turned quickly with her 40 caliber pistol drawn, only to be surprised by Naci .

"Trying to sneak in on me? You will never learn."

I know," Raven confessed. "Why don't you take me in and have your way with me. You know, as some sort of punishment." She jumped into Naci's arms and gave him a soft, gentle kiss.

The two lovers entered the side door of the cabin. The heavy smell of wood burning dominated her nostrils. Once accustomed to the wood burning, Raven could smell the scalloped potatoes simmering in the crockpot sitting on the kitchen counter.

"I thought that I would grill some tenderloin if that sounds okay?" Naci offered as he handed Raven a glass of wine.

"Sounds good to me," Raven expressed as she accepted the wine. "How was your day, take care of any bad guys?" Although Raven had been with The Foundation for several years and had been fanatically in love with Naci forever, she didn't know what his days consisted of. She had repeatedly asked the details of his involvement with The Foundation, but he would not confide in her. She had decided to let him tell her on his own accord because she reminded herself that her main focus was not Naci but the work that she did for the Foundation.

Raven placed her glass of wine on the kitchen counter and wrapped her arms around Naci's neck. She began to softly kiss him. Slowly at first, her cadence increased with her tongue action moving in and out of his mouth. Raven pressed her breasts up against his muscular chest. Being so close felt good to her; it stimulated her taut nipples. She began to feel his response on her lower stomach. She toyed with him for about two minutes, then pulled her head back and pushed with her hands to separate the two lovers.

"Hey, why did you do that? I was just starting to enjoy it," Naci complained.

"Fix supper so we can eat. I'm starved," Raven said as she offered a slight grin.

"You're a prick teaser," Naci complained without any empathy.

As usual, the dinner Naci prepared was superb. He turned the cabin lights down low and suggested that they enjoy the evening in front of the fireplace. Raven agreed. The hand laid stone fireplace offered a perfect romantic setting. Raven spread out a large blanket on the hardwood floor and placed the huge floor pillows in front of the hearth. Naci added a couple of logs to the fire. Raven held her hand out indicating for Naci to sit down and enjoy the evening.

"Now, tell me Naci, what is the one thing that you desire just this minute. If you could have anything in the world, what would it be?"

Naci smiled, rubbed his chin, and said, "I'd like to slowly pour warm milk chocolate on your naked body. Now mind you, I'd be very careful and only pour it on the sensual areas."

Raven smiled and said, "Why don't you show me the sensual areas." She lied back on her pillow holding her glass of wine carefully, not wanting to spill a drop. Naci set his glass on the hearth along with the bottle of wine. He smiled and began to unbutton her blouse slowly, one button at a time until he reached the last one. Naci gently pulled the shirt aside exposing her lace bra that secured her perfect breasts. Her abs looked like those of an Olympic athlete. Naci could count the muscle bulges from her ribs to her pants. He took his right index finger and gently followed her muscle valleys indicating that this was one area of her body that he admired. "Look at these perfect abs, Raven. I would pour warm chocolate and then carefully lick it off."

Raven placed her empty wine glass on the hearth, unbuckled her suit pants, and nodded at Naci to remove them. He took the visual command and slowly removed her pants leaving her panties in place. He folded her pants and placed them over the couch arm.

"Is there anywhere else that you would like to pour warm milk chocolate on my body, Naci?" Raven asked with a sexual tone, soft and under heavy breath.

"Yes, my love, but I'd need to remove your panties," Naci directed.

"I think you're in too big of a hurry; let's take it slow. I'm in that kind of mood."

Naci looked a bit irritated since he had been horny most of the day in anticipation of Raven arriving that night. He gently massaged her calves and then her thighs. Raven enjoyed Naci giving her legs a gentle massage. Naci kept his eyes on her stomach and breasts watching for her breathing to escalate. He started kissing her upper thigh on the outside as he rubbed the inner thigh. As he kissed her thigh towards her waist, he began to smell the sweetness of her womanhood. His member began to respond. Naci loved to softly glide his tongue in her slit giving himself pleasure. However, he elected to pass up her womanhood, so he began to kiss her abdomen. This surprised Raven given the fact that he was so horny before supper. She almost felt a little hurt that he skipped her love box, but she concluded that it was only a matter of time until she would be enjoying his tongue.

Naci continued kissing her and moved up to the top of her bra kissing her exposed breasts. Raven was thoroughly enjoying his slow, deliberate foreplay. She almost started hunching her ass but caught herself because she didn't want to rush. Naci was kissing the outer folds of her lower neck when he slid his right thigh between Raven's legs. When she felt his thigh sliding upward, she spread her legs apart to allow his leg to touch her pussy. She could feel her love button pressing on his hard thigh muscle. Raven felt a tingling in her loins. She wanted so much to hunch his leg but restrained herself. Her chest began to rise higher and higher as the seconds went by. Raven could feel the love juices starting to flow. She turned her head towards Naci and demanded that he kiss her on the mouth. Their lips met with a deep, wet cadence. Raven couldn't help herself; she wanted to take it slow to antagonize Naci, but it backfired. She felt her nipples swelling by the second. Her bra became a nuisance. She broke her lips from Naci's and said, "Please, Naci, don't toy with me. Help me reach my glory. I so need you to pleasure me."

Naci smiled and said, "I thought that you wanted to take it slow. I was looking forward to pouring warm milk chocolate on your smoking hot body…."

"Never mind what I said before. Please make love to me now!"

Naci didn't need to be told twice. He slid his body down to her waist, and to his surprise, she already had her panties off. He kissed her lower stomach; she invited Naci with legs wide open. Naci kept kissing her stomach while his right middle finger found her love button and slit. As his finger slid near her love box, he could feel the wetness. Raven grabbed the back of his head and guided it down between her legs. Naci slipped his middle finger deeper into her wet box, then he slid it up to the top inside of her sweetness and began to massage her glory, putting upward pressure that delivered extreme pleasure to Raven. She began to moan louder and louder. Her hips began to hunch with each stroke that his hand made. She struggled with her bra wanting so much to free her breasts. Naci picked up on this, took his left hand, and pulled each shoulder strap down. Raven took both hands and pushed her bra down around her waist giving her mounds much-needed freedom. She instantly began to squeeze her plump breasts and rub her hard nipples. By now, Naci was giving Raven full finger penetration increasing the speed with each passing second. Naci leaned up to meet Raven's lips. She rose up and delivered deep tongue matching his motion as he delivered to her needy love canal.

Naci could feel the love juices flowing down his wrist. He couldn't take it any longer; he broke his lips from hers and replaced his hand with his tongue. Raven was now losing control of her climax. She could feel the pleasure in her groin. It delivered pleasure all the way up her torso. She looked down at her stomach; her breasts jiggled with each pleasurable hunch that she delivered. Raven could see her hard nipples waving back a forth against the wall of the cabin. Her pussy began to quiver with delight as her climax started to build. She pressed harder and harder on Naci's tongue. She released his head and placed her hands on her hips to prepare for her first climax in over a month. "Oh, oh, Naci, caress my love button…. Yes, that's it. Here I go." The climax began to explode. Raven raised her bottom up at the height of her delight. Naci pulled up, and as she peaked, he placed his member deep inside her wet love channel. Raven loved when the timing was perfect. Naci began to pump her delivering pleasure to his manhood. Raven came, but she began to need more. She loved to climax then instantly feel the pleasure start over just like the first time.

"Oh, Naci, what perfect timing. You caught my peak just perfect. It doesn't get any better than this."

Naci slid a pillow under her ass giving him the perfect height to deliver his best moves. Raven began to scream with delight, "Oh, Naci, I love you." Her brown eyes indicated her need to keep the cadence steady. Raven's tongue began to slide out of the corner of her mouth. Her breasts, moving back and forth, caught Naci's eyes and fueled his sexual craving for Raven. Her breathing was deep and heavy. Naci slapped her inner thighs with his. Sweat began to drip from Naci onto Raven's stomach. She moaned with delight. Her mouth formed a perfect circle. Naci could hear her deep moans of joy. Raven's brown eyes begged for a faster stroke. Naci knew exactly what she wanted, so he increased his speed, bringing more and more satisfaction to both.

"I'm ready to climax again, Naci," she could feel it coming. Naci could sense her spunk and started driving her slow and hard. As he drove in, Naci would slightly raise up to rub her g spot, which caused her climax to explode. "Oh, Naci, you know how to do it just right." Raven moaned. Naci could feel the river of honey flowing as he delivered and climaxed at the same time.

Both fell to each side with deep, deep breathing. "Damn, Raven, this is like working out," Naci exclaimed.

"You bet, Naci. I love you so much. I don't know how you do it, but your timing is perfect. I love our lovemaking."

Raven and Naci looked deep into each other eyes, smiling and giving each other soft, gentle kisses. Minutes passed, their eyes never separated, and their hot, naked bodies tangled together never let the lust go dead. Raven could feel her hormones tingle as their kissing began to increase. Their pecks turned into soft, wet kisses. Then their tongues began to slip in and out. Raven could feel her groin vibrate; it felt needy and horny. The tingle grew as the minutes passed. She wrapped her leg around Naci's thigh to allow room for her hand. Raven found her love button and began to caress it. Her nakedness added to the ecstasy. Raven wished that this feeling could last forever.

"Naci, my love, could you roll over on your back and let me mount you? I need just one more ride to complete this evening. I'm not quite done."

Naci smiled and said, "This is why I love having sex with you. It is a pure pleasure." Naci turned over on his back. Raven rolled over with him and mounted Naci. She raised up and began to slap her wetness to stimulate Naci. The sound brought Naci's member alive. In just about thirty seconds, his member became hard again. Raven smiled and guided it into her wet cave. She rodecl down on it driving it deep into her. She stopped at full penetration then began to hunch his shaft. Raven could feel the pleasure build when her love button rubbed the base of his manhood. Raven closed her eyes, grabbed her tits, and began to hunch with fever speed. She started to moan louder and louder. Raven smiled. She opened her eyes to watch Naci's face. He wanted to hunch but her pressing down with her body weight made it impossible. Raven started panting with her tongue protruding out the side of her mouth. She moaned and quivered. She slid her ass back and forth across Naci's midsection. "Here I go, Naci, ooh ooh. I'm in orbit." Raven raised up with clenched teeth and moaned. She quivered for about ten seconds then relaxed. Naci could feel the wetness flow down around his shaft. Raven dismounted and hugged and kissed Naci. "Thank you, my love. Is there anything else I can do for you?"

"Yes, let's take a shower, finish our wine, then see how you can bring me to my second climax."

"It's a deal," Raven said. She jumped up and extended her hand to help Naci up. They both walked into the bedroom holding hands.

"Naci, will you promise me one thing? When we are old, will you still hold hands with me?"

"I sure will, Raven. I love you."

"I love you too." Raven returned.

CHAPTER 15

Raven entered the front door of Wolf Summit. The main headquarters of The Foundation was a heavily fortified compound with an underground bunker and airstrip located in northern West Virginia. Wolf Summit had been one of many locations that The Foundation used over the years, depending what the needs were. Raven was greeted by the long-time family confidant, Ethan. Ethan was Amelia's house manager and was a former full-time agent.

"Good day, Ms. Raven. I trust that your trip was a pleasant one?"

"Yes, Ethan, how are you doing?"

"Fine, fine, thanks for asking. Everyone is in Amelia's office waiting."

Raven entered the office to find everyone gathered at the window looking out at the view that it offered.

Amelia turned when she heard the door open and said, "Good, Raven's here. Let's get to work." Amelia, along with John, Pauline, and Naci, hugged Raven before everyone took their place at the conference table.

Raven noticed two others in the room that she didn't recognize. With the experience that she had gained the past few years, she took a hard look at both elderly men.

Amelia noticed the attention that Raven was giving the two men. "Raven, in case you're wondering who these two are, let me introduce you. The one on the left is John's cousin, Harold. They served in the great war together. The big fellow sitting next to Harold is Robert. He goes by Ax." Amelia smiled, and before Raven could say a word, Amelia continued. "Now in case you're wondering why we keep these two around, don't give it a second thought, they can carry their weight."

Raven smiled and gave the two a courteous nod. She took her place at the conference table.

Harold, a bit of a smart ass, tipped his imaginary hat to Raven then said, "Where's Nadia?"

Amelia announced, "On assignment."

Harold returned, "Just like old times, she shows up at the last minute and takes all the glory."

During and since the war, the group of individuals gathered was known as "The Legends of the Vacaras." They were all high-level Foundation operatives. Many were ageless in mind and body due to their skill, never-ending youth, and medicine developed by Nadia's father during the great war.

Amelia passed out folders to everyone then said, "This is our biggest and most important job since the government cut our funding two decades ago. As you can see, former Secretary of State Hillary Benton is the target."

This reference got the attention of everyone in the room.

"Hillary has been selling information to the highest bidder on the world stage. The latest was uranium to the Russians. The President contacted me two days ago and has hired The Foundation to terminate her. This is a low profile, high priority case. He does not want the U.S. Government and especially his office anywhere near this kill," Amelia said. "She is also getting way too chummy with North Korea, Iran, and other rogue nations, so it's hard to tell what she has done to this country. She must be stopped."

"What's the time frame?" John asked.

"She is on vacation in the Mediterranean, so this is the perfect time while she is on foreign soil. The Administration can blame the Russians or anyone of his choosing. This is what the President wants."

"It looks like we are off for a little sun in the Mediterranean," Harold announced in his usual playful manner.

"Amelia, you mentioned the Mediterranean; that's a big area. Do you have a more detailed location?" John asked.

"According to what the President gave me, she is on Vladimir Putin's yacht and will be docking in ten days at the Nice, France Marina. She is spending one night at the Hyatt Regency Hotel located just west of the Marina on the beach front."

"Man, this could get ugly. Putin is ex KGB, and I'm sure he's not traveling alone," Harold announced.

"Yes, I know," Amelia agreed. "I want Ax and Ethan on the next flight to Nice to verify this intel. Ethan knows this part of the world because he spent several years as a Foundation agent in France."

Ax and Ethan nodded.

"The way I figure, the kill cannot take place near Putin's yacht because it will be heavily guarded. Once he docks and she exits, he won't give a shit what happens. We need to make our move either in transit to the Hyatt or while she is in Nice. Once she gets on her plane, it's too late," Amelia directed. "Let's pull Nice up on satellite and look the area over."

Everyone gathered around the series of computer screens hanging on the wall of the communications room. At the helm, Amelia scanned the Nice satellite. "Here's the Port of Nice Marina. Look at the yachts parked here. They are some of the world's most expensive. Notice to the west, there is a high bluff, which is a perfect location for Raven to make a kill shot with a long gun. Ethan, see if she would have a clear view of the whole marina, and if so, rent a villa."

"Okay, Amelia."

"If the bluff shot is not possible, hopefully, the Secretary will travel this front road along the beach to her hotel. Harold, you will rent a street side room in one of the hotels between the marina and the Hyatt to make the kill shot if necessary."

Harold nodded in agreement.

Amelia turned, looked at John, and said, "John, you rent a room at the Hyatt in case all else fails. You can get close to her in the lobby. If she makes it that far, I bet she will have some sort of convulsion and die of natural causes, don't you?"

John smiled and nodded his head.

"Pauline, I want you to monitor the communications equipment. Naci, I want you to take a long gun and set up in an adjacent room of the villa. I want the two of you to hit the target as hard as possible. We need to hit hard and fast." Amelia zoomed in on the marina and noticed several small cafés. "Ethan and Ax, each takes a seat at different cafés and keep us posted on the ground activities. If the Sectary takes a different route to the Hyatt, follow her. I'll stay here, as usual, and monitor the satellite to keep everyone abreast of conditions. Everyone will wear a headset and stay in constant contact with me."

"Come on, everyone, let's go to the basement and pack up our gear for shipment," John announced.

"Good. Ethan, do you have the flights booked?"

"Yes, I just confirmed them on my iPhone."

"Excellent. I'll ship the supplies with one of our carrier flights, and you can pick up the cargo once it arrives in Nice."

Ethan nodded confirming that he understood.

"Over the next few days, I want Raven, Naci, and Harold at the gun range. Let's get some rest. It's been a long day."

NICE, FRANCE 72 HOURS LATER.

Raven, Naci, and Pauline entered the one-bedroom villa that Ethan rented. It was small and private, but adequate. The position of the villa gave a perfect view of the marina. Raven opened the French doors and stepped onto the balcony. "My God, what a view," Raven observed. The majestic sun was sinking into the Mediterranean Sea. Diamonds glimmered on water's edge as the sun set. The warm breeze could be felt by all as each agent stepped onto the balcony.

"John and I spent three months sailing the Mediterranean Sea many years ago," Pauline reminisced.

Raven turned away from the majestic view and asked, "Was it for business or pleasure?"

"Strictly business. We were chasing rogue Nazi's who escaped Europe after the war," Pauline said.

"That must have been a daunting task to hunt them down," Naci stated.

"Yes, it was Naci. We did manage to cut off several escape routes, which allowed us to capture hundreds of high-level Nazi's from exile."

The warmth of the sun and breeze made it difficult to concentrate on the task at hand, but duty called.

"I can set up my tripod inside the living room. That will give us natural cover in case Putin has snipers located around the marina," Raven observed. "The horizon has the sunset framed in perfect form. An artist could not paint a more perfect view. In about an hour, it will be totally dark, and we can unload the van. That way no other satellites will pick up our unusual activity."

For the next two hours, Naci, Ethan, Ax, and the girls unloaded and set up the long guns and communication equipment. Their setup was the hub of all Foundation activity. The drive leading up to the villa was private and could not be seen from the Marina.

"I'm going to set up the commutation equipment on the balcony. The signal in here is much too weak," Ethan said. He found the strongest signal out on the far end of the balcony.

The next morning at precisely 8 am Nice time, all the agents were in place and ready for a communication test.

Pauline placed her headset on, then powered up the transmitter and receiver, which gave life to the communication equipment. "Testing, 51-51. Do you copy, Stella?"

Amelia replied, "Yes, loud and clear."

Amelia confirmed that all headsets were operational with each member of the team. She also confirmed that they were in place, which indicated excellent reception.

"Listen up, everyone. I have Putin's yacht on satellite, and it is about three miles from the marina. Yesterday, I confirmed that the subject is onboard. As far as I can tell, no one has disembarked. If so, it was at night. All we can do now is wait until the yacht comes to port."

"How will I recognize it? All the Yachts look alike," Raven quizzed.

"Putin's yacht is named Martha Ann. Its name is written on the side on the main deck level. It's about 230 feet long, dark color on the bottom and white on top. The builder is Lurssen Yachts from Germany," Amelia said.

"That's a roger," Raven confirmed.

THREE HOURS LATER-

"Heads up, everyone. It looks as if the birdie is coming home. Putin's yacht just backed into his dock. The crew is tying her up now. Do you copy, Raven?"

"10-4."

"Naci."

"10-4."

Pauline was on the balcony with binoculars. "I can see the target through the window. She is almost to the door leading to the lower level deck where she will step onto the deck."

"I see her," Raven announced.

"I have a fix on her," Naci confirmed. "She just stepped onto the dock. Raven, you take her out, and I'll take out the nearest agent to her."

"Got it, Naci."

Just as the former Secretary of State stepped into Raven's sight, a loud burst of gunfire could be heard on everyone's headset. It continued for at least thirty seconds. "Oh, fuck, that hurts," Raven cried. "Naci, Pauline, do something." Another round of fury hailed down on the villa. The gunmen were firing aimlessly into the room. Glass hitting the tile floor dominated the aftermath of the second fire-burst. "I hope that you son-of-a-bitches rot in hell." Sounds of clip changes and heavy breathing took over the frequency. Pauline dropped the binoculars, pulled out of her two forty caliber handguns, but she was trapped on the balcony. She stepped around the corner and entered the adjacent room that Naci occupied.

Naci came in from the bedroom firing two handguns at the assassins. He slid under the huge dining table to avoid the massive gunfire. Two heavily armed men firing automatic weapons were in charge. Naci turned up the dining table for cover. Due to the thick top, it gave him decent protection. Raven managed to pull herself behind the wooden bar, but her legs were bleeding heavily. She stood up to return fire with one hand and held the other hand on her bleeding leg. Raven gritted her teeth trying to bear the pain.

Again, a barrage of gunfire filled the air. Handgun fire dominated; loud screams from behind the bar could be heard. Naci yelled, "We're under heavy attack." Gunfire once again filled the airwaves. Amelia wanted desperately to give commands, but experience taught her better. The heavy breathing continued for at least fifteen seconds. "Damn it; I'm losing it, Amelia. Help me, Naci." Raven softly pleaded for help. A deadening sound cracked the airwaves then a thump.

Amelia quickly turned the satellite onto the villa. She could see the destruction on the balcony. She zoomed in on the street side to check for additional support.

The villa was completely silent as the gunmen were changing clips. Pauline knew that this was her chance. She stepped into the doorway with both hand-guns blazing. Her eyes were full of vengeance that none of her partners had ever seen. She shot one of the two assassins in front of her with her excellent marksmanship. Pauline's vicious demeanor, which only her husband has witnessed, continued as she walked in the direction of the gunmen. Her fearless approach surprised the gunman as much as it did Naci. She bore down on the remaining gunman. With his gun jammed, he looked up at Pauline as he hopelessly tried to bring his AK 47 back to life. Pauline aimed her two handguns at his forehead and opened fire. His headless body fell to the tile floor. Not knowing how many gunmen there were, Pauline cautiously moved towards the street side door. She caught a glimpse of one escaping. Pauline opened fire landing two shots in his shoulders as he ran out the door. She followed him to the doorway, not stepping outside for fear of more assassins. He climbed into a car and escaped her wrath.

Pauline didn't speak for fear of the assassins hearing her. She quietly checked each room in the villa before attending to Raven and Naci.

"Damn it, Raven. Talk to me. Pauline, do you copy?" Amelia screamed. "Naci, answer me, Naci! God, don't let them die like this. I have one assassin escaping via the street side. I'll get his license plate."

Again, there was only silence. "Harold, abort your position and get to the villa. I don't like this one bit," Amelia demanded.

"Will do," Harold returned. Amelia swung the satellite back to the villa's balcony to see what was happening. "Ethan, do you have a fix on the target?"

"Yes, Ma'am. She is still on the dock talking to her bodyguards."

Just as Ethan finished talking, he heard a pu-tink. He turned and looked at Ax who was running for cover holding his shoulder. Ethan jumped up and ran for cover in the café.

"Amelia, Ax is shot. Sniper fire. Someone has a fix on us. We're under cover inside the cafe." Ethan reported.

"Stay put, Ethan, until I can figure out where the sniper is."

Ethan acknowledged her command. The target was now in her motorcade traveling west on the ocean side route. Amelia feverishly scanned the marina and surrounding area for the hitman.

"Harold, how far out are you?"

"Almost up to the villa," Harold informed. When he arrived, he caught a glimpse of a car turning the corner north of the villa. Harold rushed into the villa. The horror that he saw was devastating. The harbor side of the villa had been destroyed by gunfire. It was if two hundred rounds destroyed everything in the room. The walls, decorations, windows, and doors were nearly obliterated. He saw Pauline behind the bar.

"Are you okay, Pauline?" Harold yelled.

"Yes, I'm fine. It's Raven. She's been shot several times, but she's still alive. Check on Naci."

Naci was laying behind the overturned table, unconscious with blood-soaked arms. The gunman focused all gunfire on the table. The avalanche of fire-power destroyed the wooden table. Harold checked his pulse then checked the extent of the damage. "They've been ambushed, Amelia. All are alive." If it had not been for the bulletproof vests, the damage would have been fatal.

"John, don't even think about it. Stay put and complete the mission. You are the last defense that we have. Ethan, make sure that those gunmen don't return. Salvage what firepower and ammo you have and monitor the street until Raven and Naci are safe." Amelia commanded.

Pauline checked Raven's bleeding. She was hit in both upper arms in the triceps areas. Her legs also took several shots. One thing that caught Harold's attention was on the bar there was a Morgan silver dollar. Harold put the coin in his pocket then quickly pulled the sheets from the bedroom and used them as bandages. He went to Naci and began first aid. Ethan's taxi pulled up. Harold stepped behind the front wall in case it was the assassin. Harold noticed a trail of blood on the floor that led out to the street. Harold thought, "Two dead and one injured."

Ethan and Ax ran into the room, only to stop when they saw the aftermath of the ambush. "At least two of them paid for this," Ethan informed Amelia.

Ethan asked, "Who needs my help the most?" Pauline answered, "Over here, Ethan, behind the bar."

After about five minutes, Pauline announced, "We have this situation contained Amelia. Naci and Raven will be fine. Ethan and I have the bleeding stopped,"

"It looks like the work of Morgan," Harold reported. "I found a Morgan silver dollar on the bar. The gunmen must have laid it on the bar before they started shooting. That way if he ended up dead or had to run, he already has his mark on this job."

Amelia responded before John could comment, "Good job, guys. John, do you have a fix on that bitch so we can get the hell out of here?"

John responded in a grateful tone, "Her car just pulled up to the front door. I'm in the open balcony just above the entrance. They won't know what hit her. They'll think that she is having a heart attack."

"Fry her brain, John. Make her suffer, then finish her off," Amelia commanded.

"My pleasure," John answered.

The automatic doors slid open. Two bodyguards entered looking for any suspicious activity. The first agent turned and nodded. Four agents entered with Hillary Benton in the middle. When she was in the lobby about ten feet, John began to mentally focus on her skull. She grabbed her head and turned it from side to side. The expression on her face indicated a moderate pain level. John then shot her a dose of pain that brought her to knees. The six agents formed a circle around her. Guns appeared, and one agent began talking into his wrist. John let up for a short five seconds, then hammered her as if he were driving rail spikes on the CSX rail line. This continued until she didn't have an ounce of life left in her. Agents called for her travel doctor. One agent turned, looked up, and stared into John's eyes. His arm went up to communicate, so John relieved him of his duties. The agent fell to the tile floor to never get up again. Chaos began to dominate the hotel lobby. John stepped back to take cover behind a large column. Each agent began to look up, as if it as a natural thing in a situation like this, so John had to terminate every one of them. Once he was done, John turned his microphone on and announced, "Heaven can't wait for Hillary. Oh yeah, the devil has the first option on her soul."

"Are you sure that she will never harm our country again?" Amelia asked.

"She couldn't possibly be alive after what I did to her and six of her bodyguards," John informed.

"Good, the State Department will spin it as a health issue, and no one will beg to differ."

"Ethan, get the van and load everyone up. We need to get the hell out of there." Amelia demanded.

"John, there is a taxi stand one block west. Use the back door to exit. I don't want anyone to ID you. Remember, you are still famous in our world."

"On my way," John returned.

"John, have the taxi drop you off at the Saint-Roch Hospital, 5 Pierre Devoluy Street. Ethan, it is only about a mile north of your location, copy?" Amelia informed.

John and Ethan acknowledged her instructions.

ONE WEEK LATER-

"Good morning, sunshine." Naci sang as he entered the hospital room. His wounds were mending but not completely healed. "How is the love of my life feeling today?"

"Much better, I'll be glad when we can go home. Keeping one of us guard here at the hospital has to be hard on everyone."

"Now, Raven, no one is complaining. We're all in this together," Naci said.

"Naci, have you seen my St. Christopher Cross that I wear around my neck? I can't seem to find it."

Naci reached into his pocket and handed it to her. "Thank you. I panicked when I asked the nurse for my belongings, and it was missing."

"You're most welcome," Naci returned with a smile.

The room door opened and all the agents entered, John, Pauline, Ethan, Ax, and Harold. John smiled and said, "Well, Raven, today's the big day. You're being released."

Her eyes lit up with excitement. She said, "It'll be good to get back to Wolf Summit and start my rehabilitation. This is the longest that I've ever been off."

The hospital room door opened, and a deliveryman with flowers entered. "Bring them over here," Raven directed. Once he set them down on her nightstand, Harold gave him a tip and escorted him to the door. John quickly examined the vase to make sure that the delivery was safe. He handed the card to Raven. She smiled and opened it. Her expression instantly changed when she read the card. It simply said "Morgan." Raven handed the card to John then she looked in the envelope and removed a 1921 Morgan silver dollar.

"Damn it, John. What's he trying to tell me? Is he the one who ambushed us?" Raven asked. Harold shot a quick look at John but remained silent about the silver dollar that he found on the bar. " This is his marker. Morgan did this to me, damn it. Now I have two SOB's to get even with."

John hesitated. The room fell silent, then John responded, "Amelia is checking all sources. She's trying to find out who did this to us. So far, she has not come up with any leads."

Raven looked at John and shouted, "Well, here's a tip. It's that fucking Morgan. Because of that bastard, I'm laid up with about twenty wounds to prove it. Hell, I'm lucky to be alive."

John shot her a mild dose to calm her down.

Raven smiled, "Damn you, John Vacara. You know that I need to vent. I can't keep this bottled up inside me."

The doctor came in and gave Raven the go ahead to be dismissed. The whole gang smiled on their way out of the hospital room. Pauline stayed and helped Raven dress.

Out in the hallway, Naci asked John, "What the hell does this mean?" Naci held the coin up to John.

"Morgan is an ex–Green Beret who served in Nam and several special ops. I have encountered him on a few occasions. His tactics are modern; he's smart, and worst of all, he doesn't value human life. I'd bet money that he doesn't even value his own life."

"In what capacity have you encountered him?" Raven asked.

"Mostly exchanging intel. He sold information, and it was always correct, nothing more. One more thing, Morgan has always been disguised, other than his physical size." John returned. "I don't know who he is."

"Have you ever physically tangled with him?"

"Yes, once. Of course, he quickly learned that I was superior and backed off," John explained. "The key is to find out who he's working for. He used to work alone, but I have a feeling he doesn't anymore."

Ethan pulled the van up to the rear entrance of the hospital. Pauline and Harold helped Raven in, and the rest entered. The van disappeared into traffic.

CHAPTER 16

SIX YEARS LATER.

Raven awoke from a deep sleep thinking that she heard something. It was a faint knock on her apartment door. She instinctively reached under her pillow and retrieved her Smith and Wesson 40 caliber. The grip felt good and gave her confidence. She eased out of bed and cautiously walked into the living room poised to take action. Raven was positive that she had heard a knock at the door. She went to the security camera monitor, but the hall was empty except for an envelope. Raven turned the camera and checked both directions down the long hallway. With no one in the viewfinder, she walked over to the door and looked through the peephole. She unlocked the door and swung it open with her pistol in combat mode. Convinced that no one was there, she picked up the envelope and quickly closed and locked the apartment door.

Fully awake now, Raven placed the envelope on the counter while she put on a pot of coffee. She put four scoops of java into the Bunn and added water. Raven then turned her attention back to the mysterious envelope. She opened it to find a note and a 1921 Morgan Silver Dollar. A chill ran down her spine. Raven stood, eyes staring, wondering, "Was that Morgan who just left this?" Raven opened the envelope:

Raven,

I trust you slept well last night. Raven, you simply are an intriguing individual. You are a world class assassin, second to only to the Myth. He was a giant in our profession. I truly miss doing business with him. I have information on Rothman that you need to have. Meet me at the Concord Mills Mall, exit 49 off I 85 at noon today. Meet me in the food court. I'll be wearing a red ball cap and a brown shirt. Bring your laptop. I have a very interesting video on a flash drive that you must see.

Morgan

P.S. Your apartment is bugged and has camera's installed. I hacked the system.

Raven read the note two more times, threw it down, and walked into the bedroom. She hunted for the cameras. Just as she was about to give up, she noticed a small glass figurine sitting on the dresser. Raven examined it form a distance and discovered a miniature camera inside. She discovered two more in the bedroom and one in the bathroom. She thought, "These bugs must have been installed by the Foundation, and Morgan hacked in. I bet that they're all over the apartment. I'll just leave them in place for now."

Raven dressed in casual clothes, which for her included a flak jacket full of pistols. She glanced at her watch, 8:30 am. She left her apartment and drove to the mall. She parked up on a bank across the street from the parking lot at the entrance to the food court. She wanted to show up early to see if Morgan would come alone. As she waited, her mind kept thinking of a story Bill had told her about a Viet Cong sniper he chased in the jungle for months. Bill said he was the smartest sniper that he ever faced. Bill only got one shot in all the months that he hounded him. When he finally captured him in his rifle scope, Bill gently squeezed his trigger and got a direct kill shot. Only to find out later, he shot a dummy. The sniper was so clever that he managed to avoid Bill's wrath by using a stuffed uniform, which was all done while Bill watched through his scope.

Raven's mind returned to the parking lot at the mall. She suddenly realized that Viet Cong sniper could be Morgan. Could it be a Chinese mercenary in Nam for hire by the Viet Cong? It only made sense, Raven thought. Bill told her several stories about this sniper. Now that she was more involved with the Foundation, she knew that the stories Bill told we not all in Nam. Most could have happened after the war. It now made sense to her.

Raven glanced at her watch, 11:50. She walked into the mall and stopped short of the food court.

The mall was crowded making it easy to stay hidden but hard to find Morgan. Years of stalking her victims gave her a sharp eye for detail. The mall was circular like a race track. There were shops on both sides except for the open food court located in the center. Raven slowly made her way to the edge of the food court. Hundreds of tables were filled mostly with women and children. Her eyes slowly and systematically scanned every table. About halfway through, she spotted Morgan. There was no doubt in her mind that it was him. Their eyes made contact indicating that he saw her first. A hot flash ran like wildfire up her spine stopping at the back of her skull. Raven thought to herself, "He's the son-of-a-bitch who ambushed us in Nice, France. With a vengeance in her eye, she approached her adversary. He was sitting sipping on a cup of coffee when she walked up to the table.

Morgan slowly looked up, and for the longest time, the two assassins stared at each other until Morgan said, "Take a seat, Raven Anderson."

For the first time in her career, Raven didn't have a clear focus on her objective. She took a seat with her laptop in one hand and the other hand inside her jacket pocket was gripping a 9-mm pistol.

Raven thought to herself, "Hell, who is this guy? He isn't Chinese."

"You are much prettier than you were in the photo's that your late uncle showed me."

"Let me turn around; maybe you'll recognize me, you bastard," Raven said with a stern tone.

As a veteran sniper and assassin, Morgan didn't react at all. He looked Raven dead in her eyes and said, "Please explain what you just said."

Raven looked to her left then to her right. Her temper started to calm down. She remembered what Bill always said to her, "You can never be in a situation if you're mad. Mad gets you killed."

"Several Foundation agents and I were on assignment in Nice, France when you and two of your thugs ambushed us. I wound up in the hospital and out of commission for six months."

Morgan said, "I'm not going to sit here and try to convince you that it wasn't me. I work alone. The only partner I've ever had in my forty-year career was your Uncle Bill. He and I go back to the days we spent in Nam together."

Raven leaned towards Morgan, teeth clenched, and said, "You left your calling card on the bar in the Nice villa, a Morgan Silver Dollar." Raven pulled the coin out of her pocket and laid it on the table. "I keep it with me as a reminder of how badly I want to kill you."

Morgan looked down at the coin then said, "The coin that I leave has my stamp on it, the letters M-M. Go ahead; look at it."

Raven picked up the coin, examined both sides, and said, "You could not have marked this coin to throw us off."

"Think for a minute, Raven. Who gains by having you dead?"

Raven thought for a minute then answered, "Rothman, or do you know of someone else through a rumor?"

Morgan smiled and said, "Raven, there are no rumors when it comes to you or I. The whole world is scared of us except for one man and woman. Do you know who they are?"

"John Vacara and Nadia Vogt."

"Exactly, don't ever cross those two. I stay clear of them." Morgan warned. "Open your laptop; I have a file and film to show you."

Raven turned the laptop on and placed it between her and Morgan. When the computer booted up, he placed a thumb drive into the USB port. Morgan scanned through hundreds of files but didn't open any. "I'll give you this to take with you. Study every file. It will help you figure who's who. Most importantly, I want to show you a film clip that was made about twenty years ago. It's of Bill and me."

Morgan clicked on the icon marked Sloppy Joe's. "Your Uncle Bill wanted this made so you would know the truth in case he wasn't around to help you. Raven, he knew that you would be the world's most sought-after assassin. Are you ready to see this?"

Raven nodded, and Morgan clicked the icon. The scene was inside Sloppy Joes in Cuba. The bar appeared empty, in disrepair and dusty as the camera panned out around the whole bar. It showed the marble counter where thousands of the World Famous Sloppy Joes were made. The famous Mahogany bar and wall cabinets stored hundreds of bottles of Rum. During the great war, Sloppy Joe's was the place to be. Air Force pilots trained in Cuba and Sloppy Joes was the main watering hole. Then the camera stopped and was placed on an adjacent table. Bill walked over to a nearby table and joined Morgan.

Bill looked into the lens and said, "Barbara Ann, you know by now that I'm gone. You are the best assassin in the world or my longtime friend Morgan would not be showing this to you. You're thinking, what if Morgan wound end up like me, dead, then who would show you this film? Well, my sweet Barbara, it is to be kept in a Swiss bank vault, and if Morgan has been terminated, this copy would be delivered to you via several descending methods. I have deposited ten million dollars into an account with you being the sole beneficiary, in which the bank's current president will deliver it to you. If you expire first, the balance of the account will go to Morgan. If both of you are gone, then it goes to charity." Bill looked to his left at Morgan then turned back to the lens and continued, "No matter what you have been told or what you have seen, this man is your only true friend. I trust him with my life. That is why I wanted you to hear this from me on film. Morgan will not steer you wrong. How do I know this? It's simple. If he shows you this film and the money is still in the bank, then you have a true friend, one you can trust. Don't feel obligated to pay him a dime; I have taken care of Morgan financially. I have given the bank a list of questions for you to answer to establish that it is you." Bill picks up a piece of white cardboard with the three questions and answers. Bill then lights the list with a lighter. "Also, Morgan will give you hundreds of files that I have collected detailing who does what around the world. I will update this file every six months." Bill turns to Morgan; they shake hands and smile. Bill places his arm around Morgan and says, "Barbara Ann, please be careful, and remember that I love you with all my heart." Bill gets up and walks to the camera, and with his arm in the viewfinder, the camera goes black.

Raven turned her head and looked at Morgan with a tear in her eye and said, "Well, I must admit that I wasn't expecting this."

Morgan smiled and said, "Now, Raven, I'm going to give you the address and phone number of the current bank president. I suggest that we fly over to Switzerland and establish your account. I know the bank president; it will make the transition much easier. I'd imagine that the account has accumulated quite a massive amount of interest."

"How do I get in contact with you now that we aren't adversaries?"

Morgan reached his hand out and said, "Give me your phone. I'll program my phone number."

Raven looked at Morgan and said, "You know that I'm going after Rothman. The Foundation has forbidden me from killing him."

"My advice is to play it slow. If the Foundation wants him alive, play along with them. They must have a reason. I'd say that Rothman knew you were in Nice because The Foundation has a leak. I'd be patient and terminate the leak first then Rothman."

Raven sat and stared at Morgan. She laughed then said, "Hell, Morgan, you have the whole world thinking you are Chinese. You are good. I'll call when I can go to Switzerland. I have a couple of contracts to clean up first, but then I'm free."

Morgan smiled, "Duty calls. I understand." He turned and disappeared into the crowd.

Raven walked out to the parking lot when her phone lit up indicating an incoming text.

Amelia: Need you at Wolf Summit.
Raven: On my way. Be there in six hours.
Amelia: Can't wait. Agent will pick you up at the airport in one hour.
Raven: K

Raven rang the doorbell at Wolf Summit, and as usual, Ethan answered. "Well, Ms. Raven, I'm so pleased to see you. Let me take your bag."

"It's good to see you, Ethan. Is Amelia in her office?"

"Yes, but I was told to give you a letter from Mr. John first. It's in the kitchen."

Raven went to the kitchen and opened it.

Raven,

I need a favor. Please meet me in Berlin. There's a flight leaving tonight from Pittsburg. Here is a ticket and a thousand dollars operating capital. This job requires physical labor so bring work clothes. The temperature this time of year is moderate. I have someone who you must meet and a personal favor to finish that requires manual labor.

Thanks a million

John Vacara

Raven walked over to the coffee maker and poured a cup. She sat down on the bar stool and thought. "Why in the hell would John Vacara want me to help him? Why not Naci?"

Raven pulled her iPhone from her pocket, dialed, and waited for the ringtone. A few seconds later, she heard a familiar voice.

"Hello, Raven, are you okay?" Naci asked.

"Yes, I'm fine. Naci, your dad left me a note here at Wolf Summit, and he wants me to meet him in Berlin," Raven checked the note for accuracy, "Do you know what this is all about?"

"No, Raven. I haven't the slightest idea."

"I wonder what's in Berlin," Raven said.

"All I know is that he and Pauline spent time in Berlin during the war. Aunt Pearl has told me some pretty amazing stories about those two; although, she has limited knowledge because she spent the war in the States. John and Pauline were mostly in Europe in those days. "

"All that I could find out is that your dad has a rare mental gift that the Nazis wanted to capitalize on, but they could never hold him long enough to figure out why he is so advanced." Raven reported.

"Yeah, that's about all I could find out too. He doesn't talk about it."

"Okay, I guess I'll find out soon enough. I love you."

"Love you too, bye," Naci pushed the off button.

Raven found Ethan and told him about the note. He suggested that she talk to Amelia before leaving for the airport. Raven thanked Ethan and went upstairs to pack.

Raven walked up to the study and knocked on the open-door frame where Amelia was seated at her desk. Raven thought, "Look at that amazing woman. I just hope to be in such a great condition when I'm her age."

Amelia looked up and smiled at Raven, "Come in, come in, it's so good to see you." Amelia eagerly stood up and hugged Raven as if she was her firstborn. Raven took a seat, and Amelia returned to her desk chair.

"Now, what can I do for you?" Amelia asked.

"John wants me to meet him in Berlin. Do you know why?"

"Yes, he wants you to meet a dear old friend of his named Hilda. She, John, and Harold go way back to the war, about 35 years ago."

"Oh, okay, but this seems important. Why is it so important?"

"John and Harold stole something of great value from the Nazis, and I think that you and he are going to retrieve it."

"It's located in Berlin?"

"No, no, John says it's on Hilda's farm outside of Berlin. Also to your benefit, Hilda knows Rothman very well. He helped her some after the war was over. That's all I know."

"I'll just have to wait until I get there," Raven commented with a smile. Anything to do with Rothman gave Raven pleasure.

"Oh, let me tell you one thing. There is a man called von Luther out there somewhere. Watch your back; he is very dangerous."

"Is he part of the Roth?"

"No, much worse. He's an ex-Nazi; they said that he was too radical to be a Nazi. He took far too many risks and would jeopardize not only his safety but those who were associated with him as well. He tried to capture John and study his extraordinary gift."

"Yes, Ma'am," Raven returned with a tone of appreciation. "I now know why John didn't ask Naci to join him. Is it because of Hilda?"

"You will need to ask John that when you arrive in Berlin," Amelia advised. She picked up her desk phone and ordered a Foundation car from the garage basement to drive Raven to the airport.

Raven nodded and gave Amelia a long hug. She left the study to wait for the car.

★ ★ ★

The plane touched down in Berlin with only a slight thump. Raven reached under the seat in front of her and retrieved her backpack. When the plane came to a complete stop, the ground crew skillfully placed the covered ramp up to the exterior door. The flight attendant opened the side door and directed the plane's occupants to slowly exit the plane. When Raven walked down the ramp into the lobby, she saw John and Pauline Vacara waiting for her.

Raven waved and then began to pick up her walking pace towards the couple. When they met, she opened her arms and gave them a family-style hug.

"What's this all about, John?" Raven asked.

"Pauline and I have been in Germany for a few weeks on business. We decided to visit our old friend, Hilda. She was instrumental during the war because she hid Harold when he parachuted behind enemy lines to look for me. I was being held by the Nazis. The notorious von Luther discovered that I have a unique mental gift, and he wanted to understand how and why I possessed such a skill. We discovered something the other day that may interest you. Hilda knows Roy Rothman."

Raven became very interested, "When can I meet her?"

"Today, so let's get moving," John informed.

The countryside hadn't changed since the war. The rolling hills dominated the landscape. Farmland somehow looked richer now that it wasn't under Nazi control. Machines took the place of horse and plow. The locals seemed happy and waved to the trio as they drove along the route to Hilda's farm. For John and

Pauline, this brought back painful memories. Although their memories were harsh, seeing Hilda's farm seemed to lighten the burden. The Mercedes turned off the country road onto Hilda's lane. The pine trees still stood tall. John could see in his mind the Tiger tanks as they drove the same road early one morning just before daylight. The massive tank's covered Hilda's upper field. He could still see Jack Man when he opened the barn door. He turned and smiled at John when he opened the second door. A distinctive blast echoed in his mind when the Tiger tank fired, and a split second later, Jack Man vanished along with the barn door. Pauline noticed John's glazed eyes and broke the silence, "Hey, John, you look as if you're a million miles away. Snap out of it; we're at Hilda's."

John shook his head, looked at Pauline desperately, and apologized, "Sorry, my mind wandered for a minute." John killed the engine and opened the driver's door.

Hilda opened the kitchen door and waved the guests in, 'Hurry, I have dinner on the table, and I don't want the food to get any colder than it already has."

The trio entered the modest farmhouse. Their nostrils filled with the pleasant aroma.

"How in the world are you, my friends?" Hilda asked with a smile on her face.

"We're fine," John answered. Hilda hugged John first then Pauline. She motioned them to sit at the table, and she turned to Raven. "Now, who have we here?" Hilda asked as she turned her full attention to Raven.

Raven smiled. She was pleasantly surprised by Hilda's warm personality. "My name is Raven Anderson. I'm a friend of John and Pauline's son, Naci." Hilda offered her arms and hugged Raven.

Hilda suddenly realized what Raven said and commented, "Naci, now that's a familiar name. How did that one come about in the Vacara family?" She quizzed.

John and Pauline looked puzzled. Pauline asked, "What do you mean, Hilda?"

"Naci was my husband, Anton's father's name," she returned. A look of sorrow dominated her face as she was reminded of Anton's brutal death on this very farm over three decades ago. He was murdered by the Nazis. Hilda looked at John with a smile and said, "I thank you for bringing justice to his murder, John. I will always be grateful.

John smiled at Hilda as Pauline held his hand with both of hers. Raven picked up on this, and it confirmed the deep love that John and Pauline had. This reminded her of Naci and how much she wanted to be with him for the rest of her life.

"So much for the past, let's eat. The food is getting cold," Hilda announced as she wiped the tear from her eye.

"Good idea," John said as he picked up the bowl of schnitzel-veal cutlets breaded and deep fried.

Hilda began to stare at her empty dinner plate; a pleasant look overwhelmed her face. "How is Harold?

"He's just fine," John returned.

"You know, if he hadn't found my barn the night that he parachuted behind German lines looking for you, John, I would not have found him cold and hungry. He was like an angel sent from heaven. I fell in love with him the minute he looked into my eyes. Harold cared about life; he could see the good in people and also could see the evil. He felt the pain that I endured when he learned of Anton's death. I will never forget

Harold. When he left, I felt as if my life had been torn again," Hilda reminisced.

"If I may ask," Raven interrupted as she was handed the large bowl. "Hilda, how did you come to know Roy Rothman?"

Hilda's eyes lit up as if she was a teenager. "He was sent by the Americans to help rebuild Germany. His unit helped me rebuild my farm including the house and barn."

"I can see by the look on your face; he may have meant something to you?" John quizzed.

"Yes, John, Roy was a very generous person with his time. He helped me through some very tough times after the war. On days that he was not needed, he would stay all day and work to make improvements around the farm. Roy was there for me emotionally. Oh God, I wouldn't have made it if it weren't for him. I was sad when the work was finished, and his unit pulled out of Germany. We spent two wonderful years together while he was stationed in Germany. He had a natural leadership quality; his men respected him."

"Do you still stay in contact with him?" Raven asked.

"Oh, my goodness, yes. He comes to visit at least once a month," Hilda returned. "I have learned to love him even though he goes off to work for his cause."

The room fell silent when Hilda made that statement. John glanced at Pauline with a surprised expression on his face. He turned to Hilda and asked, "Cause, what cause is that Hilda?"

Hilda started to talk then hesitated, "I'm not sure that I should not say anymore." The look on her face indicated that she might have said too much.

John reached over and placed his hand over hers. Her eyes met Johns with a look of confusion. She knew that she could trust John and Pauline to give her the best possible advice. Hilda placed her free hand on top of John's hand.

"I've overheard conversations that Roy has had with strangers when they would meet here on the farm. They would always ask me to leave my home so they could discuss important matters. Once, I was walking just outside the open kitchen window and heard them celebrating the death of someone called the Myth."

Raven abruptly stood up and grabbed the edge of the thick wooden dining table. Everyone looked at her. She began to tremble as the dishes began to vibrate until she picked up the one end of the table about four inches, and then she dropped it. Hilda looked at Raven with a puzzled look.

John broke the mood when he said to Hilda, "Tell us every detail of that night. It is extremely important to us that you remember correctly."

"I don't know much about that evening, as I mentioned. I heard something about the Myth; then I took a walk out to the lower field to check on the cattle. I know that he was talking to a man named Morgan."

Raven stood up. John motioned for her to sit.

John asked, "What can you tell us about this guy named Morgan?"

"Well, oddly enough, he was Chinese. He was very quiet and polite. He and Roy talked about Putin, the Russian leader. That's the only time that I saw Morgan."

John smiled, "Okay, Hilda. What I would like to ask you is very important and personal. Are you up to it?"

"You know me, John; I trust you because you terminated the Nazi who killed my Anton. I figure that I owe you," Hilda confided. "Besides, you gave me the crate of gold bars that you buried inside my barn during the war. I made a special trip to Switzerland and deposited them like the note you left inside the box said to do. That gift means that I never have to worry about money ever again. I am loyal to you, John."

"Hilda, how close or intimate are you with Roy Rothman?"

Hilda slowly shook her head at John, then glanced over to Pauline, then back at John. She continued, "I don't love him as much as I did my husband, Anton." She looked down to the floor and said, "I don't love him as much as I do you and Harold. I truly trust you, John, so whatever you are getting at or need, I figure it is the least I can do."

"So, you don't love Roy?"

"When he first showed up, we instantly became close. After a few months, I may have loved him. Remember, I was lonely. No, I don't love him anymore. I owe him something, but if he hadn't rebuilt my farm, another American soldier would have, so my loyalty is with you."

"Again, I must ask. Why don't you love him anymore, Hilda? Think very long and hard because this is very important," John persisted.

The room was silent; only the sound of the hall clock ticking could be heard. Hilda took her fork and played with her food. Her head slowly raised up with a tear in her eye. She answered, "He didn't love me back. I could tell by the way he treated me. He only wanted sex when he needed to be satisfied. He began to drink every time that he visited, and the drinking annoyed me terribly," Hilda confessed. "It's not that he's mean; he just starts talking about things that don't make sense to me. He doesn't love me. I can tell. He comes by when he needs to get away from whatever troubles him."

"Okay, that's what I needed to know exactly, Hilda," John offered. "Hilda, please think very hard; have you ever mentioned me, Pauline, or Harold to Roy?"

Hilda didn't have to think about John's question.

"No, I haven't," Hilda answered. "I was afraid that he was looking for the gold, so I didn't want to take a chance that he would connect the three of you to it.

"That's perfect," John returned with a smile. John talked for the next hour and explained to Hilda that Roy was involved with the Roth. He explained how she could help John and Pauline. She eagerly agreed.

"I have one final question, Hilda. Did von Luther ever come by and look for his share of the gold?"

"Yes, he did about twenty-five years ago. He and another German came by after the dark days that followed your escape. They too went out into the woods and dug for two days until he found a crate of gold like the one you left for me."

"Okay, good, we have two more crates to find. Do you mind if Raven and I dig for it? One belonged to Jack Man, and I want to see that his family gets it?"

"I don't mind at all, John. You needn't ask a question like that."

Raven and John excused themselves and headed for the barn. Four hours later, they returned to the house with the gold and placed it into the car. Once inside, they washed up and sat down at the kitchen table.

"Hilda, do you have any questions before we leave for Switzerland?" John asked.

"None that I can think of, John."

"Good, but remember, never mention the three of us or the Foundation to Roy. This also pertains to anyone that he brings here. To make sure you completely understand why, we need your help. Let's go over everything one more time."

They sat and went over all the details of Hilda's new responsibilities for the Foundation. When they finished, John hugged Hilda as did the others. The Mercedes turned around in Hilda's backyard and drove out the long farm lane.

John smiled and announced, "We now have our informant back on the payroll. Raven, we are now one step closer to your revenge."

Raven looked out the rear side window and stared at the moving German countryside. She didn't respond to John's comment. When the sun came out from behind a cloud, she could see her reflection in the glass; it told the truth about how she felt. John and Pauline didn't notice the troubled look on her face.

CHAPTER 17

"It's been about seven years since Raven started working for The Foundation. How's she doing?" Naci asked Amelia as he poured a cup of coffee for her.

"She has proven to be the best assassin that this organization has ever had including the Myth. She is focused and motivated." Amelia blew on the rim of the cup to cool the coffee before she took a sip.

Naci sat down beside his grandmother on the couch in Amelia's office. Just behind Amelia's desk was a huge portrait of her in her youth. Remarkably, Amelia still looked the same. It was as if she had found the fountain of youth. "I like the way the artist captured on canvass the message that he was trying to send. It is as if she is surrounded by a mystery, a sensual past, or a secret."

Amelia smiled with a comment, "I haven't heard it put quite like that Naci. I can tell you this; you are very observant. The painting was created by my husband, Nick after the war. He disappeared, and we all thought that he was dead, but as it turns out, he wasn't. I remarried Steven, a lawyer in Pittsburg, and it turned out that he and my close confidant and daughter, Jude had an affair. To make a long and boring story short, he was insane. Later, I discovered that Nick was still alive on our German operative Hilda's farm at the end of the war. So, when we returned to the States, he painted this for me."

"That's quite a story," Naci remarked. "Sometime, I'd like to hear the uncondensed version."

"I'm afraid that we haven't the time. My past is quite complicated," Amelia confessed with a smile. "Maybe I'll write my memoirs someday."

"The reason that I stopped in Amelia is that Raven hasn't had any time off. She hasn't complained, but I'd like to spend some time with her, maybe a short vacation, if that's possible?"

"Well, I try to stay out of personal affairs, Naci, but she has requested that her workload stay full. John and Pauline have tried to convince her, but she has insisted on a steady diet of work. Why don't you have a talk with her?"

"Sounds good; a few weeks would do our relationship some good," Naci said.

"Make it a long weekend. I need you and Jill in Moscow next month. I just bought the old GO-42 bunker under the city. This will be your and Jill's new station. We will have a strategic location in Europe. Once again, The Foundation's main objective has changed from the political arena, which I have hated.

We are now focused on the world of advanced hypersonic weapons. Someone in Europe is very close to developing these weapons. The United States cannot afford to have a terrorist group or the people developing it to steal this technology. Our intel indicates it is the Russians, so that's why we are moving to Moscow."

Just then Amelia's door opened. John and Pauline walked into the office and hugged Naci. "Have you heard the news Naci? The Foundation has finally moved on past this political correctness and on to more important activities just like during and after the war." John informed with a jubilant tone.

Naci smiled, "What about Raven? She has worked very hard towards getting revenge for her Uncle's death." He asked.

"It will have to wait for now. Baron David de of the Rothschild family has requested that we look into a matter for them."

"Who is the Rothschild's?" Naci asked.

"Only the richest family in the world. Their net worth is believed to be over 400 billion." Amelia said. "They got their start way back in the 16th century when they took over the gold bullion market. Today, they own wineries, oil, copper, and diamond mining. They hold a major interest in Rio Tino, a large mining company. Their largest market sector is financing. It is said that they own all the central banks in the world including the USA."

"How do you know such a historic family?" John asked.

"Baron David's parents escaped France just before the Nazis took control. I arranged their escape," Amelia said. "They were very grateful and had felt obligated to many favors for The Foundation over the years."

"What is it that they want us to do?" Pauline asked with a curious tone.

"This has taken several years of planning. The Foundation and the Rothschild's have devoted millions of dollars to protect our freedoms and rights; not one dime has come from the United States Congress as I have led everyone to believe. The Foundation's funding dried up after President Eisenhower retired. Back in the late 1950's, the political climate began to change from a conservative tone to one of a Progressive movement. By the time that President Johnson stepped into office due to the assignation of JFK, he had pushed the progressive agenda and began an ideology for the liberal moguls in Washington," Amelia explained.

John looked curious; his hand was on his chin. He stood up, glanced at Pauline, and cleared his throat, "What's in it for them? What I mean is, why fund The Foundation all these years. It must have added up to tens of millions?"

"The last three Presidential Administrations, the past thirty years of Congress, and the so-called Establishment have taken this country down the drain with the enormous amount of debt that they have mounted, especially the last administration. Their open border policy has brought the worst of the worst of illegal immigrants to this great country. The Department of Justice is a disgrace to our Constitution. The Democratic nominee has committed treason, and they would not prosecute. The Presidents have bypassed Congress using executive orders to push their liberal agenda. The so-called Republicans have abandoned the Grand Old Party. They have shifted to the left and sold out to the leftist agenda," Amelia said.

Naci interrupted, "So, now it's beginning to make sense now. Jill, Raven, and I have been taking out Federal Judges, Washington lobbyist, State Governors, corporate CEO's, Board of Directors, and anyone who supports the liberal agenda."

"Very good, Naci," Amelia congratulated her favorite grandson. "The Rothschild's and I decided that if this ideology were to continue, a financial collapse of America would be certain. The entire world's economic future is at stake. In other words, if America fails, the whole world spins into economic turmoil. Now, do you see why the Rothschild's are involved?"

Everyone began to see the big picture. Naci walked over to the window and stared out. He looked, but he saw nothing due to his deep thought. After several minutes, he turned and said, "We haven't terminated any liberal members of Congress?"

Amelia was amazed at how Naci systematically figured out the plan that she and the Rothschilds had in mind. "Well, Naci, you have hit the nail on the head. The reason that we have steered clear of those idiots we call Congress is that we didn't want to put them in the spotlight. Besides, they are so dysfunctional that taking any one of them out would be a waste of time. We will terminate them as soon as we take out our main objective."

"So, the next logical assassination would be the President and Vice President," John determined.

Amelia quickly turned her head towards John and said, "No, as much as I would like to, that would not be effective." Silence dominated the room; it was like the devil put everyone in a trance. An uncommon fear poured over everyone's usually hardened and confident faces. "There is a much bigger fish to fry."

Amelia noticed what was happening, took command, and began to shout, "Hey, hey damn it, look at yourselves. You'd think that I just announced a kill shot for one of us. Snap out of it; this is what we do for a living. We are paid assassins."

John stood up and announced, "Amelia's right; we are better than this."

Naci starred at the floor in deep thought then looked up at Amelia and said, "You want us to take out the Democratic nominee for President, Millie Linton?"

Amelia smiled and said, "Naci, you certainly have a knack for deductive reasoning. It is no wonder that you're so good at what you do."

John walked over to the window and looked out, not indicating any form of gesture. He remained silent, as did the others. John was always the leader who could relate to the day-to-day operations. It was a trait that he had acquired during the Great War out of necessity. "This is big. I'm not sure if I agree. Look what happened in Nice last year. It took months for everyone to heal. Hell, Raven, Pauline, and Naci are lucky to be alive. We never did find the bastards who did this. I know Morgan is responsible. If I could just meet up with him, I'd fry his brain."

Amelia smiled and said, "You're one son of a bitch that he will stay clear of. John, he knows that he's no match for you."

Amelia stood up, walked over to John, and faced him toe to toe. "Since when did you lose your nerve?"

"I haven't," John returned with a hardened tone. "I just think that we should take out not only the Democratic nominee but the current President and all liberal appointed judges on the Supreme Court."

"That's a tall order, one that would consider careful planning," Amelia said. "I'll take it up with the consul. I'm thinking along those lines too."

"If we go that route, we send a message to the world," John said.

"I think that we should wait until after the next presidential election. The people should have a voice," Pauline suggested.

CHAPTER 18

"Why do I get the feeling that Roy Rothman has something to do with all this?" Pauline asked

Suddenly, a knock could be heard at the office door. Amelia answered, "Come in." The door swung open, and Raven walked in. A sense flowed through the office. Raven stood not saying a word.

Amelia smiled with a slight jester, "Raven, your work has been astounding. You have done the work of three agents, and we are very proud of you. The Foundation has been directed to take another direction, and we are not going to be assigned any more of the political assignments. Those assignments have been turned over to another agency. We only have what's on our slate."

Raven's demeanor suddenly changed; her heart began to race because she thought that she would be the one to avenge her uncle's death. Finally, she could not retain her temper any longer even if it meant losing her position with the Foundation, "I have worked hundreds of jobs for this organization. Granted, I was well compensated, but I was promised revenge. Does this still stand?" She angrily asked.

Amelia answered, "Yes, my dear, you will get your revenge. Hilda has provided us with valuable intel for the past six months, and the time has come for you to perform a final assassination, The Preacher. How does that sound?"

Raven's endorphins began to flow; a pure utopia flourished throughout her body. She turned and hugged Naci uncontrollably. He felt joy for Raven that she was finally going to get her revenge, but something wasn't right about her overwhelming reaction. Naci felt like she had only one true love; the revenge of her uncle's death meant more to her than their love for one another. Sadness overwhelmed Naci.

"This sounds wonderful," Raven responded. "Hold on a minute, what about Rothman? I want that bastard too."

Amelia answered, "In two weeks, both will be in Summersville celebrating the Potato Festival; however, you are not to terminate Rothman. The new group will need him. Do you understand, Raven?"

"Good, I will follow in as a backup," Naci offered.

"No," Raven shouted, "I will do this on my own. I don't want anyone's help. I'm more than capable of terminating The Preacher."

Naci drawled his forehead, repeated. "I will be there as a backup, and that's final."

Raven was truly pissed. She slowly positioned herself in front of Naci. Her eyes were full of hate. With teeth clenched, she demanded, "I'll only say this once. If you show up, there will be two dead." She drove her knee into his groin. Her left hand went to his throat, and her right hand bent Naci's left thumb back to his forearm. "Do you understand, Naci?" Raven released both hands, and Naci fell back onto Amelia's desk.

"Damn, no wonder she got results in the field," Pauline said.

Amelia turned to John and gave him a nod. He then turned to Raven and gave her a low mental charge to her brain. She turned towards John and snapped, "What the hell?" as she grabbed the sides of her head.

Amelia walked up to Raven and with a cold stone expression, "This is what he was famous for during the war. You don't have a clue what this man is capable of. His mental feats can destroy brain function or raise a ten-ton object. Keep your composure. You will have backup, and it will be who I say."

Raven looked into Amelia's eyes with a vengeance but then realized that she was the one in control. Amelia was the matriarch of the family, leader of The Foundation, and had the final say. Raven reluctantly conceded, "I'll play it your way. You set it up, and I'll pull the trigger."

"That's my girl," Amelia smiled as she placed her left hand on Raven's cheek. "We only need one leader in the group, and my dear, as long as I'm alive, it will be me. And for your information, I don't plan on dying for a long time."

Amelia turned to Pauline and instructed, "Bring in Hilda and the Lion." Pauline nodded and opened the side door to the office. The Wolf Summit was built with several hidden chambers and walkways behind the walls for easy exit and entrance. Hilda entered the room first and greeted Pauline with a hug. The Lion entered the room with a distinctive limp.

"Everyone knows Hilda but not the Lion. Oh, yes, I forgot that Raven introduced herself to the Lion several years ago," Amelia announced.

He nodded with a slight smile at Raven, "I guess you are convinced that I told the truth that night in the hospital, and from what I hear, I'm glad because I'm still alive." The Lion confessed.

Raven shot the Lion a stern look, one a bulldozer couldn't break. The Lion quickly looked down. "I've been busy." Raven paused then continued with forceful tone, "You know, stuff like getting shot in Nice happens because people leak information. Leaking intel endangers the lives of fellow agents."

A heavy mood fell over the room for a few seconds. Harold broke the ice and said, "Well, that was insightful." By now, most Foundation agents were scared to death of Raven; only her closest allies could make a statement like that and not be reprimanded by her.

The room was now filled with Amelia's upper tier Foundation agents. The new directive was for Amelia and The Foundation to turn over this operation to another group and move on to the world of artificial intelligence. Amelia went on to explain how much the Foundation appreciated everyone's dedication and how there would be a place in the future for every one of them.

"Now, let's formulate a plan to terminate The Preacher. Talk to me, Lion. What do you have regarding the festival?"

"Well, it's a low-key event. Only about three thousand people will attend. It includes the usual parade and music, and it finishes up with the bidding of potatoes and awards."

"Sounds like pretty standard stuff," Amelia noted. "How can we get Raven into position to make the kill shot?" Amelia pulled down from the ceiling a huge print of the city streets with the location of all the buildings along the parade route.

"Hilda, what do know about Roy's part in all this?" Amelia asked.

"Roy is the Grand Marshal as he has been several times in the past. This year, he holds the honor because he donated the land, built the building, and funded startup capital for the new YMCA in town. He also rebuilt all four little league fields, so he has the support of the local community."

"Lion, what have you got on the Rothman?"

"He has invited the governor to ride with him, so this means extra State Troopers will be on hand. Also, Roy has directed more security because of all the rumors that he has heard about the new Myth. Raven's reputation is becoming quite famous."

Again, Raven shot him a cold look. The Lion stood up and said, "Look, Raven, I know your crude tactics from before you were trained. It's your reputation that has made you famous and nothing else, so quit riding me so hard."

Amelia chimed in and said, "Now, Lion, calm down. Maybe you need to back off Raven before you really piss her off, and she does serious harm to you. By the way, how did you find out about the Governor since you don't work for him anymore?"

"I have very loyal contacts among his troops. They hate him as much as we do," the Lion returned.

"Okay, let's see. The rooftops are out due to the confinement after the kill. Besides, they will be crawling with his agents. Along the parade route is too dangerous for Raven and the crowd." Amelia stood staring at the map. Hilda, where is the Preacher during all this?"

"Well, Amelia, believe it or not, the Preacher likes parachuting. He always jumps from the New River Gorge during Bridge day, so he and Roy have decided for him to parachute onto Main Street just ahead of the Grand Marshal in front of the courthouse. The parade will stop, Roy will be handed a microphone, and he will announce the new plans he has for a parachute manufacturing plant moving to Summersville."

"Also, I heard that this year it will be televised," The Lion added.

"That's great. What other surprises does anyone have?" Amelia asked. The room fell silent. After about fifteen seconds, Amelia stated, "Then I take it there are none."

"Raven, who is most important for you to kill? I'd have to guess The Preacher would be most important kill for you rather than the Rothman? Is this correct?" Amelia quizzed.

"Yes, but I want them both. The Preacher pulled the trigger, but Roy Rothman ordered the kill."

The room once again fell silent.

"Both must go down at the same time. One without the other would only warn the Roth agents; then we would have a small war in the streets," John contributed.

"I can snipe from a long distance," Raven contributed. "I can hit my mark for about half a mile with consistency."

"That's a risk though. What if she misses?" Pauline asked, "The whole attempt would be aborted. The best option is close range."

"The parade always starts at the base of the High School hill, and the route is straight to the courthouse. What if I positioned myself on the third floor of the old Mason home at the opposite end of the parade route. That spot would give me an easy shot at both. First would be the Preacher when he is in the air just above the street, and then I could zero in on Roy just after the car stops for his announcement." Raven concluded.

Once again, the room fell silent.

"I like the Preacher kill shot but not Roy's. It may endanger the lives of others since he is on the street level. It's too dangerous," Amelia disagreed.

"Just a minute, this will not work for both kill shots. We will need to go ahead of her and clear the Mason house of any occupants including Roth agents. Raven will enter and take the kill shot for the Preacher while he is in midair. She then will head to the street level. Once the Rothman discovers his right-hand man floating down to earth dead, he will abandon the car. He has an office across from the courthouse. As Amelia said, street level is much too dangerous for Raven to take the second kill. She will have to wait until another day."

Raven stood up, "I don't like it, but you are right. I can't take a chance. I might kill innocent people."

"Yes, this sounds like it will work," Amelia added. "When is the Potato Festival?"

"In two weeks," The Lion informed. "The weather calls for clear skies."

"Raven, I want you on the range from daylight to dark," Amelia ordered. "I'm sending Jill in to clear the Mason house ahead of you. You're not to enter until she gives you the clear. Also, she will stay with you to cover your back, understand?"

"Yes ma'am," Raven answered with an upbeat tone, quite different from an hour earlier. Raven looked at Jill and smiled. Jill smiled in return.

"Naci, you will work the street just below the Mason house. Eradicate any obstacles in the way including Roth operatives. Of course, silencers and knives are the weapons of choice. Be very diligent; your life will depend on it," Amelia directed. "John, I need you on the street halfway between the Mason house and the courthouse in case anything goes wrong."

John nodded his head in agreement.

"Does anyone have anything to add?"

"Yes, I do," Naci added. "I think that we should have an armored car parked below the Mason house so Raven can make her second kill shot from there. No one ever relates an armored car to an assassination. "

"Not a bad idea, I will arrange one to be delivered so we can customize it."

"Place a trap door on the floor, and it can be parked over a storm drain. Raven can make her escape unnoticed," John added, "I did that once in Germany; only it was done the hard way, the truck parked over it had no trap door."

"Everyone, we will have a briefing in a week. I want everyone involved to make a dry run to Summersville in two days. Go in pairs on separate days. Map out the parade route with motion cameras just as the parade route is traveled. Find out the starting time and then study the sun's position at the approximate time of the kill shot. Each one of you must study your position and know it like the back of your hand," Amelia directed.

The meeting was over; an excitement was in the air. Everyone was in an upbeat mood because the mission was soon to start. There would be no more of the simple political issues with judges and corporate officers. The team felt a new motivation and knew that an adventure was about to start.

"Hey, Naci," Raven shouted. "Let's take a drive. We need to talk."

Naci's heart began to race when he heard Raven's voice. "Okay, where would you like to go?"

"Oh, I don't care. Let's drive into Bridgeport and have lunch."

"Be out front in ten minutes, and I'll pull the car around,"

CHAPTER 19

Raven stood on the front porch of Wolf Summit when she heard a familiar sound. Naci turned the corner of the house in his original green Firebird. He pulled up and opened the passenger door from the driver's seat. "Hey, good lookin', need a lift?"

Raven smiled as she got in, "I haven't seen the bird in quite a while. Does it still run pretty good?"

"Yes, I keep it running in top condition with regular maintenance. I drive her at least once a month."

The ride east to Bridgeport was pleasant and uneventful. Naci geared down the transmission; the engine thanked Naci for the workout as he pulled into Panera Bread and slipped into a parking spot in the far corner of the lot. The couple ordered their lunch and retrieved to a booth.

"How's your salad?" Naci asked.

"Good and yours?"

"Not bad, better than I remembered. This reminds me of the lunches that we ate together in Morgantown during our college days," Naci reminisced. "Boy, we had some great times back then."

Raven played with her salad turning it over and over with her fork. She stopped and looked Naci in the eyes, "What happened to us, our relationship, and the love between us? I want it back, Naci. I want to be carefree with spontaneous sex and long walks."

"I'm going to be honest, Raven; you've kind of been too busy lately with your obsession to terminate the Preacher and Rothman. I fully understand how you feel. I'd do the very same thing if the roles were reversed. In a few weeks when all this is over, we can relocate to Europe for our next assignment, and everything will be much better."

"Then you still love me, even after the way I have treated you?"

"Raven, I will always love you. We go back way too far for me not to believe in your love for me. Now, remove all your doubt and cheer up. Things are going to get better for you, and we can settle into a much more stable relationship soon," Naci reassured and held his hands out to Raven. She gently placed her hands in his and closed her eyes giving thanks for the unconditional love Naci had for her.

When she opened her tear-filled eyes, she saw a different Naci, more like the one she knew before the Foundation work. The warmth in his hands and the love in his eyes convinced Raven never to doubt his love for her. The look on his face was one of the years in the past, full of energy and hope. This was the Naci she was looking for. He could see a crack in

Raven's demeanor with her body language and the tone of her voice. The shift in her reminded him of the younger days before all the tragedy fell on her shoulders. Naci knew the pain that she suffered losing the two most important people in her life. The pain was why he remained patient and stood by her while Raven learned the trade so she could take revenge. He knew how important this job was to her, and he must do everything possible to see to it that she was the one who administered the kill shots.

The long silence during lunch was good for both of them. Looking into one another's eyes was very therapeutic. The love began to return to Raven; it seemed like the time spent together during lunch helped her to sort through her anguish. Naci helped Raven channel the hatred for the Roth and resurface her deep love for him.

"Look, Raven, you have been tied up with the Foundation all these years working day and night to earn the Foundation's respect. That alone is stressful coupled with the frustration you carried for the closure of Bill's death. I think that when this is all over our relationship will return to a more normal state."

Raven began to smile while she took her napkin and wiped the tears from her face, "Naci, you've been a tremendous help to me. I can now see why I've always loved you. Sometimes, I act stupid, but I've always loved you. Do you believe me?"

"Of course, I believe you, and I also love you. I always have and always will. No matter how long it takes, I'll be somewhere waiting for you, and that's a promise." Naci poured his heart out as he leaned over and gave Raven a soft, loving kiss that she accepted. Their lips touched gently, and with each succeeding breath, the kiss became more passionate and heated. They took it to the point when patrons sitting around them noticed. When the two lovers realized the attention that they were drawing, they broke apart and sat back in their chairs. After their breathing returned to somewhat normal, Raven said, "I saw a couple of motels down the street, I think we better check into one of them."

Naci stood up and offered his hand to Raven. They exited the restaurant.

Raven unlocked the room with her card and shoved the door open. She threw the room card on the desk then looked at Naci while she removed her blouse, unhooked her bra, and then with a devilish look, she unbuttoned and slowly began to unzip her jeans. Raven ordered, "Lock that door. I don't want some sex-starved maid named Lynn to walk in on us."

Naci did as he was told. Then it dawned on him what she said, and he responded, "How in the hell did you know about her in Florida?"

"Well, to be completely honest, I didn't know that it happened in Florida, but I'll accept that as the truth," Raven admitted as she grabbed Naci by his powerful neck and pulled him to her hot, moist lips. The motion of her kissing indicated to Naci that it had been a long time; her sexual desire needed to be satisfied.

Naci didn't argue with her or even want to talk about it. He concentrated on Raven's heightened lust, her neediness, her driven desire to be with the man she has loved since childhood. Her eyes begged for Naci to make love to her. Her soft lips demanded that her lover return the lust with each motion of her actions. They kissed like love-starved teenagers as they fell hopelessly onto the bed. Raven's right hand was searching for the one thing that she craved most. She found her reward as it sprang to life. She reluctantly pushed him away, then said with a heavy breath, "Let's get out of these damn clothes and... "

Naci grabbed the back of her neck and pulled their lips back together. Her hips began to hunch as a wave of sexual warmth flowed throughout her groin. Her hands found his belt buckle. Feverously, Raven unstrapped it. Naci 's lips broke away to catch his breath and to remove his tee shirt over his head. He looked down and saw her perfect breasts. Naci couldn't keep his hands to himself. He played with them until Raven demanded no more foreplay. Raven forgot how developed his muscular chest was. She placed her hands over her head causing her chest to heave forward making her breasts seem fuller and more playful. Her taut, pink nipples begged for his attention. Naci slid off the end of the bed and unbuttoned his jeans. Slowly and deliberately, Naci pushed his pants down until his throbbing manhood sprang to life under his boxers. Raven couldn't resist; she massaged her aching nipples to bring her lust to new heights.

"Get my pants and panties off now," Raven demanded, "I need you to pleasure me."

Naci slowly tugged on her jeans, taking his time to drive Raven insane.

"Damn it, Naci, I said to get my pants off, and I mean it," Raven moaned as she shoved her thumbs down inside her jeans. She pushed both her jeans and panties down to her knees. Naci smiled knowing this would make her want him more.

"You bastard, stop teasing me. You know how needy I am," Raven cried. Naci continued his slow removal of her clothes. "Damn you, will you once do as say, Naci? Or I swear to God that you'll never see me naked again."

Naci knew that she didn't mean it. He couldn't begin to count how many times that she had threatened this before. He slowly pulled on her pants until they were down around her ankles then he stopped. Raven moaned with displeasure as she began to kick. Naci smiled and slung her pants to the floor. Naci crawled up on the bed and lay beside her as she smiled. He began to dry hump her outer thigh and kiss her at the same time. Raven gladly accepts both actions as she began to hunch with Naci. Her tongue slid in and out of his mouth as her organism began to build. Her hands explored his muscular back. She felt the herculean build of his torso rubbing her side. Her lack of recent sex had heightened her ferocious desire. Raven felt his brawny chest heaving up and down with each breath that he took. Her deep breaths began to match his causing her taut nipples to rub his chest. Their cadence picked up speed as Raven's climax began to peak. She moaned her lust and desire building. Raven's heavy breathing continued as Naci kissed her lovely breasts. He took his right hand and delightfully massaged her left breast causing Raven to groan with pleasure. He then slid his right hand down past the tiny swell of her belly. His hand slid by her mound of tawny hair, and he slid his finger to the top of her pleasure slit. She sighed with anticipation. He continued until his thumb found her love button; he gently played with it making Raven want him even more. His middle finger was swallowed up by her hot, wet pleasure center. Raven lifted with her heels, spreading her legs apart, opening up to allow Naci to pleasure her with his finger. She slightly humped up and down with her hips to increase her satisfaction.

"Oh God, Naci, make love to me, pleeeease." Raven panted. "I need your girth to stroke my warm, dark haven; the joy of my loin is erupting!" Raven placed her free hands on her hips as her long-awaited organism began to build. Raven rose on her heels. She started to quiver then a wave of warm, creamy juice started to flow. The fresh scent of her love began to take its toll on Naci's lust. He stood up and removed his boxer shorts. The freedom of his organ felt good to him. He approached Raven with a need to pillage the damp petals of her womanhood. He grabbed Raven by the upper legs and dragged her to the edge of the bed. Her beautifully-formed, succulent breasts waved with delight. His shaft filled her wet love canal. He began to pleasure her in a way that she couldn't control. Her enormous appetite to be ravished dominated her mind. Raven began to breathe heavier. Naci's thighs slapped Raven on the cheeks of her ass as he delivered pleasure with each pounding stroke. Naci looked down at Raven, her eyes closed, her face showing deep pleasure as she absorbed every inch of his powerful beast. Naci pounded her with a piston-like motion. He delivered such powerful thrusts that Raven quickly felt her climax rip through her.

"Ohhhh, Naci, please. I can't take this, I—I can't stand it any longer," Raven shouted. Her hips quivered, and she cried, "Oh, Naci, I love you. Raven bore down on Naci then her love flowed. Naci followed, reached orgasm, and both collapsed in a sea of sheer delight.

Naci and Raven held each other while their breathing and heartbeats returned to normal. Raven felt whole again with Naci by her side. The warmth of the afternoon sun flowed through the window adding to the emotion of renewed love that Raven and Naci experienced. For the first time in years, Raven felt whole again. She wished that this day could last forever. Both were in a state of mind where for the immediate future nothing else seemed important. They simply wanted to live for the moment. Minutes turned into an hour as both laid without talking. Naci rubbed Raven's back as he nibbled on her neck. Raven's sigh of relief indicated that she was content and happy. A few minutes passed then Naci asked, "How in the hell did you find out about Lynn in Florida?"

Raven turned over to face Naci and said, "A little birdie told me."

"No shit. Now, be serious. How did you know?" Then it dawned on him.

"I talked in my sleep; didn't I?" Naci confessed.

She smiled and placed her left hand on his cheek. She looked at him with her soft brown eyes as she slowly scanned his face. Raven would close her eyes then reopen them to purposely drag the moment on and to agonize Naci. She always managed to push him to the last second before he would become irritated. When she sensed that he was close to getting angry, she ended her stall tactic and said, "Yes you did, blabbermouth."

CHAPTER 20

"We haven't had any time to get to know one another, Raven," Jill mentioned as she turned the BMW south on Interstate 79. The fall morning air felt crisp as she turned the climate control up two degrees.

"I know, Jill. This surveillance trip to Summersville is the perfect opportunity for us to talk."

Jill looked over at Raven and smiled. She looked in her side mirror then pushed down the left turn signal before the BMW entered the passing lane.

"So, Raven, you've made quite a reputation in the few short years as an operative. From what I've heard, your quick wit and marksmanship are what have kept you alive."

"I think that sometimes I catch a lucky break. The events in the field are in my favor," Raven returned.

"When you first became an operative, The Panther would send me to tail you, not to protect you but to observe your methods. I must say that you don't give your opposition any doubt or reason to question your method. You are quick, clean, and cover your trail very professionally. How did you figure this out so quickly?"

"My uncle raised me. At the time, I didn't know that he was a highly sought operative for the Foundation. I always believed that he was only a sniper in Nam. I had no idea that he worked for the Foundation until after the Preacher terminated him. Bill would talk for hours about his missions as a sniper. Every story that he told fascinated the hell out of me. In my mind, I could vividly see each movement that he made. My visualization of his every move down to the last detail was etched into my memory. Similar situations came up after I was trained and sent on assignments. I would refer to the hundreds of situations that he faced and use it to my advantage. It was like I already had the experience. Little did I know, he was also telling me stories that related to his job as an operative," Raven answered.

"That is fascinating, Raven. I believe you're a natural. I'm afraid your reputation has succeeded your Uncle's. The good thing is that you haven't been exposed to any Roth agents. They don't know anything about you, only hearsay, and that's a good thing. The Panther has been very careful to keep you hidden from them. After this Saturday, your life will change forever. Your cover will be protected on the first kill shot when you take out the Preacher as he parachutes down in front of the courthouse. However, your second kill shot will expose you to the Roth agents. When Roy Rothman realizes that his right-hand man has been assassinated and you confront him on street level for a few seconds, his agents will see you. This exposure is what we need to figure out today as we run surveillance. Keeping our identity a secret is high priority" Jill explained.

"I know. I've given this considerable thought. I think the best option would be to not confront him just after he has discovered the Preacher is dead. Instead, I could follow him and take the kill shot in a less conspicuous location," Raven concluded.

"That's a possibility. Let's drive the parade route and explore all the possible options his driver could take as an escape route," Jill added.

"Okay."

When they arrived in Summersville, the new partners scouted the entire city. They spent the day taking notes of all possible options. Videos were taken to be reviewed back at Wolf Summit. All collected data would be examined by Amelia, John, and Pauline for final decisions about the most important kill of the entire program.

On the trip back to Wolf Summit, the girls discussed the best possible solution to present to Amelia, John, and Pauline. They built a bond, and both were pleasantly surprised.

Raven broke the silence about half way back to Wolf Summit when she asked, "Jill, I must bring up Naci and you as partners. Do you mind?"

"Not at all, shoot."

"Naci and I go back to our teenage years. We are extremely close and intimate. I trust him completely."

A long silence dominated the interior of the car. Raven kept quiet as she thought about how she could frame the rest of her questions. After a few minutes, she asked, "What I want to know is if can I trust you? After all, you have a very demanding personality and always get what you go after," Raven slowly turned her head towards Jill with an indication that she wanted an honest answer.

Jill picked up on her demeanor and smiled, "Raven, I will be completely honest with you. Now that we are partners and will rely on each other, we must confide in one another. When I first met and worked with Naci, I was fascinated with him. Yes, I was attracted to him. His dedication to the Foundation is second to none. He is an extremely talented agent who is smart. So yes, I was fascinated with him and would have, and I repeat, would have, slept with him. His body is so sexy, and to be honest, I daydreamed about him. In my mind, I wanted to make hot, passionate love with him, but I ran into one slight problem."

Jill hesitated; her head stared out the passenger's window. Raven kept silent and let Jill speak on her terms. After a few minutes, she turned her head and to her surprise met Raven's eyes. Jill looked down for a split second then returned her eyes to Raven's. She continued, "The problem was called Raven. In South America, we stalked a drug lord for termination. We spent four days planning until the unexpected happened. Our mark came down with the flu and was confined to his home for ten days. We were directed by the Panther to sit tight and continue when the mark became mobile again. We moved to the next town about fifty miles south to protect our identity. The days were hot and boring; the nights were worse. We patronized bars and restaurants to kill time…."

Raven interrupted, "Jill, before you go any further, please don't tell me nothing happened because I don't want you to lie to protect Naci. I must be up front with you. I know you and Naci had sex, and before you deny it, please hear me out. The way I know for sure is that Naci talked in his sleep. I was never really sure if he had sex with you or if he just wanted to, but just now, I heard the quiver in your voice when I stopped you from finishing."

Raven focused deep into Jill's eyes. After a few seconds, Raven turned her head back to the interstate. Silence dominated as the BMW cruised down Interstate 79. Jill broke the silence, "You are remarkable. I screw the man you love, and you can put personal feelings aside. I am completely confused; how could you not be pissed at me?"

"I'm okay with this, Jill."

"You didn't let me finish. I came on to him; I have needs, but he tried to resist, but he finally caved. I am to blame. You must believe me. I felt guilty. I could not see one ounce of hate in you; how do you do this?"

Raven turned her head towards Jill, "It's not that I don't love Naci, I do very much, but one thing that I have learned over the past five years is that life is very precious. First, I lost my mom, and then suddenly, Uncle Bill was murdered. I was so upset that I drove Naci out of my life, and don't ask me why because I truly don't know. About a year later, I came to my senses and suddenly realized how much I loved him, and no matter what happened, I will never let you or anyone else come between Naci and me. I don't blame Naci for having sex with you. Hell, I'd almost have sex with you. If I were a man, I'd try to nail you the first chance that I got."

The car once again fell silent until Jill spoke, "So, you don't have any personal animosity towards me?"

Raven shot a direct glance at Jill and said, "Do I have animosity? I only would if I thought that he was falling in love with you or you purposelessly tried to take him away from me. In those cases, I will kill you and not think a thing about it. I'm so glad to have Naci back in my life. I don't care how or what you think. Just cover my back this Saturday, okay?"

Jill smiled and eagerly replied, "I won't let you down - promise."

Raven took her right hand and placed it on Jill's shoulder a gave her a firm squeeze. Remember, I always work alone, but this time I'm forced to work with you. So, don't cramp my style. For the remainder of the drive, the duo focused their conversation to the parade on Saturday.

CHAPTER 21

Naci pulled the F 350 King Ranch onto the exit ramp to the Interstate 79 rest stop. The parking lot was almost empty, but Naci parked at the far end of the row of diagonal parking spaces just to have plenty of room to check something out.

"In a hard way, Naci?" John asked.

Naci nodded as he exited the Super Duty, "We're being followed. I just wanted to be sure."

John naturally placed his hand on his concealed gun, "Let's head into the restroom and see what follows us."

Naci entered first and then John. The men's restroom was empty. John entered a stall and stood on the commode. Naci stood up to a urinal. Both men readied their pistols. Naci looked to the left when he heard footsteps. The stalkers kicked the doorstop and released the door to the closed position. The two men walked up to Naci and stood firm. Naci smiled to himself then turned around and pointed two 40 caliber automatic pistols at both men. Surprised, they took two steps back.

"Now, we can do this the easy way gentlemen, and you can tell me why you're so interested in me," Naci instructed.

The two henchmen responded, "Now, sonny, don't do anything to cause a commotion. We just want to talk."

"I'm listening."

"We were sent here to ask why you suddenly showed up in Summersville?"

"Well, tell the Preacher that it's none of his or Rothman's business," Naci returned with a firm tone.

"The Preacher isn't going to like it when we tell him that you weren't very cooperative. Besides, that's not the only reason we're here."

Naci interrupted, "We'll let's see what can I do to convince the Preacher that you are telling the truth. Oh, I got it." Naci smiled then kicked one of them in the knee causing him to scream and fall to the floor as he held his swelling knee. The second henchman took an unexpected swing and caught Naci on his blind side and knocked him back into the urinal. His head hammered into the metal stall divider mounted on the wall. John witnessed this and came to the rescue. In a stupor, Naci didn't see his father in action. John's mental gift allowed him to take control of the situation. He mentally shot a firm shock to the assailant's brain causing him to grab the sides of his head and stumble to the floor. John then mentally picked him up and slammed him down on the tile floor. John stepped out of the stall and helped Naci out the door and into the truck.

"How did I get out to the truck?" Naci asked. "I remember; that son of a bitch cold-cocked me. I should have expected it."

"I put him in his place and helped you to the truck, Naci. Are you alright?

Rubbing his temple, Naci returned, "I'll be fine when it quits hurting." Naci rubbed the side of his head and leaned forward. He turned his head to help ease the pain. Naci faced the passenger door glass and opened his eyes. It seemed to help ease the pounding. He noticed a man exiting a car. Naci looked closer and thought his face looked familiar. Naci shouted, "Hell, there's the Preacher. Why is he here?"

John looked through the side window and agreed that it was the Preacher. He placed the Ford into reverse and slowly backed out. Then he placed the transmission into drive and eased back onto the interstate.

"This is not good. I don't like to encounter the enemy so close a kill. Those two thugs will have some explaining to do when he walks into the bathroom," John predicted. The truck cab was silent while both men thought about the past few minute's events. John commented, "I don't think that they will tell the Preacher it was us. If he knew that we were this close to his territory, he would have personally greeted us in the bathroom. They may have wanted to go rogue, so they acted tough. We didn't give them much of a chance to ask after their initial contact with us."

"I think that you're right, John. I may have jumped the gun. I guess that I was a bit eager because you and I have never been in a situation like this before," Naci surmised. "Maybe we should work together so I can calm down,"

John smiled, "I guess Saturday we'll just try to keep calm or all of us in the agency will be forced to call you itchy fingers."

The two agents looked at one another and laughed. A few minutes passed, then Naci became serious and asked, "Tell me something. Back at the rest stop, I could have sworn that just before I blacked out, I heard the second man scream. Just as his scream died down, he hit the floor too hard to have fallen. Could what the agents at Wolf Summit said be true; do you have a gift?"

John didn't respond for a few minutes as he thought. The truck cab remained silent for what seemed like an hour to Naci. Finally, John began to talk, "I don't know what you've heard, but let me explain the truth about my past. A few days after D-Day, the back of my skull was crushed. I was left for dead when my platoon pulled back. The Germans found me alive and took me to Berlin and performed an experimental operation on my pituitary gland. That was when I met Nadia. She is the surgeon who operated under the direction of Author von Luther. She was a double agent hired by Amelia, but I didn't know that until after she helped me escape from the Wilhelm Institute. Your uncle Harold parachuted behind German lines to find me because he also has the same rare mental gift as I have. However, his gift is not as advanced. Because of the operation, I must be treated with a salve that is inserted into the base of my skull periodically. Without the serum, I will die. The serum does accelerate my skill level. What you thought you saw is true, but I am much more advanced than you know."

Naci thought for a moment and asked, "Why is there so much secrecy about your gift? I've even heard Amelia mention it. I have read the articles found in the microfilm documents at the library, but when I asked about it, Pauline always told me that it was a publicity stunt to help sell war bonds. She said that they made a folk hero out of you. Why not just tell me the truth?"

John replied, "Your mother and I didn't want the attention anymore. Your generation doesn't know the war as we do. Living it and reading about something of this magnitude makes a huge difference in how society perceives history. Just think about how difficult your life would have been if everyone were to know my past."

"You are exactly right. I would have gone through hell, "Naci admitted.

John and Naci agreed to keep this between themselves. There was no sense in making a sideshow out of John's mental gift. The remainder of the trip was spent discussing their findings in Summersville about the parade on Saturday.

★ ★ ★

Amelia walked into the conference room on the first floor of Wolf Summit; she began the meeting with her usual strong cup of coffee. Amelia looked around the conference table and announced, "Well, I see everyone is here and eager to start. Let me begin by reminding you all that this mission is not only extremely important to Raven but also sensitive to the Foundation. When the Foundation leaves one agenda and moves on to another, I insist that we clean up any unfinished business. For this reason, I decided to terminate the top operatives of the Roth, The Preacher and Rothman, who we all know are responsible for the death of the Myth. So, that being said, let's begin with John; what do you have?"

John opened his folder and began to read, "Naci and I examined the complete parade route and decided that there are no possibilities of any deviations from the established route. There is simply no alternate routes that they could take due to the size of the town. We visited the official town hall to verify the start time and the order of the participants in the parade. As usual, the Rothman is Grand Marshal, and his car is the first exhibit after the local High School band. The buildings along the parade route are modest in size, most with flat roofs, excellent for snipers. Naci and I were in and out of town in less than two hours to keep suspicions to a minimum. I would like to add one thing; Naci and I encountered two Roth agents about thirty miles north of town at a rest stop. At the time of the engagement, we didn't realize their intent, but after further review, it is believed that they wanted to go rogue."

Amelia suddenly looked up and asked, "Why didn't you think that they wanted to go rogue at the time of engagement? Explain engagement?"

John used to Amelia's interrogation methods, before the war, dating back to his youth as manager of their Truck Farm. He gave her request the respect that it deserved and responded, "When in the field, I always defend first and then ask questions. The agents weren't capable of talking when we left them."

Amelia then commented, "I hope that your little exhibit doesn't bring attention to the Roth due to a couple of tired and pissed Roth agents."

John in his usual manner quickly shot back, "We used our best judgment at the time." John defended his son's reaction by being vague.

Amelia in her usual manor asked, "Why are you being so gray with this small incident, John? Normally, you borderline brag when asked about your encounters in the field."

Pauline interrupted with a smile and said, "May I point out, Amelia, that John is getting older, and perhaps, he is more experienced. He simply doesn't have the energy to tangle with you anymore."

Amelia smiled and returned, "Perhaps you're right, Pauline. John shouldn't tangle with me. I knew there was a reason that I have always been fond of you." Pauline's interruption shadowed John's blunder after he backed himself into a corner. Amelia saw through Pauline's rescue. However, because of family, she dropped her interrogation.

Amelia now moved on with the meeting and asked, "Jill, what do you and Raven have to report?"

"First, we checked out the Mason house. The owners are in Europe for the summer. Raven phoned their aunt who she used to babysit for. That way, our true intentions were not revealed, and we found out that the house will be unoccupied during the festival. The aunt thinks that Raven is working in Atlanta and didn't suspect a thing. Next, we filmed the parade route. We have sent the film to everyone. I will now present it on powerpoint. You can see that we sat in the street located just outside of the Mason house and filmed at the precise time of the parade. The day that we filmed, the weather conditions were the same as forecasted as well. As you can see, the sun will not be a factor."

After the video ended, Amelia commented, "It looks like a simple kill shot. Is there a manhole where we can park the armored car?

"Yes, and I checked the tunnel underneath. Raven and Jill can travel about two hundred feet west, and I'll be there to pick them up," The Lion explained.

"Good. On the morning of the parade, park the armored car over the manhole and make sure that Jill has a key."

The Lion nodded indicating that he understood.

"Raven, the night before, you load the armored car with guns and ammunition just in case you and Jill need it. On the morning of the parade and after you terminate the Preacher, leave the Mason house, enter the armored car, and lock the door from the inside. If everything goes according to plan, Lion will remove the van the following day and bring it back to Wolf Summit," Amelia directed. "Remember, John only steps in for the kill if Raven for some reason cannot make final shot. I want everyone to wear headsets for complete communications. I'll be here in the command center watching on live satellite. Does anyone have any questions?"

The room remained silent; everyone knew the high priority that this mission was to the Foundation and Raven. Jill caught Raven's eye and asked, "Are you up for this?"

"You bet. I've been waiting a long time for this day, and with you at my back, I'm not the least bit worried."

Jill looked at Raven with a smile and sincerely said, "I think we make a darn good team."

John looked, leaned over to Pauline, and whispered, "I think that we have found Raven a good partner. Look at the way they have bonded?"

Pauline nodded her head in agreement and whispered, "Yes, I agree. The Foundation is headed into a new direction in the field of hypersonic weapons, but whatever it brings our way, I'm glad that those two are on our side."

CHAPTER 22

Naci rolled over and stretched his arms over his head. He noticed Raven sitting up in bed looking at her phone.

"What time is it?" Naci asked with gravel in his voice.

"It's 4:30, time to get moving."

"How long have you been awake, Raven?"

"Oh, only about half an hour," Raven said as she jumped out of bed and walked into the bathroom to start the shower.

The hot water flowing across her face gave new vigor to her body. The therapeutic warmth helped prepare Raven for the day's event. Somehow, this assignment seemed different. She couldn't pinpoint why, but this kill shot was perhaps the hardest one out of the dozens that she has made since joining the Foundation. The fear came from the uncertainty of what Rothman was going to do when he saw his top agent float down in front of him dead. The question of what he would do bothered Raven.

"Hey, Raven, what's wrong? You seem down. This kill shot will be a piece of cake for you," Naci pointed out as he stepped into the shower. "You have the support of the best agents in the world. So don't worry; everything will be fine."

Raven turned and delivered Naci an appreciative look as she answered, "I know, but its Roy Rothman I'm worried about. I've had conversations with the Lion. He knows him, and he's not going to take the killing of his top agent lightly."

"Remember, I'll be there also. I promise that I won't let anything happen to you," Naci reassured.

"It's not me I'm worried about. I can take care of myself, and I'm positive that Jill can handle herself."

"Then what is it?" Naci asked as he gently held her shoulders.

"Rothman is smart; he's not going to be riding in an open car and take this big of a risk without protection. I'm afraid that we're going to start a street war in our hometown, and innocent people could get hurt."

"Amelia will keep an eye on things with satellite. She has had agents monitoring Summersville 24/7 for the past two weeks. I don't know if you know this, but every assignment all of us have been ever on has been monitored. If Rothman has moved in agents, we will know when we are in position."

"Okay, but I'm still concerned. I have one other question,"

Naci looked at Raven and smiled, "What?"

"Don't take this the wrong way but, Naci, I must ask; how old is Amelia?"

Naci was taken back by the question. He didn't quite know how to respond. "Her age is deceptive, but if you're worried about her capabilities, don't be. Last month, she was sitting in an outdoor café in Rio Di Jinero when two male agents confronted her; they are both dead. I saw this with my own eyes. Don't be concerned about Amelia. She is dead serious about her job."

Raven looked at Naci and said, "Let's get showered. It's a big day, you know."

Daylight began to creep onto the horizon. The crisp fall air let to frigid morning temperature. This kind of morning brought everyone's natural instincts to a razor edge.

"What's our ETA?" John asked Naci via headset.

"Twenty minutes," Naci returned.

Raven and Jill entered Summersville on West Webster road. John and Pauline were already in position, parked in an ally adjacent to Main Street, which was on the parade route. The Lion was positioned to pick up Raven and Jill. Hilda was at the bottom of High School Hill at the beginning of the parade route. Hilda looked down at her watch, 6:15.

Amelia walked into the control room with her usual cup of coffee and asked, "Was there anything abnormal on the satellite last night?"

The command center manager answered, "Yes, we saw Roth agents taking rooftop positions at five am this morning."

"Hold on a minute," Amelia directed the agent. She placed the headset on and sat down in her chair; computer screens on the wall consistently were moving from building to building on the parade route.

"John, can you hear me?"

"10-4."

"Pauline?"

"I'm online," Pauline returned.

"Where are you? Place your hand outside of the car," Amelia directed.

Pauline did as told, and Amelia confirmed. She did the same with Naci, Lion, and Hilda.

"Raven, what's your twenty?"

"We are pulling into the Mason driveway."

Amelia looked over at the manager and demanded, "Any activity last night around the Mason house?"

He replied, "Negative."

Amelia rotated the satellite towards the Mason house and said, "It's safe to go in, but take extreme caution. Roth agents could have been inside for days."

"10-4," Jill acknowledged.

She could see Jill entering the residence with her gun in hand. Raven also entered with her two trusty forty calibers in the ready position. After ten long silent minutes, Jill confirmed on the mic, "All's clear."

Raven returned to the car and retrieved her collection of Barrett M107A1 sniper rifles. She climbed the antique stairs to the third-floor front bedroom. Once inside, she laid her favorite rifle case on the bed and opened it. She loaded the clip and placed a shell into the chamber. Raven felt the warm rush of adrenaline begin to flow -the 27-pound rifle felt extremely light. She pulled up the dresser chair and opened the window. Raven took her binoculars and knelt to see how far up she could aim. She focused in on the area in front of the courthouse where the Preacher would be landing. She placed the rifle in the corner beside the window. She closed only the shears to prevent any attention to the window. Raven returned to the bed and got the three other rifles ready. Jill placed herself in the other dormer to spot for Raven. Raven handed Jill two sniper rifles and placed her second one in the opposite corner of the dormer that she occupied.

"We're in position and ready," Jill announced for all to hear on her headset.

Amelia scanned the rooftops and announced, "I see two armed agents on rooftops with rifles on the west side of Main Street and two on the East side. Do you copy, Jill?"

Jill leaned forward and separated the widow shears as she searched with her binoculars. "Yes, I can see them all, Amelia."

"I hope you brought your rifle, Jill," Amelia said with a stern tone.

"Yes, we have four with us," Jill returned.

"Okay, Raven, once you take out the Preacher, you take the two on the East side, and Jill you take out the two on the West side, copy?"

Both agents acknowledged.

"Lion, do you copy?"

"10-4."

Hilda, can you hear me?"

"Yes, Amelia."

"Make sure that Rothman doesn't see you. He would certainly be stunned if he saw you, "Amelia warned.

"He shouldn't unless he comes behind the stores on the East side of Main Street."

All communication went silent. The waiting was the toughest part of a mission. Minutes seem like hours as nerves became more on edge. Raven and Jill were monitoring every movement on the rooftops and streets. The crowds began to gather. The sun was now up and to Raven's back, which made for clear skies and a clean shot. Jill noticed that the agents she would terminate were on their cell phones and notified Amelia.

"The Roth agents located on the rooftops are on their cells. Is there any way to tap their conversations?" Jill asked.

"We're working on it now, Jill. I will keep you posted." Amelia returned.

John and Pauline noticed a van pull up just in front of where they were sitting. The driver opened his door, which allowed John a good look at him.

"Say, Pauline, doesn't the driver of that van look familiar?"

"Yes, he does. Now, where have we seen him before?" Pauline asked.

The man entered the building from the ally while his partner remained in the van. Minutes later, he returned to the van and drove off.

Pauline took a series of photographs when the suspect returned to the van. She emailed them to Amelia.

"Amelia, we have some pictures of a suspect coming to you. He looks familiar to us. Can you ID him please?" John informed.

"Yes, we have the photos. You're right; he does look familiar. Isn't he a Russian separate, one of Putin's former KGB agents?"

"You're exactly right. We tangled with him in Morocco last summer. Now, why do you suppose Rothman is tangled up with those cats?" John asked. "This looks fishy."

"I don't know. This could be bad news. Of course, they may be here for another reason, or we could be in for a surprise."

"John, you better go on the roof and apprehend the Roth agent. Bring him to Wolf Summit for questioning, copy?"

"Got it," John returned.

"Jill, did you copy. Monitor only; do not kill," Amelia ordered.

"Only if John needs help," Jill returned.

"Do not attempt to fire. John will not need your help. I repeat; don't fire." Amelia raised her voice to clarify.

"Amelia, we have picked up the phone conversation with the agents on the rooftop. He's speaking in Russian, something about taking out Rothman," Communications reported.

"Not if we can help it," Amelia returned. She updated the field crew. Amelia then pushed the intercom and said, "Ethan, get your best agents ready to deploy to Summersville; things are getting hot."

"Yes, ma'am. I'll be in the command center in a few minutes to be briefed."

"All agents on parade detail, I have backup on the way. ETA should be just under one hour."

Ethan opened the door to Amelia's office without the usual formalities of his position. Even though he was a house man, butler, and aid, he was an asset to the Foundation. His loyalty to the Foundation and his ability to absorb instructions with precise detail were his trademarks. It was often said that he and Amelia thought alike. Amelia briefed him, and he used the private stairs to the underground hangar. He and six agents were in-flight in less than ten minutes.

"John, I have Ethan and six agents on the way."

"Good, we're going to need all the help we can get. I hear black hawk helicopters, but I can't see them. What do you have on satellite, Amelia?"

"Nothing, I'll pull the view out for a wider angle. Yes, I see them now. Crap, I see four helicopters, but they're not ours. I'd bet money that they're Russian. Wait." Amelia zoomed in the satellite to take a closer look. After a few seconds, she shouted, "They are KA-52 Alligators. This is not good."

Amelia turned her headset to another frequency and began to talk. None of the agents in Summersville could hear the conversation.

The Summersville High School Marching Band began to start playing indicating the beginning of the 45th Annual Potato Festival.

"Do you hear the music, Jill?" Raven asked as she was looking with her binoculars for the single-engine plane.

"Yes, Raven. I'll help look for the Preacher as he jumps from the plane," Jill offered.

After about ten minutes, Jill laid down the binoculars and looked through her spotter's scope. She focused in on the Grand Marshal car and then cried out, "Amelia, you got a copy. Zoom in on Rothmans car, not only the Governor is with him but also the fucking President."

"Yes, we just got a call from the Secret Service informing us. The president being here changes everything, everyone. Do not terminate Rothman, Raven. I repeat. Do not terminate Rothman, Raven. Copy?"

The frequency went silent. Jill looked over at Raven from the third-floor Mason house and said, "For God's sake, answer Amelia, or I'll take the rifle away from you."

Raven stared out the window and said, "Amelia, I can do this. It is not a long shot."

Amelia interrupted and shouted, "Jill, after Raven terminates the Preacher, if she loads another shell into the rifle chamber, kill her."

Jill looked over at Raven then answered, "Affirmative, if she loads another shell, I will terminate Raven." Jill pulled out a forty caliber Glock and loaded the chamber with a distinctive click then shot a sharp stare at Raven. "Raven, don't make me kill you. There will be another day to take vengeance on Rothman."

The marching band's music grew louder; Raven shot a smile at Jill and nodded then looked back out the window. Jill did not spot for Raven. She did as she had been told and focused on her new objective: to make sure that Raven does not kill Rothman.

Raven scanned the skyline with her binoculars. From the East, she spotted the single-engine plane, and at the precise moment, the Preacher stepped out of the craft to descend towards the Nicholas County Courthouse. Raven's adrenalin increased; she took a deep breath and calmed herself down. Like dozens of kill shots in the past, Raven gripped the rifle with her right hand and used her left to hold the binoculars. The preacher opened his shoot, which now made it possible for Raven to find him in her scope. She dropped down on one knee and began to search the blue skyline for her target. In a few seconds, she found him floating to earth facing her. She gave the scope a final focus and then placed her right index finger on the trigger.

Raven's heartbeat slowed to an unusual slow beat; the music faded away as she slipped into her zone. She could see his face now, and a tiny flash of hatred shot up the back of her neck, but she managed to control it. She laid the crosshair on his chest and then asked, "Jill, do you have him in the spotter's scope?"

"Yes, go for it," Jill shouted over the music.

Raven gently squeezed the trigger, and the rifle kicked back with the force of a mule. She looked through the scope and saw a limp Preacher with half his head blown off.

Jill announced, "Perfect kill, Raven. That's one dead son of a bitch."

The two Foundation agents reloaded their rifles and terminated the Roth agents on the rooftops.

Amelia witnessed the termination of the rooftop Roth agents then announced, "Good job, girls. Now, head for the armored car as planned and wait for my direction."

Raven looked at Jill who was now pointing the Glock at her and said, "Relax, I'm not stupid. Do you know why?"

Jill didn't flinch a muscle.

"Because if our roles were reversed, I'd do precisely what Amelia said to do," Raven offered with a smile. She stood up, grabbed the rifle, slung it over her back, and picked up the spent carriages. Raven placed the binoculars up to her face just in time to see the Preacher fall dead onto Main Street. The band stalled in position and finished the song in anticipation of Rothman giving the speech to announce the new parachute factory coming to Summersville.

"Come on, Jill. Lets' get to the armored car; it's our safest place now," Raven said. The two female agents closed the back door of the Mason house and entered the armored car locking the door behind them.

"We're in and safe waiting for orders, Amelia," Jill announced.

"Ethan, do you copy?" Amelia shouted.

With the engine noise in the background, Ethan replied, "Yes, Ma'am. We're about a minute away. Raven, I could see the kill shot from our vantage point, great shot."

"Enough chit-chat, We're by no means out of the woods," Amelia demanded.

"John, do you have the KGB agent confined?"

"Yes, he is incapacitated and in our vehicle."

"Good, take him to Hilda for safe keeping. After Ethan drops off his agents, he will connect with you for support."

CHAPTER 23

Caution dominated Main Street. The secret service took cover and rushed the president to a parked limousine on a side street of the courthouse. Because of the hectic state of hysteria, the President's car could not move. State police pulled the Governor from the convertible and surrounded him. Hell broke loose from the rooftops as KGB agents appeared and began firing at the President. Secret Service agents were falling like sitting ducks at a carnival.

Amelia screamed, "Ethan, go to the rooftops on the west side of Main Street. Eliminate the KGB firing on our President and the Governor."

The Russian helicopters began to fire at Ethan's black hawk and reigned extensive damage forcing it to land in a vacant lot behind the courthouse. Once the chopper landed, the seven agents evacuated just in time to clear the explosion. The parade crowd began to run causing mass confusion.

Amelia zoomed the satellite from rooftop to rooftop. She alternated between the rooftops and zooming out to locate the Russian helicopters. They had the Secret Service, State Police, and Foundation agents pinned down. Amelia could see that the KGB had the upper hand.

"Raven, take the Armored Car back up the street behind the Mason house. There is a knoll that appears higher than the rooftops. You and Jill get started by disabling those Russian Alligator helicopters. Lion, did you load any anti-aircraft missiles into the armored car?"

"Affirmative, twelve of them."

Raven turned the truck around and drove to the exact spot that Amelia described. Jill opened the rear doors and jumped out. Raven slid Jill an anti-aircraft missile then pulled four more to the rear of the truck. Raven jumped out and stepped to the right of the truck with her weapon. Jill let off the first round, and it was a direct hit.

Amelia shouted, "One down and three to go!" Raven matched Jill's shot for kill number two. By now, the two remaining Russian aircraft turned and flew behind Town Mountain for protection. Jill jumped back into the truck and retrieved Raven's sniper rifle and tossed it to her. She fell to one knee and wrapped the sling around her left forearm then placed her left elbow on her knee and began to pick off the rooftop Russian agents. With all the confusion, the agents never figured out where the shots came from.

Amelia scoped the rooftops and announced, "Raven, you got them all, but wait. Look out behind you; a van pulled up with four agents and is opening fire on you two." Jill jumped back in the armored truck and drove it into the black van. She then backed it up so Raven could jump in.

"Get in, Raven. Damn it," Jill screamed. Raven did as she was told. She jumped in and closed the doors.

"Thanks, I owe you," Raven said with an appreciative tone. "What now, Amelia?"

"Get around the Russian van and continue up the hill then turn right. It will place you out on a street that leads back into town."

As the armored truck drove past the black Russian van, Raven opened the two rear doors and delivered an anti-aircraft missile that vaporized all four Russian agents.

"Good thinking, girls," Amelia praised. "Attention, everyone, I need a head count now, so listen up." A short pause took place to clear the airwaves.

"John?"

"I'm okay."

"Pauline?"

"Good shape."

"Naci?" A long silence followed. "Naci, come in. Do you copy?" More silence.

"John, work your magic, and I mean don't hold back. Naci is your son and one of us. He means the world to me. Do you copy?"

"I'm on it," John answered. John had never heard emotion in Amelia's voice until today, even throughout all the years before including during WWII, Korea, and Nam. When John was captured by the Nazis, the family always said that she stayed strong in public, but of course, in private could have been different. Maybe she was showing signs of age.

"Ethan, what's your twenty?"

"I'm under some utility truck taking rooftop fire. Four of our agents are dead. I need back up."

"I thought that Raven got all the agents. Let me double check." Amelia roamed the area and couldn't see anymore agents on the roofs. Then she realized, "They must be in an upper floor window. Ethan, stay put. I'll put Raven on it. Do you copy me?"

"Where are the agents at, Amelia?" Raven asked,

Amelia rotated the satellite lens around to the back side of the courthouse and found the window with the agents in two adjacent windows. "Jill, continued along the street until you see the courthouse off to your right. There should be two windows on the backside with snipers."

In a few minutes, Raven shouted, "I found them, will terminate." Raven once again displayed her exceptional skill and terminated both agents with two shots. By now, the streets were completely stagnated with hysterical people and cars trying to flee the town.

"Amelia, we can't mobilize anymore. The streets are jammed," Jill reported.

"I see that. Just stay put in the armored car," Amelia directed.

Amelia zoomed the satellite out to find the two escaped Russian Ka-52-Alligator choppers. They seemed to have disappeared. She scoured the hillsides with no luck. She zoomed farther out until she spotted two choppers flying East. Amelia zoomed in and determined that they were the ones she was looking for.

"I think our two Ruskie choppers have had enough for now."

"Hilda, are you okay?"

"Yes, Amelia. I still have the Russian agent in John's car."

"Keep the doors locked. Do you have a weapon?"

"Yes, I've got a handgun."

"Good."

"Lion, are you okay? Where are you?"

"I'm still at the location where Raven and Jill were supposed to travel through the man hole and meet me," Lion reported.

"How's the crowd where you're located, Lion?"

"There isn't one. I'm quite a ways from Main Street."

"You're going to have to get on the street to find Naci, Lion. Copy?'

"10-4."

Just then, Amelia's cell phone that was lying on her desk rang. Annoyed, Amelia walked over to it and looked at the screen. It displayed that it was an unknown caller. Any other time, she would have ignored it, but during a crisis, it could mean a lead.

"Hello, Amelia speaking."

There was a short pause then someone a foreign accent began to talk. "Miss, uh, how do you say? Amelia, I have something of value to you," a heavily accented voice spoke.

Amelia had been the recipient of hundreds of calls like this throughout her career. She kept calm and answered, "Yes, what is it? I'm in a bit of a hurry."

"One of my agents managed to capture one of your agents because he killed three of our most valuable men today during one of our missions. You see, it made me almost very angry. So, here what I do for you. Do you listen now?"

"Yes, I'm listening. Go on," Amelia said in a calm voice.

"I want very much to have Rothman. You trade, okay?"

The phone went silent then Amelia answered, "I don't make deals unless I see what you have to trade. He could just be a run of the mill agent who isn't much use to us."

"So, it is true. You are a ruthless bitch, but this time, he is blood. We've been following him since last year in Morocco. You see, he killed my son, so now, what you say to me?"

Amelia was stunned. She had no idea that Naci was the subject of such a circumstance. There was no way to tell whose son or daughter was an agent and how influential their parents were. It was a chance that you took in this business.

"I need a name. Who am I talking to?"

"Ah, that's more like it. My name Nikyle Roustinof."

"Okay, Nikyle, let me speak to him."

"Most pleasure."

"Hello, Amelia, I guess I screwed up?"

"Nonsense, Naci, you had no idea whose son or daughter we were terminating. It's just a calculated risk. We'll find you, "Amelia reassured. Keep nodding and talking to me while I activate your tracer."

Amelia walked over to her computer and typed in Naci's tracer code. The location came up almost immediately. He was still in Summersville; she zoomed in and found the address.

"Naci, we have your twenty. Keep Nikyle busy with jargon. We'll have someone there shortly. Hand the phone back to him, and Naci, be smart. These guys have nothing to lose."

"Okay, Amelia… She wants to talk to you," Naci handed the phone back to Nikyle.

"What are the terms, Nikyle?" Amelia demanded.

"You bring me Rothman, and I'll give back son. Fair?"

"Okay, Nikyle, give me an hour to find Rothman. You've made a mess of Summersville," Amelia returned.

"One hour is okay."

Amelia returned to her headset and announced, "Heads up, everyone. I've located Naci. The Russians have him, and they want Rothman for a trade. I know where Naci is, and I spoke with him. Raven, do you know where Hill Street is?"

"Yes, I do."

"Is there an abandoned building somewhere on it?"

"Yes, an old flower shop," Raven returned, "We can walk from here. In fact, everyone can walk. It's only about a block from the courthouse."

I'll text the address, but be careful; they are ruthless. In fact, we should surround the place then sit tight until he calls in an hour," Amelia directed.

CHAPTER 24

Amelia's cell phone rang and interrupted a sea of silence at Wolf Summit, "Hello."

"Ahh, my favorite agent, Amelia of the famous Foundation. Is this correct?" Nikyle asked.

"Yes, it is. Look, we're having trouble locating Rothman. I need more time."

"This is most unfortunate. I need him tonight. Can I count on you?"

"Yes, you can. In fact, let my son, John, join you to give good faith that we will hold up our end of the bargain," Amelia offered.

"I've heard about someone in the Foundation. This is not him?"

"Yes, he is our best agent. This should be fair, right?" Amelia reasoned.

"Send him in alone." The Russian directed.

"Okay, but call me in one hour. We'll have Rothman.

Amelia ended the call on her cell then turned her headset back on and directed, "John, you have the green light. Go in and fry that stupid son of a bitch."

Fifteen minutes passed, and John still wasn't out with Naci. Amelia started to worry; then she realized that John must be extracting information from his mind. During the war, he became very good at mind reading. That was after the Nazis changed his life forever when they performed experimental brain surgery. The experiment was one hundred percent successful but only after thousands of humans lost their lives due to the years of experiments.

"Can you copy, Amelia?" John asked. "Naci and I are coming out of the flower shop. There is now one less Russian to worry about."

"Good. Is Naci alright?"

"Yes, he's fine. I would have him talk to you, but Raven has the two-hour clamp on him. She may never let go," John gestured.

"What did you find out about our Mr. Nikyle Roustinovf?"

"He went rogue. He wanted freedom from his suppressors. He had no significant intel to offer, so I went easy on him. He'll come around in three or four days," John reassured.

"According to the satellite, the town is still pretty much a mess because it's only been a couple of hours since all hell broke loose. I still don't like the other two Russian helicopters that disappeared. I'm afraid that they'll come back. You need to take cover until all Secret Service and State Police clear out," Amelia directed.

"We can hold out at my home place. I'm sure Beth won't mind," Raven offered.

"Sounds like a plan," Amelia said, "Everyone copy?"

Beth welcomed Raven and Naci into her modest home. Raven introduced the rest of the agents as they entered the kitchen.

"Now, listen, everybody. I'll have some lunch ready as soon as I can," Beth announced. "What in the world is going on in town? Mrs. McGee phoned and told me that she heard Summersville has been attacked. From what she described, the town is pretty much a total loss."

"Yes, I'd say that's pretty much it in a nutshell," Raven confirmed. "Just so you know, Beth, I terminated Bill's assassin this afternoon. He was called the Preacher." Beth looked at Raven with a tear in her eye, then closed both eyes and whispered, "May God rest his soul for he has taken my Bill from me. I will never love another like Bill." Raven opened her arms, and they hugged.

Naci looked around the kitchen. He could not remember where Hilda, Lion, and Ethan were.

"Did something happen to Hilda, the Lion, and Ethan?" Naci quizzed.

"Yes, they returned to Wolf Summit," Amelia chimed in on the headset. "The rest of you stay put for further instructions."

"Well shit, we just picked up one of the Russian KA-52 Alligator Helicopters traveling west at low altitude." By watching it on the live satellite, Amelia could see that he was flying at a low altitude to look for Foundation Agents. "Stay put, everyone. He most likely will fly past your location.

Just then an F-35 American fighter jet traveling at mac 1.8 appeared on the far horizon and laid out the helicopter in a fiery ball of flames. The Russian craft didn't have a chance.

"Well, so much for that everyone. It looks like we only have one aircraft to worry about now, "Amelia announced. She zoomed the satellite out to monitor the entire region. In less than five minutes, Amelia witnessed the fourth Russian Alligator to be taken out by American fighter jets. "I'm not sure that you can hear the jets flying above you, but the fourth Russian helicopter is now down."

Raven helped Beth with lunch serving cold cuts, chips, and drinks. Everyone seemed relaxed and satisfied that the mission was not a complete failure. They were happy with the termination of the Preacher and unknown count of Russian operatives. Raven showed a different demeanor than just a few days before. She felt like a huge weight had been lifted. She and Jill had bonded throughout the mission.

Raven looked at Jill. "Hey, I haven't had a chance to thank you for your support today," Raven said sincerely.

"No problem, Raven. I'm glad that you made the kill. I'm sure that it brought closure to your uncle's death," Jill said with a sincere tone and smile. The two agents gave one another a long, caring hug.

"I hope that Amelia gives us a chance to work together in the future," Raven commented as she and Jill separated when Naci walked up.

"I heard that Jill. Does this mean that I better start looking for a new partner," Naci said with a smile.

"I don't know, Naci, but have you ever thought the three of us? We might just make a pretty good team," Raven added.

Naci smiled and gave Raven a long, loving hug. Raven felt whole again with Naci in her life and her uncle's death partially avenged. She knew that the kill order was given to the Preacher by Rothman, and Rothman was still alive, but somehow, Raven was grateful for the Foundation's support to help terminate the Preacher.

Just then, Naci's cell phone rang, "Yes, Amelia. We'll return to Wolf Summit ASAP."

"Well, everyone, it looks like we need to wrap this up and head back to Wolf Summit," Naci announced.

They all thanked Beth for her hospitality. Raven gave her a long hug and promised to return for a long visit in the next few months.

The sun was setting just as Raven and Jill turned on Route 50 West in Clarksburg when Raven's phone announced an incoming text.

Panther: Need you for a job in Charlotte tomorrow.

Raven didn't answer immediately; she stared at her phone screen. "Jill, do you know who the Panther is?"

Jill glanced over at Raven, "No, I'm not sure very many if any agents know."

"I know. I have a gnawing desire to find out, but I have been put in my place for asking," Raven confessed.

"Raven, I tried to find out also but have surrendered to the fact that they will tell me when they want me to know who the Panther is," Jill returned.

Raven: Do you want me in my apartment or at my locker at the airport?
Panther: Airport.
Raven: K.

Raven entered the conference room on Amelia's request.

"Good job in Summersville, Raven. You had me worried for a minute when I directed you not to terminate the Rothman. I'm glad that you followed orders. I couldn't afford to lose a top agent, especially an agent who is as young and talented as you are."

"Thank you, Amelia. That means a lot coming from you."

"I would imagine that you are tired. We'll do your briefing and reports tomorrow, then you and Naci can take a few days' rest," Amelia suggested.

This took Raven by surprise and said, "Amelia, the Panther texted a few hours ago and wants me in Charlotte tomorrow morning for a job."

Amelia shot a quick and stern look at Raven. With eyes drawled, she asked, "Are you sure, Raven?"

Raven took her phone out and showed Amelia the text that she received from the Panther. Amelia read the Panther's text over and over. She pulled her phone out and texted the Panther.

Amelia: Raven in Charlotte tomorrow for a job. What gives?

Several minutes pass with no response. Amelia texted again.

Amelia: Call me. Seems to be a mix-up.

Again, several minutes pass with no response. Ten minutes later, her phone indicated an incoming text.

Panther: Correct, Raven in Charlotte tomorrow morning, tied up cannot call.

Amelia walked around her desk and over to the window. She stood with her back to Raven. After a few minutes, Amelia decided, "I don't like this one bit. I'll send Jill and Naci with you. Something just isn't right. The Panther never changes the plan without contacting me."

Raven looked worried. She had never heard Amelia use a worried tone. Out of respect, Raven didn't ask any questions. She could see that Amelia was deep in thought about the Panther.

The Foundation plane touched down at Charlotte Douglas International Airport. As usual, the tarmac was backed up with planes waiting to cross runways and dock up to individual gates. After twenty minutes, the plane pulled up to the Foundation's gate.

"So, this is your territory? I don't believe that I've been to Charlotte before. If time permits, I expect a tour of the Queen City," Jill said to Raven as they walked down the ramp to the gate.

Raven looked at Jill and smiled, "It would be my pleasure."

Raven led the trio to her usual locker numbered 51 and opened it only to find it empty, "That's strange. There isn't an envelope with instructions." Raven pulled out her phone and texted,

Raven: I'm at the airport. No instructions??

She pressed send.

Raven closed the locker, "Let's get a cab and go to my apartment. Sometimes, the Panther leaves the envelope on my kitchen counter." Naci and Jill agreed.

The ride north on Interstate 85 took the trio to the 485 beltway that offered an excellent view of downtown Charlotte. The ride only lasted ten minutes. The cab pulled up to the luxury apartment building. A doorman opened the rear cab door. Naci tipped the driver then exited the cab. He handed the doorman a twenty and smiled.

"Thank you, sir. Enjoy your stay," The doorman smiled and opened the huge stainless steel door for the Foundation agents. They entered the elevator, and Raven took her apartment key and placed it into the key slot. One minute later, the elevator door opened into the kitchen. Raven led the trio over to the kitchen island where she placed her pocketbook.

Jill looked around and teased, "My, don't we live large, Raven."

"Yes, much too large if you ask me," An unfamiliar voice from the open living room gained the trio's attention. Naci gave out a growl as he pounded his fist down on the island. At the same time, Raven pressed the button to raise up her collection of firearms. The four intruders were taken by surprise. They raised their guns and in disapproval, warned, "If you three were smart, you would give up." As soon as the countertop was high enough, Raven reached under the rising granite and retrieved a Smith and Wesson 9mm. She began to unload the clip. One of the Russian agents instantly fell to the floor with a hole in his skull. Naci and Jill also retrieved similar weapons and began to defend themselves. Thick soundproof walls prevented this skirmish from escaping Raven's apartment. After several minutes of gunplay, the three remaining agents escaped through the front door to the hallway. Naci and Jill chased after them. Raven pulled out her phone and called Amelia.

Raven's world went fuzzy as the floor suddenly came up to her. Then total blackness dominated.

★ ★ ★

"Hello, Raven," Amelia answered. "Hello."

Amelia waited for Rave to speak but could hear only a gravel Russian voice in the distance, "Take the bitch down the elevator. I'm going g after the other two."

Amelia pressed her cell phone up to her body. She then pressed the intercom on her desk and yelled, "John, Pauline, in my office on the double. Raven is in serious trouble."

"We're coming," John returned.

Naci and Jill ran down the hall after the three intruders. They turned into the stairwell. Naci stopped, looked down the descending steps, and fired at the trio, "Hell, by the time we get to the street, they'll be long gone."

Naci and Jill returned to the hall just in time to see Raven's assailant enter the elevator with her over his shoulder. Suddenly, a Russian stepped into the hall and came face to face with Naci and Jill. He raised his gun to fire. Standing behind Naci, Jill reacted and killed the agent with her pistol.

"Damn it, Jill, they have Raven," Naci screamed. Jill ran to the elevator and slammed the down button, and to their surprise, the other elevator door opened. Jill and Naci quickly entered and pressed L.

"Come on, come on," John repeated as the two agents slowly rode down. "I just hope that no one else needs a ride down." Naci pulled out his cell phone, pushed favorites, and hit Amelia's name. "Damn, no service."

The elevator door opened in the lobby just in time for Naci to see the men exit onto the street. Naci raced to the door with Jill behind him. A black van pulled out onto the street. Naci flagged a passing cab, and the duo jumped in. "Follow that black van. Here's three hundred dollars. There will be three more if you catch it." Naci shoved it thru the screen at the driver. The driver glanced down in the driver's seat and then pushed the fuel pedal down to earn the other three hundred.

Naci pulled out his cell phone and called Amelia.

Amelia felt her phone vibrate on her cheek as she was trying to listen to Raven's phone call. She took Naci's call and yelled, "Hello, Naci, what the hell is going on?"

"Don't talk; just listen. Get on your satellite and follow the black van leaving Raven's apartment in Charlotte," Amelia pressed the intercom button and ordered the communications room to pull up the satellite of Charlotte. She got up from her desk and ran to the communication room.

"Amelia, Jill and I are in a yellow cab following the van."

Amelia slid into her chair in front of the wall monitor. "Yes, I have Charlotte. Just a minute," Amelia typed in Raven's address, and the image zoomed into view.

"What direction is the van traveling?"

"West, and we just went up the ramp onto the outer beltway," Naci reported.

"Yes, I have you on satellite," Amelia observed. John and Pauline entered the control room. Amelia turned and pressed the intercom button, "Get a black hawk ready for flight. John and Pauline will be there in five."

"Yes ma'am," the intercom speaker bellowed.

"What's going on?" John asked.

"Raven has been kidnapped from her Charlotte apartment by Russian agents. I know why; they think that we have the code map for hypersonic weapons."

"Let's go, Pauline," John turned towards the door then stopped. "Where are Naci and Jill?"

"They are following the black van in a cab."

"Okay, got it, Amelia. Don't worry; we'll bring them all back safe and sound," John promised.

John and Pauline suited up and ran out to the waiting black hawk on the airstrip behind Wolf Summit. John took command of the attack helicopter. He felt a little rusty at the controls, but he picked up his touch in a matter of minutes. John took the black hawk up to three thousand feet and turned south with full throttle.

"Naci, I have John and Pauline in a black hawk headed your way. It will take about an hour."

"Thanks, Amelia," Naci returned.

Raven woke up and rubbed the back of her head. She felt a tender spot and began to get mad. Then her head began to throb. She looked at her kidnapper with a confused look. She could remember the gun play in her kitchen. She looked around the empty metal box van and noticed that he didn't restrain her, "What a dumb ass," She thought. Raven felt the vibrations of the drive train of the van as it traveled the beltway around Charlotte. "What the hell?" she thought. "Where am I?" Raven focused on the van, the driver, and its passenger. She then realized that she was being kidnapped but didn't understand where to and why?

The van exited the beltway and drove north on Interstate 77. Traffic was moderate to heavy. The farther north they traveled, the thicker the traffic became.

Fifteen minutes later at exit 30, the traffic came to a complete stall with top speeds of five miles per hour. The cab driver skillfully managed to close the gap between the cab and the black van and caught up with the van in the stalled traffic. They were only about two hundred feet behind. Jill jumped out of the taxi and began to run between the cars. Naci yelled, "Damn, Jill, what are you doing?" Jill either didn't hear Naci or simply ignored him. Naci opened the cab door and handed the cab driver the other three hundred dollars then began to run towards the van. Jill caught up to the unsuspected kidnappers in the van. To her complete surprise, the rear door of the van opened when she turned the handle. Jill jumped in with her gun pointed at the Russian in the passenger seat. Jill yelled, "Put your weapon down on the floor and shove it to Raven." The kidnapper hesitated, looked over to the driver, then turned his head back towards Jill and Raven. He smiled then growled and started to raise his gun up. Jill anticipated his stupidity and fired one shot ending his life. The traffic began to clear, so the driver floored the pedal and turned the van into the median, which threw Jill and Raven to the back of the van. They almost slid out the open rear door, but Raven managed to grab an empty spare tire mount and Jill at the same time keeping them from sliding out of the moving van. Naci on foot just about caught up to the van before it pulled out into the median.

Naci quickly turned around, walked up to a white SUV, and pointed the gun at the driver's head. He then yelled, "Get out or I'll shoot." The driver didn't hesitate. He opened the driver's door and ran to the rear of the vehicle. Naci took control of the SUV dropping the gear shift into drive and flooring the vehicle in pursuit of the black van.

"If you can understand me, just pull over, and give yourself up," Raven demanded. "You know the traffic will knot up again, and Jill will shoot you in the head when you are forced to stop." The driver didn't respond. He looked into the rear-view mirror and smiled. Raven knew then that he understood every word. He just didn't care.

The van followed as the white SUV managed to leave the median and regain traction on the smoothness of the asphalt roadway. By now, traffic was light enough to bring both vehicles up to a top speed of seventy miles per hour.

Naci dialed Amelia on his cell phone, "Hello, Amelia."

"Yes, Naci," Amelia quickly answered.

"Did you see where I changed vehicles?"

"Yes, I have you in pursuit, driving a white SUV. Is that correct."

"Yes, you're on top of it," Naci returned.

The van traveled up to exit 50 in Statesville and turned east on Broad Street with Naci right on its bumper.

Amelia yelled into Naci's phone, "There is a huge white cloud over you, and I've lost all visual. I repeat; I've lost all visual."

Naci drove with one hand on the wheel and the other holding his phone when suddenly a car pulled out in front of the borrowed SUV. Naci could not react in time and plowed into the driver's side causing a four-car pileup. Amelia could hear the loud crash through the phone.

Amelia screamed, "Naci, are you alright? Naci, answer me."

Naci's phone was now on the floor, and Naci's face was buried in the airbag.

The driver of the van began to sharply weave left to right. The erratic driving caused Raven and Jill to be tossed to the right side of the interior wall of the van. The two females were knocked unconscious. The Russian driver adjusted the interior, rearview mirror and verified that the two agents were out cold. He continued to drive until he pulled up to a warehouse where he sounded the horn. The large door opened, and he pulled the van into the warehouse. The driver placed the van into park and quickly moved to the rear of the van to find Jill's gun.

"Naci, are you okay?" Amelia's voice poured out of Naci's phone speaker. She repeated the question over and over. Naci managed to open the driver's door and pull himself out. He was stunned but still aware of the situation. He heard Amelia's voice and regained his senses. He located his phone.

"I'm okay, Amelia, but afraid that I've lost the black van. Do you still have it on satellite?" Naci asked.

"No, remember there was a huge cloud overhead? Were you in an accident?" Amelia asked.

"Yes, a car pulled out in front of me, and I t-boned it."

"Go to the nearest corner and give me the street names," Amelia directed.

"Good idea," Naci returned then he checked on the driver of the car that he hit.

"Call an ambulance, Amelia. The driver is alive but has a broken left femur." Naci commanded. "I'll get you an address."

After Naci reassured the driver and told Amelia the address for the EMT's, he continued on foot.

"The only thing that I can do is wait for John and Pauline to arrive. I will phone you a location suitable for them to land."

"Okay, Naci," Amelia replied.

CHAPTER 25

"Hmm, such pretty and sexy woman agents, I must agree," the Russian commented as he stood face to face with the restrained Raven. She could smell his vodka scented breath just inches from her face. His unshaven face reminded her of an Alaskan bear hunter. He walked around to Jill and looked her over from head to toe. Both girls were tied up to the opposite sides of a wooden post with their hands above their heads. "My, aren't you sexy, my dear American beauty. You are especially, uh, how do you say, appealing to my sensual appetite, no?" The Russian agent began to unbutton her blouse. He carefully unbuttoned each one down to where her blouse was tucked into her jeans. Then the agent placed both hands inside her unbuttoned shirt just above her waist onto her hard stomach. His rough, callused palms gently slid up to her breasts. Remarkably, Jill began to feel a warm sensation in her groin. This remarkable incident reminded her of the fantasies she had as a teenager. She would daydream of being captured by foreign agents, then make passionate love to one of them until he pleased her in every way possible. He slowly moved his hands up to her firm round breasts and gently cupped each in his hands. Her breasts overflowed his hands as he softly caressed them giving himself pleasure. Jill caught on to this and began to breathe heavily. She slowly turned her head to the side, closed her eyes, and slightly slid her tongue out of her mouth. The Russian found her taut nipples and noticed her erotic behavior. He leaned to his right, placed his lips on Jill's, and began to kiss her. She reluctantly responded giving him deep tongue lashes in return for his trust. He pressed his swelling bulge into her crotch, and she responded by wrapping her right leg around his waist driving her heel into his ass. He broke the kiss and leaned back. Jill smiled and motioned upward with her head. She returned her head to the level position then glanced up only with her needy eyes; if he untied her arms, he could have his way with her.

"Untie my hands, and you will get a piece of ass worth dying for," Jill commanded. "I will fuck your brains out." Jill moaned a sigh of relief when she saw the lustful expression on his face.

The Russian smiled, then leaned into Jill rubbing his chest on her perfect breasts while he untied her hands. Jill added the icing to the cake when she whispered, "God, hurry, and untie my arms so I can ravish you before I cum." He stepped back as her arms slowly lowered and rested on his shoulders. Jill continued to destroy his guard by rubbing her tongue on the side of her mouth. She continued to push him back with her arms until she had room and momentum to jump up and wrap her powerful legs around his neck. Within an instance, her cat-like move resulted in her taking control. Her body weight acted as a fulcrum, and she placed one hand on his jaw and the other on the side of his head. With one powerful jerk, Jill broke his neck and road him down like a calf in a rodeo.

"Nice job, Jill," Although Raven couldn't see, she could hear his neck bones crush, and his body hit the concrete floor. Jill raced over to Raven and untied her hands. Raven looked at Jill's unbutton shirt and remarked, "Nice rack. Can I touch them next?"

"Aren't you afraid that I'll break your neck too?"

Raven rubbed her sore wrist as she slowly lowered her arms, "Nah, us girls need to stick together if we're going to survive." The two agents hurried over to the parked van. Raven turned the key and started the engine. Jill opened the passenger door and dragged the dead Russian out. She jumped in and noticed Raven smiled at her.

"What?" Jill asked as she closed the door.

"You enjoyed teasing that poor bastard. Oh, hurry before I cum," Raven mocked.

"So, it resulted in our freedom, didn't it?" Jill asked with a smile.

"Yes, you were convincing. God, you had me aroused. I'm kind of disappointed that I didn't get to watch you in action," Raven teased.

"Just put this thing in gear before someone finds us. We've killed a half dozen of their agents today; that's bound to tick someone off."

Raven did as she was told and floored the van as she steered around the dead Russians and the posts that they were tied to. The tires squalled as the van made the turn. The two agents couldn't hear the black hawk land just outside the warehouse. The van pulled up to the exterior door and stopped. Jill jumped out and pushed the large green button to activate the door opener. She then quickly returned to her seat. When the door opened, the two agents could see the Black Hawk sitting with the engine in idle mode. The two pilots in coveralls and helmets looked familiar to the girls. The two rear doors swung open, and two men appeared carrying automatic pistols. The turbine jet engine began to whine as the pilot increased the engine speed. This distracted Raven long enough for the two men to move to in front of the van. The larger man ordered, "Slowly get out if you want to live."

Raven and Jill looked at each other with a worried look. They couldn't believe their luck.

"We don't have a choice. Don't try anything foolish they have the upper hand." Raven surmised.

Jill reluctantly agreed as she opened the door and stepped out. The two armed men escorted the girls back to the helicopter. Once all four were in, the whine of the massive engine began to lift the machine up. Raven tried to keep her bearings on the flight path, but the smaller man placed a blindfold over her eyes then one over Jill's.

Raven thought to herself, "What a sorry ass way to end up. Amelia, John, and Pauline are going to be so disappointed in me. Naci, damn it, he will be disappointed the most. I won't give up without a fight. When this bird lands, Jill and I will figure out something. It'll be a cold day in hell before we give up. I've been in similar situations."

After about fifteen minutes, Raven could feel the aircraft losing altitude. She heard the engine change sounds as it slowed down. It seemed to turn a hundred and eighty degrees then it touched the ground with a slight bump. The engine whined as it slowed to a halt. She could hear switches being flipped and doors open. The girls were led out of the aircraft.

"Okay, girls, this is the end of the line for you two."

Raven stopped in her tracks and yelled, "I recognize that voice. It's you, Lion, isn't it? You turncoat son of a bitch." Her temper escalated as Raven started throwing up her right foot in hopes to land a blow hard enough to break his leg. Lion was on the defense. He knew that Raven was capable of anything. Raven yelled again, "Take these restraints off, you bastard, and I'll teach you a lesson before I kill your sorry ass."

The two armed men escorted the girls onto the porch and into the building. As soon as Raven entered the building, she recognized the smell. She turned and tried to head-butt her captor. With a dull thud, she felt the pain stab thru her forehead. Raven felt good that she at least made someone suffer, if only for a few minutes. "What the hell is going on? This is my cabin."

Then Amelia ordered, "Oka,y Lion take off the blindfolds so the girls can relax."

Once the blindfolds were off, Raven and Jill looked around the cabin with a worried look.

"Would you please explain what is going on, Amelia and why did your agents restrained us? They could have told us they were Foundation agents. Why does the Lion have that disguise on?"

Amelia walked over to Raven and advised, "Now, think a minute. You two just killed six or eight Russian operatives, probably their best. Do you think that it would have been wise to try to convince you who we were?" Silence fell across the cabin.

"Where's Naci, Raven?" John asked.

"The last that we saw him, he was chasing us in a car somewhere south of Statesville on Interstate 77."

Amelia interrupted, "Naci was in a small accident, but he's fine, John."

Raven walked over to the huge windows and looked out over the Piedmont view. After a few seconds, she offered, "You know a person can see for about thirty miles. If you look to your right, one can see Pilot Mountain on a clear day. Pilots flying into Charlotte in the old days used it for a landmark." Raven spun around and noticed John and Pauline in the jumpsuits; this confused her. She looked at them then asked, "If you were the pilots, why didn't you just show us who you were? Believe me; we would have been happy to see you two."

Amelia explained, "Remember, we needed to move you two out of there. We don't know how many more Russians were around. The last thing that we want is Russian agents seeing our operatives."

"Then why were the Russian agents in my Charlotte apartment waiting for me?" Raven asked, her temper returning. "Why did the Panther lead me into a trap?"

Amelia looked stunned and replied, "I simply don't have an answer, Raven. I just don't know."

Confused, Raven snarled, "I thought that I could trust the Panther."

"They want the code for Advanced Hypersonic Weapons Systems." Amelia returned.

"Why me? Do they think that I carry it around in my purse?" Raven said. For the first time, she challenged Amelia's authority and judgment.

"Well, not exactly in your purse."

Raven looked puzzled. She stared at the floor for a few seconds, raised her head then snapped, "You didn't implant the code in me?"

"No, nothing like that, but in our defense, we didn't know it until this morning when the state department told us who had it," John added.

"Well, if I have it, then where is it? I certainly don't know."

"Bill gave you something very important to keep. What is it?" Amelia asked.

Raven placed her hand on the St Cristofer's cross hanging around her neck. A silence fell over the room. Raven looked at Amelia.

"Please, let me see it," Amelia said.

Curious, Raven removed the cross from her neck and handed it to Amelia. Amelia placed the cross in her hand. She then took her opposite thumb and index finger and slid the bottom of the cross open revealing a secret opening that contained a small 8-gigabyte memory card. Amelia removed the card, closed the cross, and handed it back to Raven, "I'd imagine you want this."

Raven nodded.

Pauline walked over to Raven and placed her hands on her shoulders and said, "Now, what you are about to see, I want you to promise to control yourself, okay?"

Raven stared at Pauline with a strange look, one of confusion and at the same time curiosity. She needed time to process this, so Raven stood in silence. "I know that this is a lot to throw on you at one time. Believe me; we didn't know where the code was until a few hours ago, Raven. You must believe me."

Raven thought about the time in Nice, France when Pauline saved her and Naci's life and of all the training that she gave her in preparation for this job.

"Alright, you've convinced me, Pauline. I promise."

"That's my girl. Now, I want you to look at that man over by the fireplace and remember that he is one of us," Pauline warned. She gave him a nod and what happened next astonished Raven. He slowly loosened his tie and unbuttoned the top button of his dress shirt. He took both hands and pulled off a lifelike mask. His identity was revealed to Raven. Once the mask cleared his face, horror poured over Raven.

"What the hell? That's Roy Rothman," Raven yelled. She turned to Pauline and said, "I trusted you. Why did you lie to me? He's the son of a bitch who ordered that Bill killed."

"Calm down, Raven. He and your uncle were friends and longtime partners," Pauline explained.

Roy interrupted, "Raven, I'm going to tell you something to help convince you. Do you remember when you were a teenager, you and Bill were deer hunting and you bagged your first deer?"

Raven reluctantly nodded,

"I was there. I'm the one who flushed it out so you could shoot it. You were so stubborn that you tried to carry it yourself, but he had to help you. Now, how did I know that if I wasn't there?

"Bill could have told you that story," Raven added.

"Okay, either way, he still would have told me. I couldn't have known any other way."

"Maybe."

"I was walking up on the ridge above you. We always kept an agent around Bill to help protect him because of the code."

"Explain what happened the day he was killed. Where was your backup that day?"

Roy looked at Raven with a heavy heart and sad expression and said, "The Preacher had an informant; we didn't know. The Preacher knew every step Bill took that day."

Raven stood in shock as she discovered that not only was Roy Rothman standing in her cabin but also she was finding out that Bill's life was taken by something as ridiculous as an informant. She stood thinking, evaluating, and cursing.

"I'm sorry, Raven."

"Shut up, Rothman. I'm thinking," Raven demanded. This brought the attention of everyone in the room. Roy didn't respond. Raven thought back to the day that Bill was murdered. She thought about reading his letter that he left for Beth. It said: "The Preacher doesn't speak the gospel. The Lion's roar seems harmless, but his breath smells.

The hatred began to show on Raven's face; her heart began to pound. Jill picked up on her aggravated state and readied herself in case Raven needed help. Raven walked over to the Lion and said, "Remember the day that I visited you in the hospital; I leaned over your bed and whispered in your ear that if I found out you were lying, I'd make those gunshot wounds seem like scratches."

The Lion looked around the room to verify who was listening. He began to back step Raven as she physically began to overpower him. He didn't take her warning in the hospital seriously and was now confronted with Raven. He pleaded, "I don't remember." Again, the Lion looked around the room to gain approval. Silence dominated for several seconds. "In fact, she is fishing for a goat. I didn't tell her that I was a double agent," the Lion cut himself off.

The words "double agent" brought attention to everyone in the room.

Raven grabbed him by the neck and in one quick motion kicked him in the groin. The Lion bent over in pain. She placed her hands on his shoulders, and with an effortless jump, she wrapped her legs around his neck and rode him to the cabin floor. She squeezed him so hard with her legs that he couldn't breathe. Desperately, the Lion started pounding the floor. Finally, he started nodding like he was ready to talk. Raven released her hold on the Lion. Once the grip of her powerful legs diminished, he gasped for air. The Lion rubbed his neck. With cat-like reflexes, Raven jumped to her feet.

The Lion turned over, raised up on his hands and knees, then hesitated. Raven was back in the defense mode with Jill at her side. A bond had developed between the two agents, a bond that Amelia saw. The Lion looked up at Raven and Jill then slowly got up to his feet. Amelia did not take her eyes off the Lion.

"They paid me a lot of money; it was too good to be true. I felt so guilty that I turned on Bill and caused his death," The Lion confessed. "The money, damn money. Raven, I'm so sorry."

"Why in God's name did you turn on Bill? He was a lifelong friend." Raven asked. "It's not the money; you are well compensated for your services. I know that for a fact. Beth showed me Bill's account balance. Money can notbe the reason. What are you not telling us, Lion?"

Raven walked up to the Lion and bitch slapped him several times. He didn't even try to defend himself.

He was beyond embarrassment, a total disgrace to the Foundation. Raven only stopped her assault because she just thought of something, "I've done some research on you, and you have a young girlfriend who has two children. Could it be that someone in the Roth has blackmailed you? Did they threaten her or her children for intel on Bill's location that day?"

The Lion stood motionless with his head down. His despicable actions caused a human life to be terminated.

Raven added, "You are a sorry excuse for an agent. You and your girlfriend do not deserve to live."

Amelia spoke up, "You have sold out the Foundation, Lion. Why didn't you come to me? I have connections. I can fix anything, but you chose to become a trader. You're a fool. Raven, you have the Foundation's permission to terminate this horrible bastard."

Raven was surprised by her reaction and shot Amelia a strange look. Raven thought, "Why would Amelia not try to extract intel from him?" Then it came to her; Amelia gambled that Raven would catch on and act like she was going to end his life so he would talk.

Raven smiled and walked over to the fireplace and pushed a button under the mantle. A stone slid to the right exposing a handgun. She retrieved the forty-caliber military issued Berretta. She loaded the chamber with a distinctive click then walked over to the Lion.

"Get up, you sorry ass. Let's take it outside. I don't want to clean up the mess inside the cabin." Jill opened the kitchen door as Raven, and the Lion exited the cabin. Everyone followed them outside to the shooting range. Jill picked up on her intentions and tied the Lion to the post that held the full torso metal target.

Fifty feet from the metal target, Raven stood in the outdoor shooting shed. She unlocked the ammunition cabinet, retrieved six loaded clips, and laid them on the counter. She placed ear and sight protection as did everyone else. Raven held up the handgun and emptied the first clip on the adjacent target. The Lion stood firm; he didn't flinch at all. Maybe, he was ready to die. Maybe, the guilt was more powerful than his fear of death. Raven replaced the empty clip and loaded the first round into the chamber. She raised the Berretta and this time fired one shot next to his right ear. The bullet took a chunk off. The Lion jerked and let out a moan. Raven raised her gun up and shot his left shoulder, which knocked him back and caused him to yell.

"Okay, you win. I'll talk," The Lion cried. "The Preacher threatened to kill my girlfriend if I didn't cooperate and rat Bill out."

Raven let out a scream and raised her Berretta. "No, no, you son of a bitch. Bill didn't deserve to die that way." Raven lowered the gun and pumped a round into his right kneecap. She turned to Amelia and asked, "Do we need more information from him?"

Amelia knew her pain and offered, "Yes, let him live for now, but the minute that he is of no more value, you will have the privilege of his death."

John untied him and carried him back to the basement of the cabin. Pauline followed only to stop at the Black Hawk and retrieve his black bag. John tied the Lion to a chair in the basement and looked at Pauline and said, "Get the serum out. Give me a dose."

John sat down at the table with his forehead resting on his folded arms. Pauline opened the black bag and retrieved a bottle of disinfectant. She swabbed a small section at the base of his skull. Pauline took out a small pointed razor. She carefully slit a tiny section of skin and taped it back. This revealed a small tube that led to his pituitary gland. Pauline then opened a small vile and placed the contents into the tube under the skin. She used the wooden applicator to pack the ointment all around the tube, then released the flap of skin and glued in back into place. Pauline tapped John on the shoulder to indicate that she was finished. He gave Pauline a long, loving kiss and gratefully said, "You saved my life again, hon."

"No, Nadia did forty years ago. I just keep it going," Pauline said with a smile as she walked over to the Lion. "Now, we can do this the hard way or the easy way. We need information, and we need it now. Do you understand?"

The Lion raised his head with a somber look and smirked, "I don't owe the Foundation one damn thing. Besides, if I talk, you will just kill me, so why make it easy?"

"John, I think he wants to do it the hard way," Pauline speculated. She slid over to the table, pulled out a chair, and sat down. "I believe you're up, my love."

John smiled and stood up. High energy returned to his body and mind. His surgeon, Foundation agent and longtime friend, Nadia, performed a lifesaving operation on him during World War II. The success of the operation, along with his inherited mental gift, made John the world's foremost mentalist. His incredible skill level has never been matched by another human. In fact, only a hand full of people knew about John's mental power. The Lion was about to experience first-hand how information was extracted in the old days.

★ ★ ★

Amelia and Roy walked up to the cabin and stepped onto the porch. Amelia took his hand and motioned for Roy to follow her. They walked to the mountainside of the cabin with the view. Roy asked, "Have you heard from The Panther?"

"No. As a matter of fact, it's been a few days," Amelia returned with a puzzled look. "Why?"

"I'd like to have some positive news. Do you think that John and Pauline can get any information from the Lion?"

Amelia smiled, and said, "I guarantee it."

★ ★ ★

John walked over to the Lion and stood before him. The Lion didn't acknowledge or look up at John. John placed his right hand under Lion's jaw and forced it up. "I don't want to enter your mind, but if you don't cooperate, you will leave me no choice."

The Lion looked at John and smirked, "You will never get me to talk. My loyalty is with the Roth."

"Since you refuse to talk, I won't need your cooperation," John assured.

Silence dominated the basement. John needed to know who was behind the Roth movement, who kept it organized and where the money came from. The best way was for him to mentally enter the Lion's mind. Pauline retrieved a chair for John to sit on. Once he sat down, Pauline stood behind him with her hands on John's shoulders to support him during the entire session. After about thirty seconds, John's body went limp indicating that he entered the Lion's mind.

CHAPTER 26

Naci stood on the corner of Broad and Second Street wondering how he was going to find Raven and Jill. The day was growing old and would soon be dark. The traffic volume was beginning to slow when he heard the whine of a foreign car pull up behind him. Naci leaned around just in time to see the passenger's door lift. An extremely beautiful, mature lady sat behind the wheel and said, "Get in. I'll take you to see Raven."

Naci hesitated because she knew Raven's name. He quizzed, "How do you know her name, and who are you?"

"I'm Nadia; I know your parents. Now, get in before more of the Russians decide to take revenge for the past few day's events."

Naci smiled, not for the good luck in Nadia's sudden appearance, but because he finally met the one woman who could explain how is own father acquired such mental power. Naci clicked the seat belt as the automatic door closed. Nadia released the six hundred horsepower engine in first gear. She expertly steered the Lamborghini to the onramp that led north on I-77. Traffic was light, and Nadia took advantage taking the Italian machine over 140 mph.

"Are we in a hurry?" Naci asked as Nadia place the car into sixth gear. "I noticed that we just passed a state police car parked under the overpass and he didn't pull out in pursuit of us."

"If you don't run this machine to its fullest potential, it will begin to give mechanical trouble," Nadia returned with a slight accent. "The reason that he didn't come after us is that I contribute large amounts of money to the North Carolina State Police Department, so I have what you Americans say, privileges."

"What is John's mental potential, Nadia? I know that you operated on him back during the war?"

"Naci, I would like to brag about him, but I promised to him and Pauline that I would never divulge his secret to you or anyone else."

"How many others are like him that you know of?" Naci asked.

"Several, but no one that you would know except your uncle Harold. He's not quite as gifted as your father. He didn't have the operation, just the shots."

"Why doesn't he talk about his gift to me?"

Nadia didn't answer; she pressed down on the fuel pedal taking the sports car to 160 mph. The trees along the roadside became a blur. The hills and dips seemed to level out. At times, it felt as if the car became airborne. Naci noticed exit 65 and then a few minutes later they passed exit 79. At this rate, they would be to Raven's cabin in less than twenty minutes. Naci starred at Nadia and imagined what she must have been like forty years ago. Her full-bodied hair had to have been luscious to touch and smell. From what he could tell, her body even today was more sensual than most younger women. Naci thought of what a temptation she must have been to John. "How did he manage to keep his hands off her. Hell, she's more beautiful than Jill," Naci thought.

Naci turned, looked at Nadia, and asked, "Give me the same operation as you did John."

Nadia geared the car down to the speed limit and took command of the right lane. "What did you say?"

"I want you to perform the same operation on me," Naci said with enthusiasm. He had the look of a teenager eager to learn from a pro.

"Look, Naci, if I hadn't done the operation, your father would have died, and you wouldn't be here. I only do the operation under certain circumstances." Nadia schooled.

"I don't believe you. It would help in our line of work; it may even save my life." Naci defended.

Nadia turned up the ramp at exit 93 then stopped the car. She looked Naci in the eye and said, "It would ruin your love for Raven. It works on your ego, Naci. It makes you invincible. Soon, you would start to think that you don't need anyone. It turns a person into a maniac. John and the others do a remarkable job of holding the mental powers at bay. The results of the operation are different in every person I have operated on. Over the years, every single person outside of the top tier of the Foundation who I operated on, we've had to terminate. Now, we have a very intensive training program to become eligible for the operation.

It could take years for a candidate to qualify, and even then, it is a very difficult decision for me to make. The operation is to take a human and condemn them to a life dependent on the serum. So, you see, Naci, just asking for the operation isn't as easy as one might think." Nadia placed the transmission into first gear and pulled the sports car up to Zephtur Road then stopped. She shot Naci a commanding smile then turned left across the interstate and drove up to the mountain retreat.

The Lamborghini pulled through the compound gate and traveled up the tree-lined road. The lane led to the open fields and the log cabin. It was built on the crest of the ridge overlooking the thirty-mile view. Nadia stopped the sports car to admire Raven's hideaway, and to their surprise, a shot could be heard. Nadia and Naci saw a figure fall to the ground just beyond the shooting range. Raven moved toward the fallen body and cursed, "You low life son of a bitch, I wish you an eternal life in hell. When I join you in hell, I will ravish a hell on you again." Raven fired the remaining shells held in the Beretta's clip ending the Lion's life. Satisfied, she walked back to the cabin. Nadia turned off the engine, and with the push of a button, both doors opened. Naci stood behind the car until Raven walked close enough to recognize him. She began to walk faster until she was at a dead run. Naci raced around the back of the car and met her with a hug.

"Oh God, Raven, I'm so glad that you are alright. I've worried so much, but hell, I knew that you could take care of yourself."

"With the help of Jill and your parents, I made it back here," Raven said. "I see you that found a ride; who's the beautiful woman that picked you up?"

"Raven, you're not going to believe me; it's John's longtime partner, Nadia."

"The Nadia?" Raven exclaimed with a surprised expression of excitement.

"Yes, the one and only," Nadia said as she put her hand out.

Raven grabbed her hand and shook it, "It's a pleasure to meet you, Nadia. I'm sure that you have a million stories, and I would like to hear every one of them."

"Well, that would be quite a feat. We'll see if I can remember all of them," Nadia returned with a smile. "Come inside, everyone. I'm sure that Amelia wants to see her favorite grandson."

The trio entered the cabin and joined the others in the main sitting room with the hand laid stone fireplace. Amelia turned around and gave a big smile when she saw Naci. "Come over here, Naci and give granny a hug," Amelia demanded. Naci wasted no time and met her with open arms. The room was silent as the matriarch of the Vacara family indulged her delight with her grandson. "I'm glad that this is over with the Roth and we are all safe and sound."

The room was silent. Everyone was grateful that they were all safe and unharmed. Raven stood at the edge of the large opening between the dining room and the living room of the cabin. She couldn't stand it any longer and asked, "Okay, I've kept quiet as long as I can. If I'm going to continue working for the Foundation, I must know why Roy Rothman is apparently on the Foundation's side, and yet our rival is called the Roth, named after Roy Rothman?"

Amelia smiled, "Alright, you do have a valid question. You see, Raven, Roy has always been a Foundation agent. We started the organization known as the Roth. He went to the liberals in Congress and solicited their support. It all went as planned, and after several years, we thought that we had every congressman responsible for illegally allocating money for the Roth. Roy made the sting, and we closed the case. But after a few months, it regained momentum and started back up. We didn't get everyone responsible in Congress. Obviously, Roy couldn't be the contact so we needed to wait until another plant could be installed. Earlier today, John extracted from the Lion a list of those in Congress who are now behind the Roth. We will move in on this list of members tomorrow morning."

"So, Roy, you didn't order Bill's death?"

"Hell no, Raven; he was like my brother. You terminated the two top Roth agents, and now, we have the fresh list and will terminate the remaining ones starting tomorrow. We will arrest the members of Congress who are funding the Roth."

Raven drawled her eyes and looked Roy dead in the eyes. Raven said, "I seriously doubt that you will arrest anyone. In fact, I'd bet my life that the Roth organization will never die as long as you are alive."

The room fell dead silent. Amelia was pissed and said with a raised tone, "How can you say this, Raven? Roy has been a loyal agent since the beginning?"

"Has it ever occurred to anyone how I became such a good agent in a short time? I found an owner's manual, for lack of a better word, that Uncle Bill left for me. He didn't give it to me directly, but he left a series of clues that took years to figure out. It even included the Panther's identity. Once I located the manual, he detailed all the operatives and the significance of each. He defined the origin and motives of all upper tier personnel, including Amelia," Raven divulged while walking around the cabin looking at each person present. She circled the room and ended up back at Roy Rothman. "Now, what do I do with you, the king of traitors?"

Amelia interrupted, "What proof do you have? Where's the manual?"

Raven turned, walked over to the interior wall, and pressed a hidden button. A section of the wall opened. Raven retrieved the manual and handed it to Amelia.

She sat down and began to examine every page. "If you will notice, every kill Uncle Bill made is detailed by his hand-written notes. It includes who ordered the kill, the location of the kill, date, time of day, weather, and the amount of money that he was paid. Also, you'll notice that the Myth listed detailed acts of treason, which include those committed by the Preacher, the Lion, and most importantly, Rothman."

Amelia slowly turned page after page, reading and examining the detailed reports that the Myth recorded. She looked up at Rothman after reading one detailed report and said, "You reported that agent Cox committed suicide as the cause of his death. Bill reported that you killed him at point blank range, then you placed the handgun in his dead hand to make us believe that he took his own life. Cox committing suicide never made sense because of his mental stability, and all mental testing never showed him suicidal."

"That's not true. Bill could not have seen what happened. He was in Europe." Rothman defended.

Amelia pulled up the death report on her iPhone, looked at Roy, and responded, "No, Roy. He was not in Europe; he was in DC that night, and you and Cox were in Baltimore."

Raven interrupted and said, "Amelia, look at the numerous times that Uncle Bill noted Rothman took bribes from different congressmen. Hell, he was a making a living on just the bribes. Also, you will notice that after each event, he made a note that he contacted The Foundation."

The tension in the room mounted by the minute. Amelia looked at Rothman and said, "According to what Bill wrote, you are a traitor. He has photos of you with congressmen handing you money. Here's a photo of you and Boris at an outdoor café. There's another photo of you with China's heads of state, and according to what Bill wrote, you were never involved with the Chinese. If memory serves me, I don't recall having you with the Chinese."

"This isn't true, not one damned word of it." Rothman pleaded then pointed to Raven. "She's the bitch who made up this whole thing, that, that manual. She thinks that I ordered Bill's assassination; that's why she is accusing me of all this."

Amelia continued reading the manual. After a few minutes, she looked up with a horrified look and said, "Raven, your uncle said that Roy Rothman had hired three Chinese assassins who impersonate Morgan."

John began to see it Raven's way. "There are Morgan impersonators; it's no wonder I couldn't kill them. There could be dozens on Rothman's payroll," He concluded.

Rothman stood in silence until he said, "I'm not even going to comment on the manual that the Myth left behind. Surely, Amelia, you don't take this seriously?"

"I will need to examine this further before I pass judgment," Amelia returned.

Raven snapped her head around to Amelia and said, "I've read the manual, and I will stand with Uncle Bill. I met with Morgan, and he showed me a very interesting film that he and Uncle Bill made twenty years ago in Havana at a bar called Sloppy Joe's. First, the film identified who Morgan is. Second, he gave me a thumb drive loaded with files indicating who's who all over the globe. I know the truth, Amelia. Not a soul in this room is going to convince me that Rothman isn't a traitor.

"I have only one more thing to say, Amelia. Divulge who the Panther is or I will. Naci and Jill deserve to know."

Raven was silent, as was everyone else in the room. Amelia shot a glance over at John, and he gave her a nod of approval to disclose the true identity of the Panther.

"Raven, why is it so important to you that Naci and Jill know the identity of the Panther?" Amelia asked.

The day that the Preacher killed Bill, we were sitting in the Stonewall Diner for lunch. Bill made this comment; he said, "Raven, there is a Foundation agent named the Panther. You must find out who this agent is on your own. If you can't, then as long as the Foundation keeps you in the dark about the identity, you haven't become one of the top tier of agents for the Foundation. Once you have the experience, demand that they tell you who the Panther is or walk out and never look back."

The room was silent. A minute passed then two. No emotion or effort to divulge the identity was displayed. Jill stood up and walked over to Raven's side. Naci was positioned beside Amelia. He glanced over at her then joined Raven and Jill. Amelia showed concern because she never once thought that Naci would walk out on the Foundation.

She cleared her throat and said, "You three are willing to give up your future with the foundation? Hell, the three of you are the up and coming Foundation. Look around; we have the experience to teach you to become the world's top agents. If you walk, you will be considered rogue, and I don't have to tell you what we will do. The three of you need the Foundation. If we don't stand together, dark ages could be ahead, not only in America but also all over the world. The future is not any brighter than it was before World War Two."

"I stand my ground, Amelia. Not once did Bill give me bad advice, and I will not back down. The manual proves this. If you want the Foundation's future to be in our hands, then you have no choice but to tell them who the Panther is. Let me terminate Rothman. Then maybe, just maybe, I'll join your little club."

Amelia stared at Raven as if she was sizing her up for an entry-level agent. Raven's stubbornness weighed heavily on her decision, but Amelia decided to reveal the Panther's identity.

Amelia turned around and nodded her head up and down to the remaining persons in the room, indicating for the Panther to come forward.

John, Pauline, and Nadia never moved a muscle. The threesome stayed put, which indicated that Amelia was the Panther.

Amelia's eyes focused on Raven, Naci, and Jill. "I must confess that this is a very difficult moment in my life; however, due to the circumstances, you three must know the truth," Amelia confessed, "Nadia, stand up and acknowledge that you are the Panther."

Nadia stood up and walked to Amelia's side, "Yes, I'm the Panther. Amelia appointed me as operating commander of the Rock Foundation. My years of field experience and my skill level as a brain surgeon qualified me as the Panther. I have operated on every person in this room who has had it done. My father performed the operation on me years ago. Because of our advanced mental capacity and my endless research on the serum I've developed, it is predicted that we will live forever. Once each of you proves that you can handle the responsibility, you will receive the operation, and then you will be a top-tier Foundation agent."

Amelia stepped up and asked, "I need to know once and for all; are the three of you with us?"

Naci responded, "I'm in one hundred percent."

Jill responded, "I'm in."

Raven began to get mad; she looked around the room at everyone and then walked up to Nadia and asked, "Why in the hell did you send us to Charlotte this morning only to walk into a bunch of maniac Russians in my apartment?"

"Not a soul in this room knew what I was doing except Amelia. We needed to flush out Russia's top agent named Boris. He took the bait, and Jill broke his neck in the warehouse."

"Hold on a minute." Raven quipped. "How did you know that she killed Boris?"

Nadia smiled and returned, "I'm the one who rented the warehouse and set Boris up with a promise of five hundred pounds of gold if he could bring me you, the new Myth, the one who is taking the original Myth's place. I convinced the Russians that she was a threat to their organization. You see, they believed the original Myth was still alive and you, Raven, are his daughter and partner. The Russians are terrified of him, and they sure wanted their hands on you. I watched the whole thing from an office high above the warehouse floor."

"Weren't you afraid of sending all three of us into a trap like that?"

"Not at all. I've fought enough Russian operatives to know that they are no match for the three of you. Remember that I was just a few feet away and could have helped," Nadia reassured. "Amelia was on board with this, and after all, it was her grandson."

The room fell silent; Raven began to shake her head from left to right repeatedly. After a couple of long minutes, she turned to Naci, "I'm sorry, Naci." A look of horror poured over his face. She slowly glanced around the room at each person present. She paused and looked at Pauline then continued until she came back to Naci. The room was dead silent. Raven placed both hands on Naci's face and gave him a long, soft kiss. A tear formed in her left eye; her lips began to quiver as she reluctantly pulled away from Naci. "I'm so sorry, Naci. It can't be like it was for us." Raven turned away and drawled her pistol and pointed it at Rothman and said, "You are the son-of-a-bitch who ordered Uncle Bill's death, and now, you will pay."

"Raven, no, don't you terminate him," Amelia warned. "Let me finish reading the manual; don't do it."

"For God's sake, Amelia, he's the bastard, as are his Chinese thugs who ambushed us in Nice, France, or have you forgotten?"

John stepped forward and warned, "Raven, I can fry your brain in an instant. Now, put the gun away."

Raven turned toward John with a deadpan look on her face. John heated up her handgun to the point that she couldn't hold it any longer. She dropped it rubbing her hand.

Naci screamed, "Raven, don't do anything foolish. They'll incapacitate you."

Raven's temper was at its boiling point. She walked over to Rothman and stood toe to toe. Beads of sweat formed on her forehead; her fists doubled, shaking, not in fear but pure anger. She leaned into Rothman's ear and whispered, "I will kill you, but you will suffer a day and night before you die; I fucking promise you. I know the truth, and you know the truth. You will be looking over your shoulder until I end your miserable life."

With a look of hatred, Rothman said in a low tone, "Raven Anderson, you don't have the guts to hunt me down and kill me."

Raven smiled and said in a low tone, "I'd say the same thing if I were in your shoes. But you know I'm right,"

Raven turned to Naci and said, "As detailed in the manual that Uncle Bill left me, I have a lot of valuable intelligence that Morgan and I can use. The partial copy Amelia has proved Rothman is a traitor. I have the original, and it's about three times bigger. I'm done with The Foundation."

"Raven, no, don't walk out on us. You will be signing your death certificate," Naci warned.

"The only reason that I agreed to join The Foundation was to avenge Uncle Bill's death. You have the proof in his hand-written manual who killed him. I have hundreds of files and don't forget the film. Of course, I will not show you the film because it would divulge Morgan's identity. Your family stopped me from terminating Rothman, so I'm canceling my commitment to The Foundation. Hell, for all I know, Rothman has had the same operation Nadia performed on John. I'm not doing your dirty work any longer; you can find someone else."

Naci pleaded, "Raven, don't go. I will hunt you down. No agent walks away from The Foundation."

"Then pick up my gun and shoot me Naci. But I'm warning you, don't miss. This is much bigger than our love. I made a promise to myself after Uncle Bill's death that I would hunt down and kill the ones responsible. Guess what, you and this Foundation haven't done anything to help me. Hell, I don't care how much Rothman is worth to you; I want him dead. I will give it one month, then Rothman is fair game."

Raven and Naci stared at each other for what seemed like an hour. Naci looked at Amelia for guidance. She could see the tears running down his cheeks. She motioned to everyone in the room to stand down and let Raven walk.

Raven stopped at the door, paused for a few minutes, and reached into her pocket. She threw her cell phone on the floor. Without turning around, Raven said, "Here's my phone with your tracer. I'll have the chip that was planted in my shoulder removed so you can't trace my location."

As she left, Raven said, "And by the way, Rothman just bailed on you, he's the one on the run, and I'm the one who will kill him." Everyone looked at each other and around the cabin; Raven was right. Amidst all the commotion, Rothman escaped. Rothman was gone. Just then, Nadia's car started with a roar, then the engine noise faded. "I will return with Rothman in a coffin," Raven said.

Raven opened the cabin door, stepped out, and never looked back. Tears flowed down both her cheeks.

Naci stood in horror. His heart was broken because he knew that Raven meant every word. Raven vanished along with Naci's heart.

Amelia looked at John and said, "Do not put a contract on Raven; she might just be right."

CHAPTER 27

ZURICH, SWITZERLAND ONE MONTH LATER

Morgan dialed Raven's phone. "How was your flight, Raven?" Morgan asked.

"Fine, I arrived last night."

"Where did you stay?"

"At the Renaissance Tower," Raven answered.

"Ah, yes, did you have the Pike Perch Filet? I hear that it's fantastic."

"Yes, the waiter recommended it, and I thought it was delicious."

"Let's meet for lunch at the Restaurant Belvoirpark. It's an incredible place to eat, and it's located across the street from the bank. Your Uncle and I have eaten there many times," Morgan informed.

"Our appointment is a 2. Let's meet at noon." Raven said.

"Good, I'll make the reservation," Morgan offered.

"Thanks, see you then."

★ ★ ★

Raven walked up to the Belvoirpark Host and announced that she was there to meet an elderly gentleman.

"Your name, please?" The Host asked.

"Raven Anderson."

"Yes, Ms. Anderson, please follow me."

Morgan stood up and offered Raven a chair by pulling it out for her to be seated. "I hope you don't mind eating outdoors. It's such a beautiful day."

"Not at all, Morgan. I want to thank you for all your help over the past several months. You certainly have made my life a lot easier."

"My pleasure and don't trouble yourself thinking that you're obligated to me. Bill saved my ass more than once. I owe him for the rest of my life."

The waiter stepped up and filled the water glasses. "Uh, what do you pleasure to drink, madam?"

Raven smiled and said, "Bring your finest German beer."

"And what may I serve you, sir?"

Morgan smiled, "The same."

The waiter nodded and said, "Certainly." He returned within minutes with the brew.

"Tell me, Morgan, what do you recommend to eat? Make it light," Raven asked.

The waiter set the beer down and said, "Are we ready to order?"

Morgan said, "Yes, the lady will have fresh tuna with blue potatoes and broccoli. I will have beef filet cubes, beetroot risotto, beans, and capers. Also as an appetizer, I would like to have a serving of Beef Head Barbacoa."

"Would the lady care for an appetizer?"

Raven shook her head no.

Morgan smiled and said, "Well, Raven, what's been keeping you busy for the past year? I know we haven't had much contact. I heard that you took out the Preacher."

Raven smiled, then her expression turned bad, "Yes, the Preacher is dead and so is the Lion. I haven't taken out Rothman."

Morgan asked, "Why not?"

"Because I was under contract to The Foundation, and they wouldn't let me."

"Was?" Morgan replied with a surprised expression.

"Yes, I gave Amelia enough proof to prove that Rothman was a traitor then I walked out on them. I gave Rothman a month until I was going to hunt him down. Bill had kept a diary, but I only gave them part of it. I didn't show them the film of you and Bill. I didn't want to expose your identity. They still think that you're Chinese."

"Did they explain that if an agent goes rogue, they terminate them?" Morgan asked.

"Yes, I understand. But because of Bill, I have enough evidence on the Foundation killing top members of Congress, Heads of States, and Federal Judges to keep me alive for the rest of my life."

Morgan smiled and said, "Bill was right; you are smart."

"Not me, Morgan, Bill was the smart one. I'm just the beneficiary of his intelligence."

The waiter placed the Beef Head Barbacoa appetizer on the table along with two small plates.

Morgan rubbed his hands together and said, "It's been awhile. Let's dig in, Raven."

Raven put her hand up, palm facing Morgan and waved, "No thanks, I think I'll pass, I'm watching my weight."

Morgan laughed as he swallowed his first bite. "Here, Raven, try just one bite. It's very good." Morgan spooned a small portion onto the spare plate and slid it to Raven. She placed a small amount on her fork, glanced at Morgan, then place the delicacy into her mouth. Raven grinned, chewed, and swallowed. She took her napkin and wiped the corners of her mouth.

"Not bad, Morgan, I was pleasantly surprised. How is this prepared?"

"Several ways but for this version, they take a skinned beef head, rub their favorite oil and spices on it, wrap it in palm leaves and tin foil, and smoke it for about ten hours. They then tear off the facial meat and serve it with one of many favorite sauces. The most tender area is the thick muscle in the back of the jaw."

The rest of the meal followed. Raven and Morgan continued to discuss her future now that she wasn't with the Foundation.

"What are your plans once you terminate Rothman?"

Raven sat quietly then answered, "I'm not sure. I certainly don't need the money. I could stay on my own or retire. I just haven't thought about it."

"How about joining up with me? I may just learn a thing or two working with the Myth 2.0," Morgan said.

"2.0? How do you figure that?" Raven jested.

"That's the rumor. You're a legend and don't think for one second that you're not."

Raven sat and smiled then asked, "Morgan, what made Bill so good at his profession?"

"Well, Raven, I'd say that it was his skill set. Some say that he was as good as it gets. He was deadly with any weapon he used including his fists. He was extremely intelligent; he was super observant, and he paid attention to detail. He trusted only one person, me," Morgan said.

"When you found out about his death, why didn't you come after the Lion and Rothman?"

"I made a promise to Bill. If you were a player and his death occurred, he wanted you to avenge his killer. I'm simply carrying out his wish."

"I'm glad. Thank you. Oh, look at the time. We better go to our appointment," Raven said glancing at her watch.

Morgan stood up and said, "The offer will be open. I want you to join up with me. Just think about it, Raven."

"Okay."

Raven and Morgan entered the Lienhart & Partner Bank at precisely two pm. Morgan took Raven to the office of Franz Lienhart for introductions. Morgan and Raven followed Mr. Lienhart's private assistant to his office.

"Come in, come in, Morgan and have a seat." Smiling, Mr. Lienhart held his hand out and shook Morgan's hand.

"Mr. Lienhart, I would like to introduce Ms. Barbara Ann Beirne, Bill's niece." Raven and Mr. Lienhart shook hands. "Mr. Lienhart is the Banks largest stockholder, and with deposits as large as yours, he always makes it a point to be the first to welcome you," Morgan informed.

"It's a pleasure, uh Ms. Beirne, to finally make your acquaintance. I would like to express our deepest sympathies to Bill's untimely death. We are so sorry." There was a small pause, and the office fell silent. "However, on a lighter, note Ms. Beirne, I was beginning to think that you didn't want, or should I say need, this account."

"Please, Mr. Lienhart, please call me Raven. I also am pleased to make your acquaintance. Yes, I'm very grateful for this account and trust me, I knew that it was in good hands. I wasn't worried."

The office door opened and a middle-aged man walked in. "Ah, yes, Ms. Raven, I want you to meet Dr. Duri Prader, CEO of this institution. He is a long-time executor and will oversee your account. If you please, take a seat and make yourself comfortable."

Raven and Morgan sat down while Mr. Prader laid out several documents for them to sign.

"This may take a few minutes to lay out. Ms. Raven, Morgan is one of our largest and longest depositors so naturally, when he brought your Uncle to us some twenty plus years ago, we were delighted."

The signing of all the papers took about an hour. During all the paper shuffling and her signing on the lines marked with an X, Raven glanced over as Morgan as he signed his duty as executor of the account over to her. Raven kept thinking about how lucky she was to have such a good friend as Morgan. He could have simply never told her of this account, assassinated her, and all this would have been his. He had offered work, so maybe, he needed her services, Raven thought.

"Well, that last signature should wrap things up," Mr. Prader said. "Here is my card. If you ever need anything, please contact me."

"Yes, Mr. Prader. I do have one question."

"Certainly, how may I help you?" Mr. Prader asked with a smile.

"What is the account balance?"

With a smile, Mr. Prader said, "Ms. Beirne, if you will turn to page twelve of your booklet, you will find the answer. We listed it in U.S. dollars so you would understand the amount."

Raven opened her portfolio to page twelve. She stood in complete shock. A smile grew on her face; the account balance read, $29,765,251.39 U.S. Dollars.

"I had no idea. How did the original investment grow into this amount?"

Mr. Prader said, "We are very good investors, and our tax rate is much lower than you're accustomed to. You have signed documents applying for dual citizenship. I will take care of it. However, you need a residence here in Zurich."

"Yes, I understand," Raven answered.

"You have the copies of the application for citizenship. We will submit the application for you; however, please find an apartment while you are here, perhaps tomorrow. When you have found a place, ask the realtor call me, and I will handle all the financial arrangements. There's no need for you to bother; it's a part of our service. The address will facilitate your citizenship status."

Morgan offered, "I can show you around Zurich tomorrow. I'm sure we will have one picked out by the late afternoon."

Raven nodded yes to Morgan and smiled at him. Raven thought, "I'm not an emotional person when I'm around men other than Naci. Morgan has been good to me. I wonder what is his angle is or if he is simply that good of a friend to Uncle Bill. Damn it, Raven, he just handed me 29 million dollars, and I have no possible information he needs unless it's Foundation intel he's after. That's not it. He worked with Bill and the agency; he knows more than I do. Unless, unless, he's my…."

Morgan shook Raven and said, "Earth to Raven, are you ready to go? These gentlemen have other appointments."

"Yes, yes, I'm sorry." Raven got up and followed Morgan out to the outer office.

The next day, Morgan and Raven met with a local realtor who had three apartments lined up to show Raven. Morgan had called the day before to get things set up. Since she would not be living there or even visiting very often, it was easy for Raven to choose. She and Morgan were finished before lunch and were at a street side café when Morgan asked, "What now, Raven? Where are you off too?"

"I think you know the answer to that. I'm going after Rothman. Do you happen to know where he is these days?" Raven asked.

"I hear he's Wyoming, elk hunting. He's based out of Jackson Hole," Morgan reported.

"That's exactly where I don't want to be, in open country," Raven replied.

Morgan thought for a minute then stated, "Isn't one of your strongest attributes the long gun. You could make the kill shot and be miles away. He'd never know what hit him.

"No good, I promised Rothman that I'd make it a slow death, a day and night. Besides, I want to see his face when I pull the trigger for the kill shot.

Morgan slowly nodded his head up and down, "Yes, you can't disappoint Rothman."

You don't happen to know where he'll be next?" Raven asked.

Morgan smiled and said, "It just so happens that he has a meeting next week with some politicians. The topic is, now get this, Climate Change. He thinks that they are going to let him on the ground floor on the carbon tax market. They want to start a market where corporations must buy carbon stock, like wall street trades. This will only benefit the extreme wealthy like George Soras and other global financiers. Rothman will offer to do some dirty deed for them like knocking off some hack or conservative political adversary opposed to the idea."

"Where is this meeting?" Raven asked.

"Double Tree Inn, Washington DC-Crystal City. It's located near the Pentagon. It's a great location for an assassination. It has a revolving rooftop bar and restaurant," Morgan explained.

"I think I've been there; the food is carried up via elevator from the downstairs kitchen," Raven said.

"If you want, I can reserve a table for myself. We can wear electronic communication, and I can pinpoint his exact table before you get there."

"Yes, I can intercept a food carrier, ride the elevator up, and with your help, kill Rothman. We can be on the elevator on our way out before anyone can call the police." Raven speculated.

Morgan and Raven's eyes met. She leaned across the table and stuck her hand out to Morgan and said, "Partners."

Morgan smiled, grabbed Raven's hand, and shook. "What a day, I think we have the perfect combination, your youth and my experience. I only wish Bill were here to join us."

Raven's eyes met Morgan's as she said, "I do too. You know what though? We'll do just fine, just fine."

CHAPTER 28

DOUBLE TREE INN, WASHINGTON DC.

Morgan adjusted his hidden earpiece and whispered into his watch, "Raven, do you copy?

"Yes, Morgan loud and clear."

"Are you still in the room?"

"Yes, I need to make a dry run up to where you're located to check the timing. Do you see any Foundation or Roth agents?" Raven asked.

"I'm at the bar; my back is to the revolving restaurant. I'll turn around and check. When Rothman comes in for dinner, I'll take a table after he is seated so I can have a better view," Morgan said. "I don't see anyone yet. Hell, he may not eat here tonight."

"Has he even checked in yet?"

"Yes, I hacked into their computer network. He arrived last night; he just hasn't eaten here yet."

Raven hesitated and asked, "What room?"

Morgan answered, "I was afraid that you would get around to asking, Room 522."

Raven was silent. A couple of minutes passed then Morgan's earpiece sounded, "Can you hack the restaurant's reservations for tonight."

"Let me check. I can use my phone," Morgan used his expert computer skills to find the reservation list for that night. "Yes, he is scheduled to eat in one hour."

Raven thought, "Any Foundation agents on the reservation list?"

Morgan checked, "None that I can see. Wait, who is N. Fennell?"

"Fuck, that could be my ex-boyfriend, Naci Vacara. Most likely, Jill Carter will be with him. Hell, the whole crew could be there tonight."

"Sit tight; I'll make a reservation for myself. Then I'll be down. I have an idea; use the inter-room doorway and meet me in my room," Morgan announced.

Morgan opened his door, went straight to the closet, placed a duffle bag on top of his bed. When he opened it, six tranquilizer guns were etched into the foam liner. He loaded all six and hid them inside his suit jacket. "Go to the service elevator by the kitchen and wait for my signal. I'll keep you posted. When Rothman sits down and orders, I'll tell you to come on up. When I see you with your blonde wig and sunglasses, I will tranquilize all the Foundation agents. On my cue, come into the dining room past the bar and terminate Rothman. Raven, be prepared; this could get bloody if Rothman has pigeons perched around the dining room."

Raven nodded and checked her 9mm Glock. She opened her bag and placed two extra handguns under her jacket. She then filled her pockets with loaded clips.

Morgan returned to the restaurant and took his seat. He used his phone and hacked the security camera system to shut down the cameras. Perched behind his menu, he scanned the room looking for agents. He saw Naci and Jill along with two other agents with them. Rothman and two senators entered the rotating dining room and were escorted to their table. Morgan whispered into his watch, "Raven, Rothman is seated at the center table; he's not hard to find. There are four Foundation agents at another table; I'll take care of them. I see two Roth agents seated next to Rothman. Do you copy?"

"On my way."

Morgan glanced over at Naci and made eye contact with him. Naci turned towards Jill and motioned with his eyes to look at Morgan. They laughed indicating that they didn't pick up on Morgan as a possible threat or agent. Morgan knew he had to put Naci out first. The last thing that he wanted was Naci in the way and possibly shot. Morgan slowly laid two tranquilizer guns on the table and covered them with his napkin. He then motioned for a waiter.

"Yes, may I help you, sir?" The waiter asked.

"I'm in a bit of a hurry. Could you please take my order now?" Morgan didn't want the waiter to be in his way when Raven entered the dining room.

The waiter gladly retrieved his black ticket book and said, "Certainly, what will you have?"

Morgan responded, "Let's see. I'll have the beef filet, medium well," Morgan hesitated then continued when the waiter looked at him with a smile. "Baked potato, sour cream, and fresh cut green beans. Hold the salt please." The waiter finished writing, extended his hand out asking for the menu. Morgan obliged and handed it to him.

Although the main floor of the restaurant was revolving, the bar area and waiter station were stationary. The skies were clear, and the sunset was only minutes away. The bright red sky offered spectacular views of the city. This was perfect timing. Most patrons were enjoying the sunset, and due to the bright sky, the rotating dining area was poorly lit. These circumstances offered excellent protection for Raven and Morgan. Minutes passed, Morgan kept his eyes glued to the service elevator located behind the bar area that waiters used to transport the food from the kitchen.

Morgan whispered, "How much longer? The lighting is perfect here; the sunset is providing excellent cover."

Raven answered, "The elevator has stopped, and the door should open any second."

Morgan stood up with the tranquilizer guns under his folded arms. The elevator doors opened; Raven stepped out with a covered tray in one hand and the folding tray holder in the other. Morgan smiled at Raven and stepped ahead of her. Their timing could not have been better. Naci's table of four was located on the outside row of the dining area next to the view; all four were seated and admiring the sunset. Morgan placed two darts, one in Naci's neck and other in Jill's. Both agents slumped over. Morgan laid the two empty guns on the table and repeated the same procedure with the two agents seated next to Naci and Jill. By now, Raven stepped up to Rothman's table, unfolded the tray holder, and placed the covered tray on it. The three men didn't notice Raven. She lifted the tray cover, quietly placing it next to the food tray. She then retrieved two handguns with silencers and shot the two politicians on the top of their heads driving the bullets down through the spinal cords assuring instant death. Rothman's eyes instantly searched for the killer. He reached for his gun and started to stand up when he saw the barrel of her handgun. Smiling, Raven removed her sunglasses. His face reflected horror. "I promised you a month ago that your death would take a day and night. Well, I lied." Raven picked up the tray cover, placed it over Rothman's head, and placed two rounds into his skull. She quickly covered his head. Rothman slumped over face down on the table. The tray cover was on top of his head, dripping with blood. Once satisfied that Rothman was dead, Raven scanned the dining room for possible threats. Morgan had just finished terminating the two Roth agents and motioned for Raven to evacuate to the elevator. When she went by the bar, she noticed that the bartender had picked up the phone. It was clear that he had witnessed Raven's actions and was attempting to notify the police. Raven saved him a phone call; she terminated him with one squeeze of the trigger. Morgan followed Raven to the elevator walking backwards to take one final look. The elevator door opened, and both assassins stepped in. The door slowly closed. Raven stepped up to Morgan and gave him a gentle hug and said, "Thank you, Morgan, for providing closure to Uncle Bill's death. I am truly grateful."

While in the grasp of the hug, Morgan replied, "Thank you, Raven. I too am grateful for the closure."

Morgan gave Raven a pat on the back as he noticed the elevator stopped at the kitchen level. He pulled back from Raven's hug and motioned to Raven with his eyes that the elevator was about to stop. She smiled at Morgan with her teary eyes, and the door opened. Morgan and Raven stepped out, turned, and walked to the stairwell. They took one flight up and then jumped on a hotel elevator to their floor. Both entered Morgan's room where Raven removed her sunglasses, blonde wig, waiter's jacket. She stuffed both down into a carry bag then placed the sunglasses back on.

Morgan said, "Did you wipe down the room and double checked for personal items?"

Raven nodded yes. Morgan pulled his sleeve back and glanced at his watch, "We have five minutes to evacuate the property before the cameras automatically turn back on." The duo quickly exited the room and headed for the parking garage.

Morgan opened the Jaguar trunk with his remote. He handed Raven his bag, and she placed them in the trunk while Morgan started the car. Raven shut the trunk and joined Morgan. The Jag pointed its nose out of the parking garage to street side and turned onto Arm-Navy Drive.

Raven leaned back into the seat with a smile that she thought she would never have. Morgan looked over to her and asked, "Why the big smile?"

Raven turned her head towards Morgan and said, "The feeling of revenge. I just can't help it. I feel whole again. We won; Rothman is dead." Raven looked up and said, "Uncle Bill, I did it; the miserable son-of-bitch is dead."

Morgan shifted gears and said, "Raven, my dear, I too am happy. I feel better now that Rothman is dead."

The car was silent for the next five minutes then Raven pulled out a cell phone and began typing.

To Panther:

Rothman is dead. Tell Amelia and John that their little boy Naci is fine. He and his girl Jill might be a little groggy for a few hours. I believe they need more training, too easy. They're not ready for the big leagues. Leave the tough jobs to me. Oh, if you haven't figured it out; this is Raven. I'll be in touch.

Raven rolled down her window and tossed the cell phone. Morgan smiled and said, "Let me guess; you texted either Amelia or Nadia and gloated."

Raven smiled and said, "You know, Morgan, I'm beginning to like you more and more.

Morgan said, "I feel the same, Raven, my dear. Where to next?"

Raven thought for a minute, "I hear Italy is beautiful this time of year!"

The End.

Made in the USA
Lexington, KY
18 June 2018